SHE TOOK A DEEP BREATH AND DARTED IN THROUGH THE DOOR

Hacker had been drinking for at least the four hours since Twig had arrived at the supply post. The posse must now be more than an hour from here.

She was also going to get him out before anyone noticed that his term of office had been her.... ...ood, one of his ....en called a bar. Facing ...man as tall as he, but much he....... with a long, black beard.

"Hey!" shouted the black-bearded man, and his voice was a deep and growling bass. "Hacker, look! Don't tell me it's that wild kid, the one the Plant raised! It is! I'll be damned, but it is!"

"Leave her alone, Berg!" said Hacker thickly. "Twig—Twig, you get out of here. Wait for me outside."

"No, you don't," said Berg, grinning. "You're staying, Hack. I've got some people coming to see you. Your term as Congressman from this district ran out yesterday. You got no immunity now."

"Hacker!" she whispered desperately in his ear. *"Run now!"*

She ducked around him and came up facing Berg. The big man stared at her stupidly for a moment and then her right hand whipped in a backhand blow across his face, each finger like the end of a bending slender branch, each nail like a razor.

FORWARD!

GORDON R. DICKSON

Edited and with an Introduction by
Sandra Miesel

BAEN
science fiction
BOOKS

FORWARD!

This is a work of fiction. All the characters and events portrayed in this book are fictional, and any resemblance to real people or incidents is purely coincidental.

A Baen Book

Baen Enterprises
8-10 W. 36th Street
New York, N.Y. 10018

First printing, July 1985

ISBN: 0-671-55971-0

Cover art by Paul Chadwick

Printed in the United States of America

Distributed by
SIMON & SCHUSTER
MASS MERCHANDISE SALES COMPANY
1230 Avenue of the Americas
New York, N.Y. 10020

ACKNOWLEDGMENTS

These stories have appeared previously, in a somewhat different form, as follows:

"Building on the Line," *Galaxy Magazine*, November 1968. © Galaxy Publishing Corp.

"Babes in the Wood," *Other Worlds*, May 1953.

"Napoleon's Skullcap", *The Magazine of Fantasy & Science Fiction*, May 1962. © Mercury Press, Inc.

"Rescue Mission," *The Magazine of Fantasy & Science Fiction*, January 1957. © 1956 by Fantasy House, Inc.

"Robots Are Nice?" *Galaxy Magazine*, October 1957. © 1957 Galaxy Publishing Corp.

"The Dreamsman," *Star Science Fiction #6* edited by Frederik Pohl, © Ballantine Books Inc. 1959.

"The R of A," *The Magazine of Fantasy & Science Fiction*, January 1959. © 1958 by Mercury Press, Inc.

"One on Trial," *The Magazine of Fantasy & Science Fiction*, May 1960. © Mercury Press, Inc.

"The Queer Critter," *Orbit*, November-December 1954, © 1954 by Hanro Corp.

"Twig," *Stellar #1* edited by Judy-Lynn del Rey, Ballantine Books, 1974. © 1974 Random House Inc.

"The Game of Five," *The Magazine of Fantasy & Science Fiction*, April 1960. © Mercury Press, Inc.

"Guided Tour," *The Magazine of Fantasy & Science Fiction*, October 1959. © Mercury Press, Inc.

CONTENTS

Editor's Introduction

by

Sandra Miesel

We humans have been making progress far longer than we have been dreaming about it. The process itself is as old as life—our blood still carries the salt of primordial seas. But the theory of progress is younger than the written word.

Primitive man watched the turning wheel of the seasons, enthralled by their recurring patterns. Discoveries accumulated, civilization appeared, but continuity was prized more than change. So rigid was custom that metal tools were cast to look like stone or stone pillars carved to look like logs. Innovations were disguised as "reinterpreted" traditions.

Discontent with the world as it was stirred nostalgia for paradise, for a lost Golden Age far in the past. Some hoped the cosmos would dissolve into primal chaos and begin anew. Cyclic myths became the rule in cultures from the Mediterranean to the Far East. Of course, in an eternally repeating universe, no real advancement is possible: it matters not whether resurrection follows death, or death, resurrection.

Meanwhile, as the Bible took form, it inspired an alternative view in which life was a purposeful pilgrimage through linear time. Moreover, material creation was real, wholesome, and destined to be trans-

1

formed. Eastern Christianity in particular stressed humanity's glorious potential. "God became man so that man might become God," said St. Athanasius, anticipating by sixteen centuries Teilard de Chardin's daring vision of creature and Creator meeting at evolution's Omega Point.

Antiquity's achievements overawed the Middle Ages: "We are but dwarves standing on the shoulders of giants." Yet this period bustled with technologies unknown to the ancients and vast energy was expended on taming wild country for settlement. In proud contrast, the Renaissance—which saw itself as another age of giants—openly praised invention and rewarded exploration. The object of life was the pursuit of excellence in mind and body as well as spirit.

Secularized versions of these Judeo-Christian ideals have become the guiding principles of modern Western civilization. Belief in progress waxed strongest between the Enlightenment and the First World War, the era of the First Industrial Revolution. In its most confident phase, the evolutionary sensibility fostered by Darwin and Marx proclaimed that mankind was perfectible and utopia was attainable. The Golden Age now lay ahead rather than behind. Nothing could prevent its imminent arrival.

Naturally, these assertions have stirred opposition: no sooner are machines built than Luddites arise to smash them. Even if we were all equally eager for advancement—which we are not—we would be wise to question the means and rate of proposed changes. But because our century has seen too much land ravaged and too many people slaughtered in the name of "Progress," the very concept is now condemned by some.

Future debate on this issue must be moved to the forum of the heart. Only transfiguration within can equip us to master transcendence without. Let psychic evolution match physical improvement. Let each developing power generate a corresponding ethical curb. Let yesterday's Unconscious make peace with tomorrow's Conscious. Then, at last, our species will be fit to bear the weight of glory.

*Mankind is forever pulling out "on the Long Trail—
the Trail that is always new." Yet the trailbreaker's
forward progress is never a feat of body alone.*

Building on the Line

I

Crack-voiced, off-key, in every way like a fingernail drawn across the blackboard of his soul, the song cauterwauled in John Clancy's helmet earphones:

"... Building on the Line, Team. Building on the
Line!
"Building Transmit Stations all along the goddam
Line!
"Light-years out and all alone,
"We have cannibalized the drone;
"And there's no way to go home
" 'Till we get the Station working on the goddam
Line!"

Clancy closed his mind to the two thousandth, four hundred and—what? He had even got to the point where he had lost count of the times Arthur Plotchin had sung it. Was that a win, he wondered, suddenly—a point for Plotch, in finally driving him to lose count? Or was it a point for him, in that he had managed to shut out the singing, at least to the point of losing his involuntary count of the times Plotch had sung it?

A bright light hit him in the faceplate, momentarily blinding him; and the singing broke off.

3

"Heads up, Clance!" It was Plotch's voice, cracking like static now in the earphones. "Keep your mind on your work, dim-bulb! Time to fire the wire!"

Clancy deliberately did not answer, while he slowly counted off six seconds—"*One-Mississippi, two-Mississippi* . . ." It was one of the things he could be sure rubbed Plotch the wrong way; even as he knew Plotch was sure by this time that the endless repetition of the *Line Song* was like sandpaper to Clancy's raw nerves.

"What?" Clancy said, at the end of the sixth second.

"You heard me, you . . ." Plotch choked a little and went silent, in his turn.

Clancy grinned savagely inside his helmet. With the flash from Plotch's signal-light blinked out of his eyes, now, he could make out the other's silver-suited figure with the black rectangle of tinted glass that was its faceplate. Plotch stood holding his wire gun by the other of the last two terminal rods in the almost-completed Star-Point. He was some hundred yards off across the barren rock of this hell-born world, with its two hundred degrees below zero temperature, its atmosphere that was poisonous, and almost non-existent to boot, with its endless rock surface, its red clouds always roiling threateningly overhead and the not-quite-heard gibber of uneasy native spirits always nagging at a man just below the level of his hearing.

Plotch was trying to turn the deaf treatment back on Clancy. But that was a game Clancy played better than his dark-haired, round-headed teammate. Clancy waited; and, sure enough, after a few moments, Plotch broke first.

"Don't you want to get back to the ship, horse's-head," shouted Plotch, suddenly. "Don't you ever want to get home?"

Was Plotch starting to sound a little hysterical? Or was it Clancy himself, imagining the fact? Maybe it was neither. Maybe it was just the hobgoblins, as Line Team 349 had come to call the native life-form, putting the thought into Clancy's head.

For the hobgoblins were real enough. There was no doubt by this time that some form of immaterial life existed in the fugitive flickers of green light among the bare rocks of XN-4010, as this frozen chunk of a world had been officially named. Something was there in the green flickering, alive and inimical; and it had been trying to get at him and Plotch all through the five days they had been out on the job here, setting up Number Sixteen of the twenty-six Star-Points required for a Transmit Receive Line Relay Station. Luckily, one of the few good things about the survival suits they were wearing this trip was that they seemed to screen out at least part of whatever emanations the hobgoblins threw at them.

Clancy broke off in the middle of his thoughts to switch the living hate within him, for a moment, from Plotch to R. and E.—the Research and Experimental Service, which seemed to be just about taking over the Line Service, nowadays. Thanks to an evident lack of guts on the part of the Line Service Commandant.

The work on the Line Teams was bad enough. Fifteen men transmitted out to a drone receiver that had been lucky enough to hit a world suitable for a Relay or Terminal Station. Fifteen men, jammed into a transmit ship where every cubic inch of space and ounce of mass was precious because of their construction equipment, was balanced against the weak resolving powers of the drone. Jammed together, blind-transmitted on to a world like this, where you lived and worked in your suit for days on end. That was bad enough.

Add Plotch for a partner, and it became unbearable. But then add R. and E. and it went beyond unbearable. It was bad enough five years back, in the beginning, when a fifteen-man Team would be testing perhaps a dozen new items for R. and E. Now Clancy had a dozen new gadgets in his suit alone. He was a walking laboratory of specialized untried gimmicks, dreamed up on comfortable old Earth. Plotch had a dozen entirely different ones; and so did all the others. Though who could keep count.

Clancy bent ostentatiously to tug once more on the immovable terminal rod he had just spent three hard physical hours of labor in planting six feet deep in XN-4010's native rock.

He had in fact been down with the terminal for some minutes before Plotch called. But he had been pretending to be still working, for the sake of making Plotch struggle to get him to finish up. But now it was time to tie in. These terminals were the last two of the nineteen that made up a Star-Point, as the twenty-six Star-Points, spread out over a diameter of eighty miles, would, when finished, make a working Relay Station. Tying in these last two terminals would activate the Star-Point. They could go back to the transmit ship for ten blissful hours outside their suits before they were sent out on the next job. Head down, still tugging at the rod, Clancy grinned bitterly to himself.

There was usually a closeness between members of a Line Team that was like blood-brotherhood. But in this case, if the hobgoblins were trying to stir up trouble between Plotch and him, they were breaking their immaterial thumbs trying to punch a button that was already stuck in *on* position. Clancy straightened up from the rod and spoke over his helmet phone to Plotch.

"Yeah," he said. "I'm done."

He drew his own wire gun and, resting it in the sighting touch of the terminal rod, aimed it at the rod Plotch had just set up. He saw Plotch's gun come up, glinting red light from the glowing clouds overhead, and aim in his direction. For a second the pinhole of light that was sighting beam from Plotch's gun flickered in his eyes. Then, looking at his post, he saw its illumination there, like a small white dot.

"Ready?" Plotch's voice sounded in his earphones.

"Ready!" answered Clancy. "On the count of three, fire together with me. *One . . . two . . . three!*"

He pressed the firing button of his wire gun as he spoke the final word. An incredibly thin streak of silver lightning leaped out from the end of his gun through the receptor on the side of the post before him and buried its far end in the receptor on the post beside Plotch. In almost the same second a similar streak of lightning-colored wire joined Plotch's post in reverse to his. The physical shock of the suddenly activated Star-Point field sent both men stumbling backward awkwardly in their protective suits; and a varicolored aurora of faint light sprang up about the star-shaped area of grounded Relay equipment, enclosed by the twenty rods joined by double lengths of fine wire.

Number Sixteen Star-Point of the Relay terminal on XN-4020 was in and working. Now they could get back to the ship.

But then, as if the Star-Point's completion had been a signal, the low-hung clouds just over them opened up in a sort of hailstorm. Objects came hurtling toward the surface below—objects of all shapes and sizes. They looked like large rocks or small boulders, most of them. But for one weird moment, incredibly, it seemed to Clancy that some of them had the shape of Mark-70 anti-personnel homing missiles; and one of these was headed right for Plotch.

"*Plotch!*" shouted Clancy. Plotch whirled and his dark face-plate jerked up to stare at the rain of strange objects arcing down at them. Then he made an effort to throw himself out of the path of whatever was coming at him.

But he was not quite fast enough. The missile, or whatever it was, struck him a glancing blow high on the shoulder, knocking him to the rock surface underfoot. Clancy himself huddled up on the ground having no place to hide. Something rang hard against his helmet, but the shock of the blow went into his shoulders, as the supporting metal collar of his suit—another of R. and E.'s test gadgets— for once paid its way by keeping the helmet from being driven down onto the top of his head, inside.

Around him there were heavy thuddings. One more, just beside him. Then silence.

He got up. There were no more rocks falling from the skies. All around him there was only the silent, shifting, colorful aurora of radiation from the connected terminal rods; and the motionless, spacesuited figure of Plotch was a hundred yards off.

Clancy scrambled to his feet and began to slog toward the still figure. It did not move as he got closer, in the stumbling run which was the best speed he could manage, wearing his suit.

II

When at last he stood over Plotch, he saw his teammate was completely unmoving. Plotch's suit had a bad dent at the top front of the right shoulder joint; and there was a small, dark, open crack in the suit at the center of the dent. There was only rock nearby; no sign of any missile. But Plotch lay still. With that crack in it, his suit had to have lost air and heat instantly. His faceplate was white now, plainly opaqued on the inside by a thick coat of ice crystals.

Clancy swore. The gibbering of the hobgoblins, just out beyond the frontiers of his consciousness, seemed to rise in volume triumphantly. He reached down instinctively and tried to straighten out Plotch's body, for the other man lay half-curled on his side. But the body would not straighten. It was a figure of cast iron. There was no doubt about it. Within his suit, Plotch was now as rigid as the block of ice that, for all practical purposes, he now was.

Plotch was frozen. Dead.

Or was he?

Clancy abruptly remembered something about the experimental gadgets in Plotch's suit. Had not one of them been an emergency cryogenic unit of some sort? If that was so, maybe it was the unit that had frozen Plotch—working instantly to save him when the suit was pierced.

If that was so, maybe Plotch was salvagable after all. If it really was so. . . .

"Calling Duty Lineman at Transmit ship!" Clancy croaked automatically into his helmet phone, activating the long-distance intercom with his tongue.

"Calling whoever's on duty, back on the *Xenophon!* Come in, Duty Lineman! Emergency! Repeat, Emergency! This is Clancy! Answer me, Duty Lineman...."

Static—almost but not quite screening out the soundless gibbering of the hobgoblins—answered, roaring alone in Clancy's earphones. His head, a little dizzy since the rain of rocks, cleared somewhat and he remembered that he should not have expected an answer from this ship. There was interference on XN-4010 that broke communication between a suit transmitter and the mother ship. It cut off, at times, even communication between a flitter's more powerful communication unit and the *Xenophon.* He struggled to his feet and, bending down, took hold of Plotch's stiff body underneath the armpits of the suit. He began to drag it toward their flitter, just out of sight over a little rise of the rocky ground, a couple of hundred yards away.

The ground was rough, and Clancy sweated inside his suit. He sweated and swore at his frozen partner, the hobgoblins, the R. and E. Service for its experimenting—and Lief Janssen, the Line Service Commandant, for letting R. and E. do it. The gravity on XN-4010 was roughly .78 of Earth normal, but the rocky surface was so fissured and strewn with stones of all sizes from pebble to boulder that Plotch's unyielding figure kept getting stuck as it was pulled along. Eventually, Clancy was forced to pick it up clumsily in his arms and try to carry it that way. He made one attempt to put it over his shoulder in a grotesque variation of the fireman's lift; but the position of the arms, crook-elbowed at the sides prevented the bend in the body from balancing on his shoulder. In the end he was forced to carry what was possibly Plotch's corpse, like an oversized and awkward baby in his arms.

So weighed down, he staggered along, tripping over rock, detouring to avoid the wider cracks underfoot until he topped the rise that hid the flitter from him. Just below him and less than thirty feet off, it had been waiting—an end and solution to the grisly and muscle-straining business of carrying the frozen and suited figure of Plotch in his arms.

It was still there.

—But it was a wreck.

A boulder nearly two feet in circumference had struck squarely in the midst of the aft repulsor units, and the tough but lightweight hull of the flitter had cracked open like a ceramic eggshell under the impact.

Clancy halted, swaying, where he stood, still holding Plotch.

"I don't believe it," he muttered into the static-roar of his helmet. "I just don't believe it. That flitter's *got* to fly!"

For a moment he felt nothing but numb shock. It rose and threatened to overwhelm him. He fought his way up out of it, however; not so much out of determination, as out of a sudden rising panic at the thought of the nearly thirty miles separating him from the transmit ship.

The flitter could not be wrecked. It could not be true that he was stranded out here alone, with what was left of Plotch. The flitter *had* to save them.

Then, suddenly, inspiration came to him. Hastily, he dropped onto one knee and eased Plotch onto a flat area of the rock under foot. Leaving Plotch there, balanced and rocking a little, grotesquely, behind him, Clancy plunged down the rubbled slope to the smashed flitter, crawled over its torn sides into what had been the main cabin and laid hands upon the main control board. He plugged his suit into the board, snatched up the intercom hand phone and punched the call signal for *Xenophon*.

"Duty-Lineman!" he shouted into the phone. "Duty-Lineman! Come in, *Xenophon!* Come in!"

Suddenly, then, he realized that there were no operating lights glowing at him from the control panel before him. The phone in his hand was a useless weight, and his helmet earphones, which should have linked automatically with the flitter receivers of the intercom sounded only with the ceaseless static and endless, soundless gibbering.

* * *

Slowly, almost tenderly, he unplugged his suit, laid the phone back down on the little shelf before the dark instrument panel and dropped down on the one of three seats before the control board that was not wrecked. For a little while he simply sat there, with the hobgoblins gibbering at him. His head swam. He found himself talking to Plotch.

"Plotch," he was saying, quite quietly into his helmet phone. "Plotch, there's nothing else for it. We're going to have to wait here until the ship figures there's something wrong and sends out another flitter to find out what happened to us."

He waited a few moments.

"You hear me, Plotch?"

Still there was only silence, static, voiceless gibbering in his earphones.

"We can stick it out of course, Plotch," Clancy muttered, staring at the dead control panel. "Inside of two days they ought to figure we're overdue. Then they'll wait a day, maybe, figuring it's nothing important. Finally they'll send one of the other teams out, even if it means taking them off one of the other jobs. Oh, they'll send somebody eventually, Plotch. They'll have to. Nobody gets abandoned on the Line, Plotch. You know that."

The five days of bone-grinding manual labor on the Star-Point took effect on him, suddenly. Clancy fell into a light doze, inside his suit, sitting in the wrecked control room of the flitter. In the doze he half-dreamed that the gibbering voices took on their real hobgoblin shape. They were strange, grotesque parodies of the human figure, with bulbous bodies, long skinny arms and legs and turnip-shaped heads with the point upward, possessing wide, grinning, lipless mouths, a couple of holes for a nose, and perfectly round, staring eyes with neither eyebrows nor eyelashes. They gibbered and grinned and danced around him, kicking up their heels and flinging their arms about in joy at the mess he was in. They stretched their faces like rubber masks into all sorts of ugly and leering shapes, while they chanted at him in their wordless gibberish that they had got Plotch—and now they were going to get him, too.

"*No!*" he said, suddenly aloud in his helmet—and the spoken word woke him.

III

He glanced around the ruined flitter. The hobgoblin shapes of his dream had disappeared, but their gibberish still yammered at him from somewhere unseen.

"No," he said to them, again. "If you could rain rocks like that all the time, you'd still be doing it. I don't think you can do that except now and then. Even if it was you who did it. All I've got to do is wait." He corrected himself. "All we've got to do is wait—Plotch and I. And a flitter will come to pick us up."

Plotch is dead! Plotch is dead! gibbered the hobgoblins triumphantly.

"Maybe," muttered Clancy. "Maybe not. Maybe the cryogenic unit caught him in time. Maybe it froze him in time to save him. You don't know. I don't know.

A thought struck him. He got wearily up from his seat, clambered out of the wrecked flitter and struggled up the slope to where Plotch's frozen body in its suit still sat balanced, although by now it had stopped rocking. Clancy stood staring down at it—at the thick coating of white on the inside of the faceplate, ruddied by the red light from the clouds overhead.

"You dead, Plotch?" he asked after a little while. But there was no answer.

"So, maybe you're alive, then, Plotch, after all," said Clancy out loud to himself in the helmet. "And if you're alive, then that cryogenic unit works. So you're safe. You won't even have to know about the time we spend waiting for them to send a flitter after us.—Or, maybe . . . ?"

A sudden, new cold doubt had struck Clancy. Something he half-remembered Plotch's saying about the unit.

"I can't remember, Plotch," he muttered fretfully. "Was it supposed to be good for as long as necessary, that cryogenic action? Or was it just supposed to keep you for a few hours, or a few days, until they could freeze you properly, back at the ship? I can't remember, Plotch. Help me out. You ought to remember. What was it? Permanent or temporary?"

Plotch did not answer.

"Because if it's temporary, Plotch," said Clancy, finally, "then even if you're alive now, maybe you won't still be alive by the time the rescue flitter gets here. That's not good, Plotch. It's a dirty trick; having a cryogenic unit that won't last for more than a few hours or a few days. . . ." For a moment he was on the verge of emotional reaction; but he got his feelings under control. Anger came to stiffen him.

"Well, how about it, Plotch?" he shouted after a moment into the silence and the gibbering. "How about it—can you last until the flitter gets here or not. Answer me!"

But Plotch still did not answer. And a cold, hollow feeling began to swell like a bubble under Clancy's breastbone. It was a realization of the dirtiest trick in the universe—and Plotch just lay there, saying nothing, letting him, Clancy, flounder about with it in him, like a hook in a fish.

"You dirty skull!" burst out Clancy. "You planned it like this! You deliberately got in the way of that rock or whatever it was! I saw you! You deliberately got yourself all frozen up the way you are now! Now you want me to let you just sit here; and maybe sit too long before the ship sends somebody to rescue us? Is that it? Well, you know what, Plotch?"

Clancy paused to give Plotch a chance to answer. But Plotch maintained his unchanging silence. He was finally learning how to outdo Clancy on the not-answering bit; that was it, thought Clancy light-headedly. But Plotch's learning that was nothing now, compared to this other, dirtier trick he was pulling.

"Well, I'll tell you what, Plotch," said Clancy, more

quietly, but venomously. "I'm going to take you into the ship myself. How do you like that?"

Plotch obstinately said nothing. But the hobgoblin voices chanted their gibber in the back of Clancy's head.

All that way with a dead man! Plotch's dead! Plotch's dead! chanted the hobgoblin voices. But Clancy ignored them. He was busy calculating.

They had come out due east of the ship, Plotch and he. It was now afternoon where they were. All he had to do was to walk into where the clouds were reddest, because that was where the western sunlight was. The days were sixteen hours long right now in this latitude on XN-4010, and the nights were a brief four hours. He had a good six hours to walk now, before darkness came. Then he could rest for four hours before picking up Plotch again, keeping the brightest light at his back this time, and carry on. It would be six days at least before the ship would be likely to come to a certain conclusion that he and Plotch were in trouble— and at least another day, if not two, before another flitter and two-man team could be diverted from their regular job to investigate what had happened out here. Seven days at least—and thirty miles to the ship.

Thirty miles—why, that was only a little over four miles a day. He could do that any time, carrying Plotch. In fact, he ought to be able to do twice as much as that much in a day. Three times as much. Ten or twelve miles in a sixteen-hour day ought to be nothing. It was less than a mile an hour. Clancy got Plotch up in his arms and started off, his feet in the boots of the suit jarring one after the other against the naked rock beneath them. He walked down, past the damaged flitter, no longer looking at it, and thumped away, carrying his unyielding load in the direction of the brightest red clouds.

Far ahead, as far as he could see to the horizon, the rock plain seemed fairly level. But this was an illusion. As he proceeded, he discovered that there were gentle rises and equally gentle hollows that blended into the general flatness of the area, but which caused him to spend at least a share of his time walking either downhill or uphill. His legs took this effort without complaint; but it was not long before his arms began to ache from holding Plotch's stiff body in front of him, although he leaned back as much as he could to counterbalance the weight.

Eventually he stopped and once more tried to find some other way of carrying his burden. Several times he tried to find a position in which Plotch could be balanced on one of his shoulders, but without success. Then, just before he was ready to give up completely, he had a stroke of genius, remembering the gimmick collar on his suit that kept the inside of his helmet top from touching the top of his head. Testing, he discovered that it was possible to carry Plotch grotesquely balanced on top of his head, with the top of Clancy's helmet resting against the frozen man's unyielding stomach and with a knee and an elbow resting on Clancy's right and left shoulders, respectively. The helmet pressed down upon the collar and the weight upon it was distributed to the rigid shoulders of Clancy's suit, with the assistance of Plotch's frozen knee and elbow—and for the first time Clancy had a balanced load to carry.

"Well, Plotch," said Clancy, pleased. "You aren't so bad to take after all."

The flush of success that spread through Clancy lightened his spirits and all but drove away the unending gibbering of the hobgoblins. For a moment his mind was almost clear; and in that bit of clear-headedness it suddenly occurred to him that he had not set his pedometer. Gradually rotating about, holding Plotch balanced on his head and shoulders, he looked back the way he had come.

The wrecked flitter was just barely visible in the distance, its torn parts reflecting a few ruddy gleams of red light. Gazing at the smashed vehicle, Clancy did his best to estimate the ground he had covered so far. After a few seconds, he decided that he had come approximately a third of a mile. That was very good going indeed, carrying Plotch the way he had, to begin with. Carefully holding Plotch in place now with his left hand, he reached down with his right and set the pedometer, which was inset in the front leg of his suit just above the knee, giving himself credit for that third of a mile he had already covered. Only twenty-nine and some two-thirds of a mile to go to reach the ship, he told himself triumphantly.

"How do you like that, Plotch?" he asked his partner.

He started off with fresh energy. Perched on top of Clancy's head, Plotch rode with a fine, easy balance, except when Clancy came to one of the hollows and was forced to walk downslope. Then it was necessary to hold hard to Plotch's knee and elbow, to keep the frozen body from sliding forward off the helmet. For some reason, going upslope, the knee and elbow dug Clancy's shoulders and helped hold Plotch in place, almost by themselves. All in all, thought Clancy, he was doing very well.

He continued to slog along, facing into the dwindling western light behind the fiery masses of the clouds. Like all Line Team members, he was in Class Prime physical shape, checked every two weeks in the field, and every two months back on Earth to make sure he was maintaining his position in that class. He was five feet eleven inches in height, somewhat large-boned and normally weighed around a hundred and ninety. Here on XN-4010, his weight was reduced by the lesser gravity to about a hundred and fifty pounds. Plotch, who was five-nine, lighter boned and usually weighed around a hundred and sixty on Earth, here weighed probably no more than a hundred and thirty. On Earth, Clancy would have expected himself to be able to put on a hundred and thirty pound pack and equipment load on top of his suit and make at least a mile an hour with it over terrain like this—and for at least as many hours in a row as there were in the ordinary working day. That was, provided he stopped routinely for a rest—something like a ten-minute break every hour.

Here, he should do at least as well as that. Still, the calculation had reminded him that periodic rest was necessary. He sat down, eased Plotch off his shoulders and looked at his watch to measure off a rest period of ten minutes. He looked almost genially at the figure of Plotch with its frosted faceplate, as he sat, elbows on knees, resting.

"How do you like that, Plotch, you bastard?" he asked Plotch. "It's no trouble for me to carry you. No trouble at all. Maybe you thought you'd get out of something by playing dead on me. But you're not. I'm going to take you in; and they're going to thaw you out and fix you up. How do you like that, Plotch?"

Plotch maintained his silence. Clancy's thoughts wandered off for a while and then came back to the present with a jerk. He glanced down at his watch and stared at what he saw. A good half hour had gone by—not just the ten minutes he had planned on. Had he fallen asleep, or what?

The light filtering redly through clouds was now low on the horizon ahead of him. He looked at the pedometer on his leg and saw that he had only covered a little over a couple of miles. Sudden fear woke in him. There would be no making the ship in a few days if he went along at this pace—no hope of it at all.

Suddenly his throat felt dry. He tongued his drinking tube into position before his mouth and drank several swallows before he realized what he was doing and pushed the tube away again. The recycling equipment in these light-weight survival suits could not be all that perfect. Certain amounts of water were lost in the ejection of solid body wastes and in various other ways which, though minuscule, were important. That loss had to be made up from the emergency tank built into the back shoulder plates of his suit; and with the flitter wrecked, now some miles behind him, there would be no chance of refilling that tank—which at best was only supposed to carry enough supplementary water for two or three days. He would have to watch his liquid intake. Food he could do without ... but he suddenly remembered, he had plenty of stimulants.

He tongued the stim dispenser lever in his helmet

and swallowed the small pill that rolled onto his outstretched tongue, getting it down with only the saliva that was in his mouth. Then he struggled to his feet. He had stiffened, even in this short period of sitting; and he had to go down on one knee again to get Plotch back up on his shoulders before rising.

Once more burdened, he plodded ahead again toward the horizon and the descending red light behind the unending clouds. Now that he was once more on his feet and moving, the voiceless gibber of the hobgoblins made itself noticeable again. The stim pill was working through him now, sending new energy throughout his body. Up on his shoulders, the frozen body of Plotch felt literally light. But the increase of energy he got from the pill had a bad side effect—for he seemed to hear the hobgoblin voices louder, now.

IV

He had about another two and a quarter hours before the sun started to set along the edge of the horizon; and the wide rocky land began to mix long, eerie black shadows with its furnace-glare of sunset light. He stopped at last for the night, before the last of the light was gone, wanting to take time to pick a spot where he could be comfortable. He found it, at last, in a little hollow half-filled with stones, so small that they could fairly be called gravel. But, when he laid Plotch down and checked with the pedometer at his knee, he found that the day's walk so far had brought him only a little over seven miles—although the last two hours he had been making as good speed as he could without working himself into breathlessness inside his suit—which could have been dangerous.

He lay down on the gravel. It felt almost soft, through the protection of his suit. He stared up at the darkening cloudbelly overhead. The hobgoblin voices began to increase in volume until they roared in his head, and he began to imagine he saw their faces and bodies as he had in his dream of them, imagined now in the various, scarlet-marked formations of the blackening clouds. He tongued for a tranquilizer; and as it took effect, the light and the forms faded together. The roar sank to a whisper. He slept.

He woke abruptly—to find that the sun was already well above the opposite horizon behind him. The roiling clouds were furnace-bright with a morning redness too fierce to look on, even through his tinted faceplate. He drank a little water, took a stim pill to get himself started and got himself back on his feet with Plotch on his shoulders. Turning his back on the morning light he began a new day's march.

Even through the clouds, the light was strong enough to throw shadows. He kept his own moving shadow pointing straight ahead of him, to be sure he was headed due west. Even with the best he could do about maintaining his bearings, the odds were all against his passing within sight of the ship, itself. On the other hand, once the pedometer showed he was within a three or four mile radius of the ship, he could try to reach them with a constant signal from his suit intercom. And even if the intercom had trouble, the regular scanar watch by the Duty-Lineman then should pick up his moving figure on its screen, if he passed anywhere within horizon distance of the ship.

He took his rest regularly every hour; and he was alert each time to see that he did not exceed the ten minutes he had allowed himself. Together with the exercise and the increasing daylight, he began to warm to his task—even to become expert at it, this business of plodding over an endless rocky desert with the frozen body of Plotch balanced on his shoulders. He grew clever to anticipate little dips, hollows or fissures. The hobgoblins were clamorous; but under the combined effect of the walking and the stim he almost welcomed them.

"Thought you'd helped Plotch to get away from me, didn't you?" he taunted their gibbering, voiceless voices. "Well, see what I'm doing? I'm hanging on to him, after all. How about that, you hobgoblins? Why don't you throw some more rocks at us?"

The voices jabbered without meaning. It struck him suddenly, as an almost humorous fact, that they were not entirely voiceless now. They had gained volume. He could actually—if he concentrated—hear them in his earphones; about as loud as a small crowd of buzzing gnats close to his ears.

"I'll tell you why you don't throw more rocks at us," he told them, after a while. "It's the way I figured it out back at the flitter. You've got to work something like that up; and that takes several days. And you've got to work it up for a particular spot— and I'm moving all the time now. You can't hit a moving target."

His own last words sent him off into a humorous cackle, which he stopped abruptly when he realized it was hurting his dry throat to laugh. He plodded along, trying to remember whether it was time for him to allow himself a drink. Finally, he worked out that it was time—in fact, it was past time. He allowed himself three sips of the recycled water. If he was correct, his shoulder tanks should still be about half full.

But as he went on through the day and as his shadow shortened before him until the most glaring cloud light was directly overhead, he began to feel the effort of his labors, after all. He took advantage of the sunlight being overhead to rest for a little longer than usual, until XN-4010's star should once more have moved ahead of him.

It was still too high in the cloud-filled sky for him to use it as a directional guide, when he forced himself to his feet once more. But he walked with his faceplate looking ahead and down, noting the short shadows thrown backward by the rocks he passed and making sure that he walked parallel to those shadows.

Meanwhile, the hobgoblin voices got louder. By mid-afternoon they were very nearly deafening. He was tempted to take a transquilizer, which he knew would tune them down. But he was afraid that a tranquilizer would have just enough of a sedative effect to make the now almost intolerable job of carrying Plotch over the uneven ground too much for him.

By the time the sun was far enough down the western sky to be visible as a bright spot behind the clouds ahead of him, he was staggering with fatigue. He stopped for one of his breaks and fell instantly asleep—waking over an hour later. It took two stim pills this time, washed down with several extra swallows of the precious water to get him on his feet and moving. But once he was upright he cackled at the hobgoblin voices which had once more thronged around him.

"Just call me Iron Man Clancy!" he jeered at them hoarsely, through a raw throat and staggered on toward the horizon.

At the end of the day, his pedometer showed that he had covered nearly sixteen miles. He exulted over this; and, exulting, fell into sleep the way a man might fall into a thousand-foot-deep mine shaft. When he woke, the next day was well started. The sun was a full quarter of the way up the eastern horizon.

Cursing himself and Plotch both, he stimulated himself and struggled to his feet and set out once more. That day he began to walk into nightmares. The hobgoblin voices became quite clear—even if they still gibbered without sense—in his earphones. Moreover, now as he staggered along, it seemed to him that from time to time he caught glimpses of turnip heads and skinny limbs peering at him from time to time, or flickering out of sight when he glanced quickly in the direction of some boulder larger than the others.

Also, this third day of walking, he found he had lost all logical track of the time and the periods of his rest halts. Several times he fell asleep during a halt in spite of himself; and, by the time the red furnace-glow of the sun was low behind the clouds on the horizon before him, he was simply walking until he could walk no more, then resting until he could walk again . . . and so on . . .

At the end of the day the pedometer showed that, to the nearly sixteen miles covered the previous two days, he had added only seven. There was a good eight miles to go yet before he would be— theoretically at least—in the neighborhood of the spaceship.

Eight miles seemed little after covering more than twenty. But also, it seemed to him, as he sank down for the night and unloaded Plotch from his shoulders, that the eight miles might as well be eight hundred. Literally, he felt as if he could not take another step. Without bothering to find a comfortable position, he stretched out on the bare rock beneath him; and sleep took him with the suddenness of a rabbit taken by the silent swoop of a great horned owl.

—When he woke on the fourth day, he had Plotch on his shoulders and was already walking. It seemed to him that he had been walking for some time, and the moving shadow of himself projected before him, which he followed, was already short.

Around him, the desert of bare rock had altered. Its loose boulders, its little rises and hollows, its fissures— all of these had somehow melted together and changed so that they made up the walls and rooftops of a strange weird city of low buildings, straggling in every direction to the horizon. The flat rock he walked on flowed upward off to his left to become a wall, tilted away to his right to become a roof; and among all these buildings, the city was aswarm with the hobgoblins.

V

Gray-bodied, turnip-headed and skinny-limbed, they swarmed the streets of their city; and all those within view of Clancy were concerned with him and Plotch. They were concerned *for* him, they implied, in their leering, jeering way. Their gibber still would not resolve itself into words; but somehow he understood that they were trying to tell him that the way he was going he would never make the spaceship. For one thing, he had gotten turned around and was headed in the wrong direction. His only hope of making it to the ship was to sit down and rest.—Or, at least, to leave Plotch behind, turn around and head back the way he had come. They were trying to help him, they suggested, even as they sniggered, and postured and danced about him. But somehow, a certain sort of animal cunning would not let him believe them.

"No!" he stumbled on through their insubstantial mass of gesticulating bodies. "Got to get Plotch to the ship. If I leave him, he'll get away from me." Clancy giggled suddenly, and was shocked for a second at hearing the high-pitched sound within the close confines of his own helmet. "I want him back Earthside."

No! No! The hobgoblins gibbered and made faces and jostled about him. *Plotch is through living. Clancy will be through unless he leaves Plotch behind.*

"You don't fool me," Clancy muttered, reeling and stumbling ahead with the dead weight of Plotch on his shoulders. "You don't fool me!"

After a while, he fell.

He twisted as he went down, so that the stiff body of Plotch landed on top of him. Lying flat on his back on the ground with the hobgoblin's bodies and faces forming a dome over them, Clancy giggled once again at Plotch.

"Hope I didn't chip you any, old boy." He grinned at Plotch.

He lay there for a while, thinking about everything and nothing. The labor of getting back to his feet and getting Plotch once more up on his head and shoulders loomed before him like the labor of climbing up the vertical side of a mile-high mountain. It was just not to be done. It was humanly impossible. But, after a while, he found himself trying it.

He got to his knees, and after a great deal of slow effort, managed to get Plotch balanced once more stiffly on his helmet and his shoulders. But when he came to rise from his knees to his feet, bearing Plotch's weight, he found his legs would not respond.

You see, said a large hobgoblin smirking and pulling his rubbery face into different grotesque shapes directly in front of Clancy's faceplate, *Clancy has to leave Plotch if Clancy is going to get to the spaceship.*

"To hell with you!"

Somehow, with some terrific effort and a strength that he did not know was still in him, Clancy found himself back on his feet once more, carrying Plotch. He tottered forward, wading through the hobgoblins that clustered around him. There was nothing substantial about their bodies to clog and hold back the movement of his legs, but their attempts to stop him wearied his mind. After forty or fifty steps he stumbled and fell again, this time losing his grip on Plotch, who tumbled to the rock, but lay there, apparently unbroken. Clancy crawled to the unmoving figure through the clutching mist of gray hobgoblin bodies.

"You all right, Plotch?" Clancy muttered.

He patted Plotch's stiff, suited body from helmet to boots. As far as touch could tell, there was no damage done. Then he saw that above the frost the faceplate was starred with cracks. Gently he probed it with the gloved fingers of his right hand. But, while cracked, the faceplate seemed to be still holding together.

"All right, Plotch," he muttered. He made one more effort to get Plotch on his shoulders, and himself on his feet; but his body would no longer obey him. Still kneeling, half-crouching over the figure of Plotch, he fell asleep. At first the sleep was like all the other sleeps, then gradually a difference began to creep in.

He found himself dreaming.

He was dreaming of his appointment ceremony as a Line-man back in the main tower of Line Service Headquarters, back on Earth. He and all the other cadets were dressed in the stiff, old-fashioned green dress uniforms, which, in his case, he had not put on again since. The uniforms had a high stand-up collar; and the collar edge of the cadet in front of him had already worn a red line on the back of the cadet's neck. The man kept tilting his head forward a little to get the tender, abraded skin away from the collar edge, while the voice of the Commandant droned on:

"*. . . You are dedicating yourself today,*" the Commandant was saying, harshly, "*to the Line, to that whole project of effort by which our human race is reaching out to occupy and inhabit the further stars. Therefore you are dedicating yourselves to the service of your race; and that service is found within the Line from everyone in our headquarters staff out to the most far-flung, two-man teams on new Terminal or Relay Worlds. All of us together make up the Team which extends and maintains the Line; and we are bound together by the fact that we are teammates. . . .*"

The Commandant, Lief Janssen, was still senior officer of the Line Service. He was a tall, stiff military-looking man with gray hair and gray mustache, trim and almost grimly neat in his green uniform with its rows of Station Clusters. He made an imposing figure up on the rostrum; and at the time of the appointment ceremony Clancy had admired the Commandant greatly. It was the past five years that had changed Clancy's mind. Janssen was plainly pretty much a man of straw—at least where R. and E. was concerned. It was strange that such an effective-looking man should prove so weak; and that a small book-keeperish-looking character like Charles Li, the Head of R. and E., should turn out to be such a successful battler. Theoretically, the two Services were independent and equal, but lately R. and E. had been doing anything it wanted to the Line Team.

Up on the platform, in Clancy's dream, the Commandant continued to drone on. . . .

"*. . . For, just as the human race is the Line, so the Line is the Line Team, in its single ship sent out to hook up a new Relay or Terminal Station. And the Team in essence is its two and three-man units, sent out to work on planetary surfaces heretofore untrodden by human foot. The race is the Line Service. The Service is the Line Team, and the Line Team is each and every one of your fellow Linemen. . . .*"

The speech was interminable. Clancy searched for something in his mind to occupy himself with; and for no particular reason he remembered an old film made of the hunting of elephants in Africa, before such hunting was outlawed completely. The hunters rode in a wheeled car after the elephant herd, which, after some show of defiance had turned to run away. Standing up in the back of the wheeled car, one of the hunters shot—and one of the large bull elephants staggered and broke his stride.

Clearly the animal had been hit. Soon he slowed. A couple of the other bulls, evidently concerned, slowed also. The hit elephant was staggering; and they closed in on either side of him, pushing against him with their great gray flanks to hold him upright.

For a while this seemed to work. But the effects of the shot were telling—or perhaps the hunter had fired again, Clancy could not remember. The wounded elephant slowed at last to a walk, then to a standstill. He went down on his front knees.

The other two bulls would not abandon him. They tried to lift him with their trunks and tusks; but he was too heavy for them. Up close, the hunter in the wheeled cart fired another shot in close. There was a puff of dust from behind the elephant's ear where the bullet hit. The wounded bull shivered and rolled over on its side and lay there very still.

It was plain he was finally dead. Only then did the other two bulls abandon him. Screaming with up-curled trunks at the wheeled cart, they faced the hunter for a moment, stamping, then turned and ran with the rest of the herd. The hunter and the others in the wheeled cart let them go . . .

In his dream, it seemed to Clancy that the elephant was suddenly buried. He lay in a cemetery with a headstone above his grave. Going close, Clancy saw that the name on the headstone was *Art*. There was something else written there; but when he tried to go closer to see—for it was just twilight in the graveyard and not easy to read the headstones—a dog lying on the grave, whom he had not noticed, growled and bared its fangs at him, so that he was forced to back off. . . .

Slowly, from his dreams of graduating ceremonies, elephants and graveyards, Clancy drifted back up into consciousness. It seemed that he must have been sleeping for some time; and his mouth was wet, which meant that somehow he must have been drinking water—whether from his suit reserves, or from some other source. But he did not feel now as if he had his suit around him.

VI

He opened his eyes and saw, at first, nothing but white, the white walls and ceiling of a small room aboard a spaceship. Then he became conscious of a girl standing beside the bed.

She was dressed in white, also, so at first he thought that she was a nurse—and then he noticed that she wore no nurse's cap, only a small, strange-looking gold button in the lapel of her white jacket.

"Who're you?" asked Clancy, wonderingly. "Where is this?"

"It's all right, you can get up now," the girl answered. "You're on our ship. We're Research and Experimentation Service, and we just happened to land less than half a mile from where you were. So we picked you up and brought you in. Luckily for you. You were headed exactly in the wrong direction."

"And Plotch?" Clancy demanded.

"We brought in your teammate, too," she answered.

Clancy sat up on what he now saw was a bunk, and sat on the edge of it for a moment. He was wearing the working coveralls he normally wore underneath the suit; but they seemed to have been freshly cleaned and pressed—which was good. He would not have liked to face this very good-looking girl in his coveralls, as they must have been after six days of his wearing the suit.

"R. and E.?" he echoed. For a second her words seemed to make sense. Then the great impossibility of what she was saying, struck him.

"But you can't have landed a ship on XN-4010!" he said to the girl, getting to his feet. "We're still just putting out the Star-Point terminals. The only way another ship could get here would be to home in on the drone that our Line ship homed in on; and that's been inactive since our second day here, when we started cannibalizing it for Station parts!"

"Oh, no. This ship," she answered, "uses a new experimental process, designed to bypass the wasteful process of sending out a thousand drones in hopes that one may home in on a planet that may be used as a Terminal or Relay point for a ship shifted from Earth. But here comes someone who can explain it much better than I can."

A short, round-faced man with black hair and a short, black mustache had come briskly into the room. After a second, Clancy recognized him from seeing him on news broadcasts, back on Earth. He was Charles Li, Head of the Research and Experimentation Service; and he wore a long white coat, or smock, buttoned in front, with a small gold button like the girl's in his lapel.

It was strange, thought Clancy woozily, how an impressive figure like Janssen could turn out to be so incapable of protecting his own Service, while someone like this fuzzy-looking little man could prove to be so effective. You certainly could not judge by appearances. . . .

"I heard what you said, young man," snapped Li, now, "and I'd warn you against judging by appearances. The method that brought this special ship here is a gadget of my own invention. Of course, it's a million-to-one chance that we should land right beside you, out here; but that's what scientific research and experimentation deal with today, isn't it? Million-to-one chances?"

Clancy had to admit silently that it was. Certainly most of the R. and E. gadgets in their survival suits seemed to represent million-to-one shots at coming up with something useful. But Li was already taking Clancy by the arm and leading him out into and down a white-painted corridor of the ship.

"But there's something you need to do for us," he said in steely, commanding tones, his grip hard on

Clancy's arm. "It's imperative your transmit ship be told of our arrival, as soon as possible. But the very nature of the device which brought us here—top secret, I'm afraid, so I can't explain it to you now—places us under certain restrictions. None of us aboard here can be spared to make the trip to your ship; and the nature of our equipment makes it impossible for us to send a message over ordinary inter-ship channels."

He led Clancy into a room which Clancy recognized as an airlock. His suit was waiting for him there.

"We're sorry to put you to this trouble, particularly just after recovering from a good deal of exhaustion and exposure," said the black-mustached man briskly. "But we have to ask you to put your suit on once again and finish your walk to your spaceship, to tell them that we're here."

"Why not?" said Clancy. He began to get into his spacesuit, while the other two watched; the girl, he thought, with a certain amount of admiration in her eyes.

"Yes, it's too bad one of us can't be spared to go with you," said the mustached man. "But we have no outside suits aboard the ship, and then if nothing else one would be needed for protection from the hobgoblins."

"Protection—?" echoed Clancy. He paused, in the midst of sealing the trunk of his suit. For the first time it struck him that he could not hear the voiceless gibber of the hobgoblins here.

The mustached man must have divined his thought, for he answered it.

"Yes," he said. "The special hull materials of this ship shield us from hobgoblin attempts to control us. A refinement of the shielding material in your suits. That same sort of protection we now have will be necessary for future Line Teams and whoever chooses this planet. I will have to recommend it once we get back to Earth."

"Yeah," said Clancy, putting on his helmet, but

with the faceplate still open. "I could have used some of that shielding myself, before this."

"You've done a marvelous job, Lineman," said Charles Li, "in resisting hobgoblin attack so far. They haven't been able to affect you at all, no matter how exhausted you've become. That will be going in my report, too. Well—good luck! And remember, head back the way you came."

Li reached out to shake hands. But, just at that moment, Clancy remembered something.

"Plotch!" he said. "I've got take Plotch on in with me! He'll need medical attention."

"I'm afraid it's too late for medical attention." Li shook his head sharply. "Your teammate is dead."

"No, he isn't!" insisted Clancy. "You don't understand. There was a cryogenic unit in his suit."

"Yes, I know all about that," Li interrupted, "but you're mistaken. The cryogenic unit was actally in one of the other suits. Your teammate is indeed dead. Come along, I'll show him to you."

He turned and led the way once more into the corridor, the girl and Clancy following. They went down the corridor a little way and into another room with a single bunk in it. On this bunk lay Plotch, in his suit, but with the faceplate open and unfrosted; and with his hands folded on his chest. His face had the stiff, powdered and rouged look of a body that has been embalmed.

"You see?" said Li, after a moment. "I sympathize with you. But your friend is quite dead; and carrying him, you might not have the strength to make it to your ship. You can leave him safely to us to be taken care of." Clancy stared at Plotch, he did not believe Li. He thought he detected a slight rise and fall of Plotch's chest, under his coveralls, which were now as clean and pressed as Clancy's own.

But cleverly, Clancy saw the futility of arguing with the powerful Head of the R. and E. Service. Clancy nodded his head and went back out into the corridor; he began to fasten up his faceplate.

"Don't bother to show me out," he said, grinning. "I can handle the airlock by myself."

"Good luck, then," said the mustached man. He and the girl shook hands with him and then went off down the corridor, around a bend of it, and disappeared. Clancy turned and walked heavily to the airlock entrance, walked into it, waited a second, then turned and tiptoed back into the corridor and back up to the room in which Plotch lay.

Even thawed out in his suit, Plotch was a heavy load to get up from the bunk, but Clancy closed his faceplate and got him up in his arms in the same awkward, front-carrying position in which he had first tried to carry the other away from the smashed flitter. Carrying Plotch, he tiptoed back out into the corridor into the airlock and cycled the lock open. Once outside, with the airlock's outer door closed behind him, he started tiptoeing off toward a sunlight-blazoned patch of clouds, which was only an hour or two above horizon. He was almost sure it was nearly sunset and that he was still headed in his original direction.

As he went, the weight of Plotch forced him down off his toes, to walk flat-footedly. Slowly, Plotch seemed to gain heaviness, and tremendous weariness began to flood back into Clancy. He was dreadfully thirsty. But when he gave in at last to temptation and sucked on the water tube in his helmet, only a little raspy gasp of moisture-laden air came through his mouth. Somehow, although he could not remember doing it, he must have emptied his reserve water supply. But he could have sworn that there had been some liquid still in reserve.

However, there was no help for him now. As if in compensation, he made the discovery that Plotch had frozen stiff once more in the same old position. Almost without thought, he maneuvered the frozen body back up on his helmet and shoulders in the same position in which he had carried it so far and tottered on toward the red, glaring patch of sunlight-illumined cloud before him.

His head swam. With every step, the efforts of

moving seemed to grow greater. But now he had no
strength left, even for the process of reason. He did
not know exactly why he was carrying Plotch, with
such great effort, toward the sunset; and it was too
great an effort to reason it out. All he had strength
for was to plod onward, one foot after another, one
foot after another. . . .

Several times it seemed to him that he passed out,
or went to sleep on his feet. But when he woke up he
was still walking. . . .

Finally, he had lost all contact with his body and
its strange desire to carry a frozen Plotch into the
sunset. He stood as if apart from it in his mind and
watched with a detached and uncurious amazement
as that body staggered on, tilting precariously now
and then under its burden, but never quite going
down, while the landscape danced about it, one moment being rocky plain—the next a fantastic, low-
walled city thronged with hobgoblins—the next a
dusty African plain where elephants fled before hunters in a wheeled cart. . . .

He was still walking when the sun went down. And
after that he remembered nothing . . . when he finally came to again, it was to a fuzzy, unreal state.
He was lying on some flat surface and a body was
bending over him; but the features in the face of the
body danced so that he could not identify whoever it
was. But, in spite of the unreality of it all, the smells
were hard and familiar—the interior stink of a Line
transmit ship, the smell of his own bunk aboard it, a
mingled odor of men and grease.

VII

"He'll be all right," a familiar voice said above him.
It came from the figure with the mixed-up features,
but it was the voice of Jeph Wasca, his Team Captain.

"Plotch?" Clancy managed to croak.

"What?" The blurry figure with the dancing features bent down close to Clancy's face.

"Plotch. . . ." Clancy felt the strength draining out

of him. After a few seconds, the figure straightened up, the dancing face withdrawing.

"I can't understand you. Tell me later, then," said Jeph's voice, brusquely. "I haven't got time to talk to you now, Clance. You go to sleep. When you wake up, you'll be back Earthside."

The indefinite figure withdrew, and all the fuzzy lights, colors, sounds and smells surrounding Clancy whirled themselves into a funnel that drew him down into dark unconsciousness.

When he woke this third time, he was indeed—as Jeph had promised—Earthside. He could tell it, if no way else, by the added pull of gravity, holding him down harder upon the bed in which he lay. The room he opened his eyes upon was plainly a hospital room, and there was a bottle of glucose solution with a tube leading to a needle inserted in his wrist.

He felt as if he had spent half a year locked up in a packing case with a pack of angry bobcats. Where he was not sore, he ached; and he did not feel as if he had strength enough to move the little finger of one hand. He lay for a while, placidly and contentedly watching the featureless white ceiling above him, and then a nurse came in. She put a thermometer sensor-strip into his mouth briefly, and then took it out again to examine it. Once his lips were free, he spoke to her.

"You're a real nurse?" he asked.

She laughed. She had freckles on her short nose, and they crowded together when she laughed out loud.

"They don't let imitations work in this ward," she said. "How're you feeling?"

"Terrible," he said. "But just as long as I don't try to move, I feel fine."

"That's good," she said. "You just go on not trying to move. That's doctor's orders for you anyway. Do you think you're up to having some visitors later on this afternoon?"

"Visitors?" he asked.

"Your Line Team Captain," she said. "Maybe some other people."

"Sure," Clancy said. She went out; and Clancy fell asleep.

He was awakened by someone speaking gently in his ear and a light touch on his shoulder. He opened his eyes and looked up into the face of Jeph standing at his bedside with another man—a tall man standing a little behind him.

"How are you feeling, Clance?" Jeph asked.

"Fine," answered Clancy sleepily. His fingers groped automatically for the bed-control lever at the bedside and closed upon it. He set the little motors whirring to raise him up into half-sitting position. "The nurse said you might be in to see me."

"I've been waiting to see you," said Jeph. "Got somebody here to see you." The man behind Jeph moved forward; but Clancy's eyes were all on Jeph.

"Plotch?" Clancy asked.

"He's going to be all right," Jeph answered. "They've got him defrosted and on his way back to normal—thanks to you."

"Don't thank me!" exploded Clancy. "Jeph, I can't take that guy any more! If I have to take any more of him, I'll kill him!"

"Relax," said Jeph. "I've known that for some time. I made up my mind some months back that one of you had to leave the Team."

"One of us—" CLancy went rigid, under the covers of the bed.

"Plotch's being transferred."

Clancy relaxed.

"Thanks," he muttered.

"Don't thank me," said Jeph. "You earned it. You saved all our necks out there on XN-4010—and more. That's why the Commandant's here to talk to you."

Clancy's gaze shot past Jeph for the first time; and the tall man stepped right up to the bedside. It was Janssen all right, with his gray, bristling little military mustache, just as Clancy remembered him. Janssen smiled stiffly down at Clancy.

Clancy's nerves, abraded by his sessions with the hobgoblins, took sudden alarm.

"What about?" he demanded warily.

"Let's get you briefed first," said Janssen sharply. He pulled up a chair and sat down, kicking another chair over to Jeph, who also sat down.

"Sorry to put you through your paces like this," Janssen said, not sounding sorry at all, "just the minute you get your eyes open. But when the time's ripe, the time's ripe. We've got someone else due to meet us here; and he may want to ask you some questions. I'm going to be asking you some questions for his benefit, in any case; and what I want you to do is just speak up. Give us both straight answers, just the way they come to you. You've got that?"

Clancy nodded again, warily.

"All right. Now, to get you briefed on the situation," said Janssen. "First, it seems you ran into something new out there on XN-4010. That planet's got an actual sentient life form, which exists as something like clouds of free electrons. Beyond that, we don't know much about them, except for three things; none of which we'd have known if you hadn't managed to carry Plotch on foot all the way back to the ship. One—"

Janssen held up a knobby forefinger to mark the point.

"—They can move material objects up to a certain size, with a great deal of effort—as in that shower of rocks you remember," he said. "But evidently it's not easy for them. Also, they can affect human thinking processes—up to a point. Again, though, it's not easy for them. For one thing, any kind of material envelope, like the body of a ship, or a flitter, or a suit like you were wearing, shields them out to a certain extent, depending on its thickness. For another, it seems they only become really effective if the human is the way you were, near the end of your walk—in a highly exhausted condition; the kind of condition where lack of sleep or extreme effort might have brought you to the point of hallucinations, anyway. Third— and most important—they were trying to kill off all the men of your Team. It seems they were able to understand that with the drone dismantled, the ship unmanned and the terminal not yet fully built and operative, there'd be no way for another ship out to XN-4010. In fact, the chances of our hitting the planet on a blind-transmit once more, let alone getting another drone safely landed on it, were microscopic. For some reason they didn't want us to know about their existence; and that suggests that maybe they wanted to make preparations of some kind—either for defense or offense against the human race."

He paused.

"Lucky for us," he said brusquely to Clancy, "*you* frustrated them."

"Just by bringing Plotch in?" Clancy demanded. There was something disproportionate in all this. He did not trust Janssen at all.

"That's right, Clance," said Jeph. "There's something you don't know. If you'd decided to sit down out there and wait for rescue, you'd have dried up to dust inside your suit before any rescue came."

Clancy stared at the Team Captain.

"All but one flitter and two-man crew," said Jeph slowly, "were out on jobs—and the closest one out was farther away from the ship than you and Plotch were. Clance, every one of those flitters was smashed by rock showers, and its crew killed or stranded.

VIII

Clancy swallowed for the moment forgetting the Line Commandant.

"Who ..." he could not finish the question. He only stared at Jeph with bright eyes. Jeph answered slowly, but without any attempt at emotion.

"Fletch," the Team Leader said, "Jim, Wally, Pockets, Ush and Pappy."

Clancy lay still for a moment, gazing at the wall of the room opposite. Then he looked back at Jeph.

"What kind of replacements are we getting?" he asked. He looked at Janssen challengingly.

"The best," answered the Commandant. "And I'll

keep that promise. Again, because of you and your bringing Plotch in on foot."

"I still don't see what that did—" Clancy broke off, suddenly thoughtful.

"Now you start to see, don't you?" said Jeph. "There were three of us and one flitter left in the spaceship. Twelve men and six flitters—including you and Plotch, all the other flitters and men we had—were out on work location. All of them overdue, and none of them back. What was I going to do? I could not risk sending out the two men I had left for fear the same thing would happen to them— they might not come back. On the other hand, without the Star-points all finished, there was no way we could transmit the ship back Earthside. The only thing was for the three of us to stay put and keep the ship powered. We couldn't transmit or receive, but with luck we could act as a beacon for another blind drone transmit from Earth— once Earth figured we were in trouble."

Jeph paused. Clancy slowly nodded.

"Then you came staggering in, with your load of frozen Plotch," said Jeph. "We shoved Plotch into the freeze-chamber and tried to find out from you what had happened. You weren't up to talking consciously; but I pumped you full of parasympathetic narcos, and you babbled in your sleep. You babbled it all. Once I knew what I was up against, I was able to risk my last flitter and my last two men to go out on quick rescue missions to each of the work-points. After that we went out with the men who were left for only a couple of hours on the job at a time, until the last Star-point was finished and we could transmit ourselves back here."

Clancy nodded again. He was thinking of Jim, Wally, and all the rest who had not come back, looking out the window of his room at the green hospital grounds outside with unfocused eyes. Someone else had just come into the room; but Clancy was too full of feeling to bother to look to see who it was. He was aware of Jeph and the Commandant turning briefly to glance toward the newcomer, then they were back looking at him.

*   *   *

"All right," Janssen said grimly, with one eye still on whoever had just come in. "Let's have your attention Lineman. There's a question some people may be wanting to ask you. That's how you were able to see through what the hobgoblins were trying to do to you, in making you leave Plotchin and go off in the wrong direction; once they'd gotten you to hallucinating about a new experimental type ship that didn't need the Line to shift from Earth out to XN-4010?"

Clancy scowled down at the white bedspread.

"Hell," he grumbled, "I didn't see through it! I mean I didn't start adding up reasons until later. Like the rescue ship landing right beside me; and the people on her using our Team's own word for the 'hobgoblins'; when they hadn't heard me calling them that myself."

"But you didn't leave Plotchin the way they wanted you to. And you didn't take their word for it that you were headed wrong for your ship," said Janssen.

"Of course not!" Clancy growled. "But it was just because I felt there was something wrong about it all; and I wasn't going to leave Plotch behind, as long as there was a chance they were lying about his being dead."

"All right. Wait a minute." It was the newcomer to the room speaking. He stepped close to the bedside. "Wasn't I given to understand you hated this teammate of yours—this, uh, Plotchin?"

Clancy looked up and goggled. He was gazing at a short man with a round face, black hair and a little black mustache. The man of his hallucination, only this time he was real: Charles Li, the head of Research and Experimentation Service.

Li's voice was not as deep as it had been in Clancy's hallucination—in fact there was almost a querulous note in it. But he sounded decisive enough.

"Why—I still hate him!" snapped Clancy. "I hate his guts! But that didn't mean I was going to leave him out there!"

He stared at Li. Li stared back down at him.

"I guess you haven't heard the latest interpretation

of that, Charlie," Janssen said stiffly to Li, and the head of R. and E. turned about to face the Commandant. "Our Service psychologists came up with a paper on it just a couple of hours ago—I'll see you get a copy of it by the end of the day."

Li frowned suddenly at Janssen.

"Never mind," Li said, "just give me the gist of it."

"It's simple enough," said Janssen. "The immaterial life forms on XN-4010 got control of Clancy's conscious mind. But the only way they could make him hallucinate was by telling him what he *ought* to see and then letting him drag the parts to build the hallucination out of his own mind and memory. So while they had control of him pretty well, consciously, they never did get down into the part of him where his unconscious reflexes live. And did you know that team loyalty lives down among the instincts in some men, Charlie?"

"Team loyalty, an instinct?" Li frowned again. "I don't know if I can see that."

"Take my word for it, then," said Janssen, "but it's easy enough to check." He looked down at the shorter man. "Not only humans, a lot of the social animals have the same reflex. Porpoises hold another porpoise up on top of the water after he's been knocked unconscious, so that he won't drown—that's because the porpoise breathing mechanism is conscious, not unconscious like ours. Land animals too."

"Elephants . . ." muttered Clancy, suddenly remembering. But none of the other men were paying any attention to him.

"Under an instinct like that," Janssen was going on, raspingly, to the R. and E. Service Head, "the loyalty of every team member is to the team. And every other man on it. And the loyalty of the team's to him, in return. As long as there's a spark of life left in him, his teammates will do anything they can, at any cost to themselves, to care for him, or rescue him, or bring him home safely—"

"Lief, not one of your spiels, please—" began the

shorter man, but Janssen overrode him by sheer power of voice.

"*But*," went on the Commandant, "the minute he's dead, their obligation's lifted. Because they all know that now he has to be replaced by a new man on the Team, someone to whom the loyalty they used to owe the dead man will have to be transferred. What tripped up those hobgoblins on XN-4010 was the fact that Clancy here couldn't be sure Plotchin was dead. It didn't matter how much he hated Plotchin; or how overwhelming the evidence was that Plotchin was dead, or that trying to save Plotchin might only mean throwing his own life away, too. As long as the slightest chance was there that Plotchin could be rescued, Clancy was obligated by his Team instinct to do his best for his teammate. That's why Clancy brought the man in, in spite of how he felt about him, personally, and in spite of all those aliens could do, and in spite of the near physical impossibility, even under the lower gravity there, of carting a frozen dead man, weighing nearly as much as he did, for miles."

Janssen stopped talking. All the while he had been speaking, Li's face had been growing sourer and sourer, like a man who had discovered a worm in the apple into which he has just bitten.

"Can I talk now?" demanded Li. The querulous note in his voice was mounting to a pugnacious whine.

"Go ahead," said Janssen.

"All right." The smaller man drew a deep breath. "What's this all about? You got me over here to see this man, telling me you had something to show me. Evidently you wanted to prove to me he's a hero. All right, I agree. He's a hero. Now, what about it?"

Janssen turned to Jeph.

"Shut the door, there," he ordered. Jeph complied. Janssen's eyes raked from the Line Team Captain to Clancy. "And if either of you breathe a word of what you hear in this room from now on, I'll personally see that you get posted out on a job two hundred light-years from Earth, and forgotten there."

IX

Clancy's stomach floated suddenly inside him, as if an elevator he was in had just dropped away under the soles of his feet. His premonitions of trouble on seeing Janssen had been only too correct. Here, the man who had evidently lost five years of battles with the head of R. and E. was about to take one more swing at the other Service Head, using Clancy as a club. Two guesses, thought Clancy, as to what the outcome would be—and what would happen to Clancy himself as a result.

He had escaped the hobgoblins of XN-4010, only to be trapped and used by the super-hobgoblin of all—his own tough-talking, but ineffective Line Service Commandant. There he was now—Janssen—tying into Li as if he'd been the winner all these last five years, instead of the other way around.

"I'm glad to hear you admit that, Charlie," Janssen was snapping "because Clancy here *is* a hero. A real, live hero. A man who damn near killed himself doing a superhuman job in the face of inimical alien action to save his teammate. Only he nearly didn't make it, because he was already chewed down past the exhaustion point when he started. Not just from fighting his job and aliens—but from being worn thin by a round damn dozen of your Service's useless ivory-tower experiments, built into his working suit!"

Li stared at him.

"What're you talking about?" bristled Li. "It was the collar-innovation on his own suit that kept him from being brained when that rock hit his helmet. If it hadn't been for the experimental cryogenic unit in Plotchin's suit, Plotchin wouldn't be alive now!"

"Sure. Two!" snarled Janssen. "Two gadgets paid off, but of—what? A total of twenty-three, for both men's suits? What did the other twenty-one gadgets do for either of them? I'll tell you. Nothing! Nothing, except to wear them out to the point where they were ready to cut each other's throat like half the rest of my men on the Line Teams nowadays!"

Li's face was palely furious behind the black mustache.

"Sorry. I don't see that!" he snapped. "Your man's still only a hero because the cryogenic unit gave him a revivable teammate to bring back. And credit for the cyrogenic unit being in Plotchin's suit belongs to us!"

"You think so?" grated Janssen. Li's voice had gone high in tone with the argument. Janssen's was going down into a bass growl. Both men looked ready to start swinging at each other at any minute. Janssen's gray mustache bristled at Li. "Stop and think again for a moment. What if your cryogenic unit hadn't worked? What if Plotchin had actually been dead? Clancy wouldn't have had any way of knowing it, for sure. *And so he'd have brought Plotchin in, anyway!* You think you can take his hero status away from him just because your unit worked? He did what he did out of a sense of duty to his teammate—and whether there was a live man or a dead one on top of him at the time doesn't matter."

"So?" snarled Li.

"So!" barked Janssen. "I've been lying back and waiting for something to hang you with, Charlie, for four years. Now I've got it. I'm starting to punch buttons the minute I leave this hospital. We're both of us responsible to Earth Central, and Earth Central's responsible to the taxpayers. I'm going to set the wheels going to bring my hero up in front of a full-dress Central Investigating Committee—to determine whether the excessive number of experiments your Service has been forcing upon my Line Teams might not have caused the Relay Station installation on XN-4010 to fail in the face of attack by inimical aliens, who then might have gone undiscovered and eventually posed a threat to the whole Line, if not to the whole human race."

Clancy had a sudden, irrational impulse to pull the

bedcovers up over his head and pretend they had all gone away.

"Are you crazy?" snarled Li. "You tried fighting me, five years ago, when we first got Central permission to test experimental equipment under working conditions, on your Line Teams. And Central went right along with me all the way."

"That was then, Charlie!" Janssen grated. "That was *then*, when you had all the little glittery, magic-seeming wonder-world-tomorrow type of gadgets to demonstrate on the TV screens and grab the headlines. All I had was honest argument. But now it's the other way around. All you've got is more of the same—but I've got the real glitter. I've got a hero. Not a fake hero, flanged up for the purpose. But a true hero—an honest hero. You can't shoot him down no matter what angle you try from. And I've got villains—real villains, in those alien hobgoblins, or whatever they are. I'm going to win this inquiry the same way you won the last one. Not in the Committee Room, but out in the News Services. I can get you and your experiment wiped clean out of my Service, Charlie! And I'll play hell with your next year's appropriations, to boot!"

Janssen shut up, his mustache stiff with anger. Clancy held his breath, resisting the impulse to shut his eyes. The Line Service Commandant had taken his swing; and now—how, Clancy did not know, but there would undoubtedly turn out to be a way—Li would lower the boom.

"All right," said Li, bitterly. "Damn you, Lief! You know I can't afford any threat to next year's appropriations now that the drone by-pass system is ready to go into field testing! Name your price!"

Clancy blinked. He opened his eyes very wide and stared at Li.

"But you wipe me out, and you'll regret it, Lief!" continued the R. and E. Head, bursting out before Clancy could get his brains unscrambled. "Admit it or not, but a lot of our ivory-tower gadgets, as you call them, have ended up as standard equipment, saving the lives of men on your Teams!"

"Don't deny it!" snapped Janssen. "I don't deny it and never did. And I don't want to wipe you out. I just want to get back the right to put some limit on the number of wild-eyed ideas my men have to test for your lab jockeys! That's all!"

"All right," said Li. He, too was relaxing, though his face was still sour. "You've got it."

"And we'll draw up an intra-Service agreement," said Janssen.

"All right." Li's glance swung balefully to fasten for a second on Clancy. "I suppose you know you'll be holding up progress?"

"That won't matter so much," said Janssen, "as long as I'm upholding my Linemen."

"Excuse me," Li answered stiffly, looking back at him, "I don't see that. As far as I'm concerned, progress comes before the individual."

"It does, does it?" said Janssen. "Well, let me tell you something. You get yourself a fresh crop of laboratory boys out of the colleges, every year, all you want, to work in your nice, neat, air-conditioned labs. But I get only so many men for work on the Line— because it takes a special type and there's only so many of that type born each generation!"

Clancy stared guiltily at Janssen. Clancy's conscience was undergoing an uncomfortable feeling— as if he had just been punched in the pit of his stomach.

"I know," Li was answering, with a sour glance at Clancy. "Heroes."

"Heroes, hell!" exploded Janssen. "Race horses! That's what my boys are—race horses! And you wanted to turn them into pack mules for your own purposes. Not damn likely! Not any more damn likely than I was to roll over on my back and let you get away with using a full-dress Central Investigation Committee to get permission to stick your nose into my Line Service! Open your eyes for once, Charlie! Use your imagination on something living! Can you imagine what it's like to do what these men do, jammed at best into the few clear cubic feet of a tiny transit ship you could cover with a large tent? And at worst—living in their suits out on the job for days on end, working harder than any manual laborer's worked on Earth in fifty years, always under strange conditions and unknown dangers like those hobgoblins on XN-4010?"

Janssen had to stop for a second to draw breath.

"Can you imagine doing that?" he went on. "Just to put in a Line Station for a million fat tourists to use; just about the time you're maybe getting killed or crippled putting in another Station out on some world the tourists have never heard of yet?"

"No, I can't," he said, dryly. "And I don't believe any normal, sensible man can. If the work's that bad, what makes any of your men want to do it?"

"Listen." Clancy propped himself up on one elbow. His conscience and the recognition of how wrong he had been about Janssen was finally bringing him into the fight. It was late. But better late than never.

"Listen—" he said again to Li. "You get a feeling you can't describe at the end of a job—when a working Station finally goes into the line. You feel good. You know you've done something, out there. Nobody else did it, but *you*—and nobody can take it away from you, that you've done it!"

"I see." The short man's mustache lifted a little. He turned to the door, opened it, and looked back at Janssen. "They're romantics, your Linemen. That's it in a nutshell. Isn't it?"

"That's right, Charlie," said the Commandant coldly. "You named it."

"Yes," said Li, "and no doubt the rest of the race has to have them for things like building the Line. But, if you'll excuse me, personally I can't see romantics. Or romanticism, either."

He went out shutting the door.

"No," said Janssen, grimly, looking at the closed door. "You wouldn't. Your kind never does. But we manage to get things done in spite of you, one way or another."

He glared suddenly at Clancy, who was staring at him with a powerful intensity.

"What're you gawking at, Lineman?" he barked.

"Nothing," said Clancy.

Since Life's journey is a way of growing, arriving travellers are not necessarily the same people who embarked earlier.

Babes In the Wood

The dyed lips, the carefully coifed hair, and the elaborately patterned cloak made a brave showing; but the plain fact of her youth shone through like light through a curtained window. Jory Swenson swung away from her in a rage and cursed the hook, a thin little man who licked his lips nervously and squirmed under the tongue-lashing, but would not back down.

"You gutted fool!" stormed Jory. "Are you trying to get me vaporised for abduction? She's just a child."

The hook's little eyes jumped nervously from Jory to the girl.

"What of it?" he husked. "You're going off-planet. Nobody knows. Nobody'll care."

"What if we get picked up before we get to the spaceport?" snarled Jory. He swung abruptly back to the girl. "How old are you?"

"Eighteen," she said, in a small, thin voice.

"Aaah," said Jory, "don't lie to me." He half-raised his hand, threateningly. "You're lucky if you're fifteen."

She shrank a little, her eyes watchfully on his hand, but her voice was firm in answer.

"I'm eighteen."

"I tell you!" burst out Jory "Don't give me that. When did you run away from home?"

"Last week," she said.

"And your people have been looking for you for a week then," said Jory. "That's fine."

"Oh no," interrupted the girl quickly. "They sent me to my aunt's to live. But my aunt—she's dead. She died about a month ago but nobody ever told them and she'd already said in a letter I could come."

"Oh?" said Jory. "Oh?"

"And I'm eighteen," she spoke rapidly, as if afraid he would silence her before she had done speaking. "I've got a work card with my age on. I can prove it."

"Sure," said Jory, sarcastically. The hook tugged impatiently at his arm.

"How long you going to stand here?" he demanded. "The ship lifts in two hours. I tell you this is all the woman I could find you. You take her or you don't get anything."

"Woman!" spat Jory. Then shrugged. "All right. I'm done for anyway if I miss the ship."

The hook went to the door and whistled in his witness, a man as scrawny and unprepossessing as himself. The marriage ceremony was conducted in the hurried chatter of the hook's high voice and the papers signed in a sober silence. Jory paid the little man and turned to his new bride.

"Here we go," he said. "Pick up your bag."

Without a word she lifted the battered clothing box that held her possessions, and followed him out. They stopped under the night lights of the almost deserted street and Jory rang one of the automatic curb signals for a taxi. It came almost immediately and they rode to the spaceport in silence. It was only when they stepped out at their destination and Jory was reaching into his pocket for money to pay the fare that the taxi driver spoke.

"Say," he said, leaning out the window and squinting up at Jory's face in the pale, all-pervading glow of the landing lights, "aren't you the passer that Little Tommy's looking for?"

Jory's fist, still clutching change, came out of his pocket swiftly, and he hit the taxi driver with all his force on the point of his exposed jaw. Coins sparkled and danced ringingly on the concrete; and the man slumped backwards on the seat. Jory whirled to run, but the girl stood frozen, wide-eyed and blank-faced, staring at the unconscious driver.

"No you don't!" snarled Jory. "You don't quit on me now!" And, grabbing her by one wrist, he jerked her away after him in a stumbling run for the looming bulk of the waiting ship.

They lay strapped in their cradles in a two-place cabin, waiting for the takeoff. Jory lay stiffly, his face upturned to the metal ceiling, listening to the girl cry. The sound infuriated him, the more so because he could do nothing about it, could not reach out to slap her into silence because of the straps that bound him in the cradle; and he dared not loosen the straps for fear of being caught unprotected at the takeoff.

"Shut up!" he said tightly through clenched teeth. The girl continued to sob.

"I didn't know—" she moaned. "I didn't know—"

"Didn't know what?" Jory grinned grimly, sarcastically, at the dull ceiling. "That I was a bad man? A nasty criminal?"

There was no answer but the sobs.

"Well I am," said Jory, still talking to the ceiling. "But you could have done worse, Kiddie. Believe me, you could have done a lot worse." There was still no answer and suddenly anger flamed up inside him and he felt an abrupt, furious need to justify himself.

"You little fool," he gritted. "You're lucky you got on a ship at all. There's half a dozen places that hook might have worked you into, instead—don't you know that? Do you think that just because you asked him nice to fix you up with a husband so you could get free emigrant passage, that he was obligated to just that, and not something a hell of a lot worse, but that would make him more money? At least you got what you wanted and you'll have a chance on a new world. That's more than half the Kiddies he contacts get.

"Sure, sure," he went on, calmed a little by the explosion of his own violence, and talking half to

himself, now, "I was a passer, peddling weed to dopes
in the spaceport clubs; and you were a baby going to
school. I've done my share of cutting with the gangs
and the most you ever did was sprinkle insect powder for crawlers. But there's no more of either for you
or me. We're Mr. and Mrs. Jory Swenson, neither
good nor bad, but emigrants with free passage to
Mical V and a government bonus to get us started in
the new life." A siren moaned suddenly through the
ship, warning of takeoff. Jory's lips twisted in a final
grin. "Look on the bright side of it, Kiddie."

Beneath them a vibration began to grow. It mounted
and mounted until the ceiling began to blur before
Jory's eyes, and the sudden thunder of the rockets
cut loose. A giant leaned his weight on Jory, pressing
him back into the padding of his cradle; and the
breath came wailing from his throat as black specks
danced before his eyes. The weight on him grew,
grew, and grew until the whine of the gyroscopes cut
through the din, tilting the ship to escape angle. The
wall tilted and the cradle moved on its tracks, slamming to a new position. Unconsciousness took Jory.

He floated in a haze of unreality and sickness.
There was something wrong with him—with *him*,
Jory; but he could not seem to do anything about it.
Vaguely he was aware that the takeoff was over. That
the changeover to second order flight was over; and
that other passengers moved freely about while he
still lay in his cradle. But something was wrong; for
half the time he was not on the ship at all, but back
on Calezo, running away from Little Tommy.

He was back on Calezo, peddling a package in the
Sherwood Club and Pani had come up to drag him
away from his prospect, to pull him into a dark
corner of the club and tell him to get out. Pani was a
muscle for the same outfit that Jory belonged to and
a straight sort of man. He didn't have anything to
gain by warning Jory—as a matter of fact, he was
sticking his neck out to do it, but they'd known each
other ever since Jory had been old enough to be in
business, and they got along. Cook was dead, Pani

had told Jory, and Little Tommy had taken over his outfit—which meant everybody but Jory was now working for him. Jory, he didn't like; and now with no outfit to protect him, Jory was due for it. In the gloom of the corner, the sweat had rolled down Jory's back as he listened. A long time ago he had cut Tommy bad in a gang fight and the spidery little man remembered what the spindly child had suffered.

Besides, now that he no longer belonged to an outfit, the uniforms would be after him. There was no choice. He had to go off-planet—unless he wanted to hit the woods, and for a city child like Jory, that was unthinkable.

So, in the depths of his delirium he ran again and hid, dodging and ducking through the great rabbit-warren of the city, whose depths and shadows now spelled danger instead of safety; ran and hid until a hook that wanted money more than he feared Little Tommy had found him the wife he needed to get himself passage on an emigrant ship where Government authority would be his protection.

And in his delirium, the running and hiding went on and on.

It passed eventually. He awoke at last to a space-ship cabin that was made of the stuff of solid reality and did not dissolve away into the fantasies of his nightmare. The girl was seated on her cradle, which had been dogged down and converted into a sort of couch, even as his had been flattened into a bed, and reading. She did not notice the new sanity in his eyes.

"How long have I been like this?" he said—and realized that he had not said it, but merely thought the words. He tried again; forced air from his chest with tremendous effort, opened his mouth, and moved lips.

"How long—" he croaked.

Her head jerked up, she dropped the book and bounced to his bedside.

"Oh, you're better!" she gasped—then, hurriedly—"Don't move. I'll get the doctor." She was out the

door and gone from the room before he could force
out another word.

He felt a momentary flash of irritation that she
had not answered his question but he was too weak
to hang on to his anger. She did not return immediately, and he drifted into a light doze from which he
emerged to find the ship's doctor standing over him.

"Better, eh?" said the doctor. He was a stocky,
ruddy little man and he placed one set of fingertips
on Jory's wrist, counting his pulse."

"How long—" repeated Jory.

"Eh?" said the doctor. "About a week and a half,
ship's time. Looks like you're making this trip in bed,
young fella."

"Got to get up," muttered Jory.

"No you don't," said the doctor. "You lie there and
count your blessings, the chief of which is that you're
alive at all. You must have been on the verge of
collapse when you came aboard. How much sleep
had you had during the thirty-six hours before
takeoff?"

For a second the nightmare danced again just outside the range of Jory's vision.

"Don't know," he said numbly. "None."

The doctor snorted.

"Thought so," he said, with an air of satisfaction.
"You listen to me and stick to your bed. Your wife
can look after you. Give her something to do." He
turned to the girl.

"You heard what I told him. Keep him quiet. If he
won't stay down, see me." And, with a brisk wave of
his hand, he was gone.

Jory sagged in the bed. A wave of exhaustion was
sweeping over him, smothering him, forcing him down
into sleep; but there was one thing he had to do
before he yielded. With a great effort he turned his
head on the pillow to look into the girl's eyes, and
the question came out in a husky whisper.

"What's your name? I don't remember."

She blushed, suddenly all child, and dropped her
head.

"Lisa Kent," she answered.

Lisa Kent, Lisa Kent. He hugged the sound of it comfortingly to him as he sank like a stone into the deep, obliterating ocean of sleep.

He recovered slowly, not quite understanding what had made him an invalid. From what little the doctor would tell him (for that individual was one of the uninformative sort) he gathered that the punishment of the takeoff had been not the straw, but the beam which had broken the camel's back, and that if his exhausted condition had been realized at the time of boarding, he would not have been allowed to take off. So much for that. The really important thing was that he was better now and on the way to regaining his strength. The thought that he might have faced landing on a pioneer world in a bed-ridden condition touched him with a thrill of panic whenever he let himself think of it.

However, as time went on, he found himself thinking of it less and less. For some reason, possibly because he had dreamed so much of it in his delirium, the world of his past had acquired a strange unreality. It was if the illness had set itself up as a barrier to the past and everything that he remembered during it and before were part of a half-forgotten fantasy. More and more he found himself thinking of the future from the viewpoint of the hopeful colonist that his papers proclaimed him to be. The vision of a new life painted itself in a hundred different colors for his recuperating imagination and he discovered the beginnings of a new emotion inside him—he was starting to think of the new planet as a home, his real home, the first he had ever known. The barren seed within him as yearning to put down roots.

There was a new factor, too, in the now unstrained atmosphere of the tiny cabin in the relationship between himself and Lisa—he could no longer think of her simply as 'the girl.' Although he remembered nothing of her attendance on him while he had been ill, and although she, herself, never referred to it, both of them were forced to an acceptance of the fact that they had somehow become aquainted. It was just that, although there was no common experience which either wished to refer to, it was now ridiculous for them to treat each other as strangers. Even if one or the other had wished it, his continuing dependence upon her in the intimacy of the small cabin would have denied it. And they found themselves standing on a neutral ground of neither like nor dislike, in the truce of mutual tolerance.

In the weakness and peace of his slowly mending body and spirit, Jory lay propped up on his bed for long periods of time, watching her, as a prisoner, floating in the vacuum of unlimited time, might watch a spider spinning a web. And she, indifferent as the spider, washed, dressed, brushed her hair, waited on him, or sat reading in a sort of happy unconsciousness of his gaze.

He found her fascinating. For the first time in his experience he was entering into the complete, all around the clock life of another human being: and the pageant of her actions was an unvarying source of entertainment to him. He found her responsive to things of the moment, passing suddenly from one emotion to the other with the flickering interest of the young. More child than woman, he found her; but at the same time, more woman-child than child. She seemed to have walled off everything outside the cabin, all past and all future, and to be content in the womb-like security of the present. She was happy—the doctor had been right—with the job of caring for him. It was a happiness that he first attributed to the childish satisfaction of having a doll to play with; but in this he later found he had been uncharitable. She, too, was experiencing the fascination of living a closely-knit existence with another human being.

They did not talk at first, beyond the few words necessary for him to indicate his desires and she to satisfy them. The neutral ground on which they found themselves was an uncertain one and neither was willing to take the first step toward testing its solidity. Inevitably, however, incidents occurred at intervals to throw their speech outside the limits of bare necessity; and it was across the stepping stones of these incidents that they gingerly approached each other, the suspicious wolf to the timorous colt.

The first of these incidents came upon them suddenly, catching them both unprepared in a conversation where neither knew what to say. It came about when Lisa laughed suddenly and unthinkingly at something humorous in the book she was reading, and, looking up, found his eyes upon her; questioningly, she thought. She made a little gesture with the book, explainingly.

"It—it's funny," she stammered in explanation. The expression on his face did not vary, but she sensed in him a struggle for words equal to her own.

"Oh?" he said harshly. And—after a long pause. "What was it?"

"Oh—" she said, and stared at him helplessly. His words were an invitation to read him the passage she had laughed at; and she longed to do so, but her innate timidity made the prospect seem appallingly dangerous.

"Oh—nothing much," she said, finally. He gazed at her for a moment longer, then closed his eyes, turning his head away from her. And she, like a rabbit relieved from the hypnotic stare of a snake, sank her attention gratefully back into the pages she had been reading.

However, the ice had been broken; and, when nothing more out of the way occurred during the next few days, she found herself hoping for a repetition of the brief conversation. Various plans flitted through her head but she shrank from their execution, afraid of the rebuff which she felt sure would follow. At last, when she had almost given up hope, Jory took the plunge she had been avoiding. He had been lying staring at the ceiling, following the 1800 hours meal, when abruptly, without warning, his voice shattered the silence between them.

"You don't get out enough," he said flatly.

Her heart leaped and thudded in her breast.

"You sit around the cabin here all the time," he went on, still without looking at her. "Why don't you go down to the recreation room now and then?"

"Why—" she stammered, "it's all right. I don't mind."

"You don't have to hang around here all the time," he retorted, his voice rising on a note of anger. "I don't need you that much."

Her mind hunted frantically for the proper thing to say and before she knew it the truth came tumbling out.

"But I like it here better!" she cried. Her words seemed to hang in the air between them for a long time. Then the tension in the room snapped like an overstretched string and Jory's rigid figure sagged slightly in relaxation.

"Suit yourself," he muttered.

It was not long after that that he woke in the night hours, and lay in his bed, wondering what had wakened him. For some moments he could not locate the cause; and then it came to him, a slight, steady, rhythmical noise, half-heard in the darkness.

Lisa was crying. Very quietly, very easily, in a reasonless childish way, she was sobbing to herself with her head half-buried in her pillow.

He lay staring into the blackness and listening to her. And gradually the emotional impact of the sound reached through to him. At first it was merely another noise, disturbing, but not greatly so. And then it began to take on greater meaning; a tinge of accusation seemed to grow in it, a lost and hopeless accusation to damn him for strange reasons that he was at a loss to understand, but could not deny. His own emotions twisted and writhed, growing and increasing in violence until the verbal reaction came tearing from his lips and he yelled at her.

"Shut up!"

She shut up. And the sudden silence left him a little frightened.

When he woke the following morning, he noticed that she avoided his eye, and the emotions of the night before returned in full force. She moved about the cabin as usual, taking care of the few housekeeping tasks that were required, but on this particular morning he read a reproach in every expression of her face, in every movement of her body. It was a new sensation to him, a hot and uncomfortable one, and he struggled against the illogicalness of it, struggled in silence and in motionlessness, so that he lay stiff and tight on the bed, his jaw clenched and his eyes staring straight ahead of him.

What bothered him, although he did not know it, was the urge to apologize; for his shouting at her in the night, for his unvarying harshness of word and action, and for everything else in their association for which his new-born sense of guilt accused him. He labored under a complete ignorance, however, of the apology as a social mechanism. It was, quite literally, unknown to him. Child of the gutter, youth of the streets, for him a verbal expression of regret meant only a forced acknowledgment of inferiority. So, the welter of emotions boiled within him, blindly hunting and tearing for an undiscovered exit.

He fought. He fought himself until the sweat stood out in great shining drops on his forehead driven by his own savage determination to find a solution. What he wanted to do, he did not know, but he would do it if he had to tear himself apart in the process. Borne up on the red surge of his anger, he forced himself suddenly up into a sitting position and swung his legs over the side of the bed. A wave of dizziness shook him, but he grabbed the edge of the bed and held on tightly with both hands until it passed.

He shook his head to clear it, and felt Lisa's hands on his shoulders, pressing him back.

"You've got to lie down," her voice said, frightened.

"Let go," he said hoarsely, "sit down yourself. I'm going to talk." Her hands fell from his shoulders and as his vision cleared, he saw her back away and sit down on the edge of her bed.

"Listen," he said. "You were crying last night. You don't have to cry. Hear me?" She shrank slightly into herself.

"I'm sorry," she whimpered. He ignored her, going on talking, forcing the words from his lips by pure brute force, not knowing how to say what he wanted to say, but determined to express himself by pure weight and number of words.

"We got things to talk over. There's things you've got to understand. I'm not dumb—maybe I never learned much outside of gang stuff—but I'm not dumb, and I'm older than you. You and me—you and me—" he stalled, pawing the air for expression, "we aren't either of us what we were back there. And we aren't going to be what we were, either. Hear me? We're going to be different—new, sort of, if you know what I mean. And we can't—won't—be new until we can get over being what we were. You know what I mean?" He glared at her; and she nodded, a little scaredly.

"So," he went on. "We got to get over it. You and me, we're going to land where there's hardly any real cities. Just little places. And we're going to have to do some kind of work to stay alive. Now you—what can you do?"

She looked down at her hands, lying limply together in her lap.

"Nothing," she said in a small voice.

"Look," he said, desperately, "you've been taking care of me. You suppose you could be some kind of a nurse?"

She shook her head.

"You must have had some kind of idea, when you first thought of getting married up and emigrating. You must have figured on doing something. What was it?"

Tears brimmed up suddenly in her eyes as she raised her head and looked at him.

"I was going to be somebody's wife."

"Cut it out!" he shouted defensively. "You don't have to cry. I told you that." She blinked back the tears. "All right, so you were going to be somebody's wife; and he'd take care of things like working. It's all right; I get it. I don't blame you. It's just that I got to find these things out. What else did you figure on?" She toyed with the blanket edge on her couch.

"I thought maybe he could have some kind of a job

and we could have a house of our own—and— things," she ended vaguely.

"Didn't you think maybe you were a little young for stuff like that?"

"I'm eighteen."

"Don't lie to me!" he roared at her suddenly. "I don't care what you do, just don't lie to me." She shrank back from him, white-faced, but nodding her head.

"I don't care how old you are," he went on. "Just don't tell me you're eighteen when I know you're not."

Then suddenly—so suddenly that he could never after remember how it happened—she had thrown herself at him, and was kneeling, clutching at him, her head buried in the lap of his bedrobe and bawling with utter abandon.

"I will too cry if I want," she choked out in a muffled voice.

He stared down at her in complete bafflement and dismay.

"Hell—all right—cry then," he muttered, overwhelmed. She sobbed into his bedrobe; and, after a little while, he reached out gingerly and stroked her hair in a helpless fashion.

It was at this moment that the ship's doctor had the bad luck to open the door in the normal process of making his daily call. His head came in first, and he stared at the two of them.

"Get the God damn it out!" roared Jory and immediately felt better than he'd felt in a long time. The doctor's head disappeared, the door popping to behind him.

Jory went back to stroking Lisa's hair. It felt surprisingly good beneath his hand; and, although he still had not said what he had wanted to say, for some reason he discovered that he was now conscious of a vast relief.

After that, during the remaining days of the trip, they talked. And, after the first few conversations, the speaking was mainly done by Jory and the listening by Lisa. She preferred it that way: for her story was briefly told. Nothing had happened to her beyond the fact that she had grown up and run away from parents who were not too bright and were not interested in her. Simply that; not unkind, not overbearing, but just not interested. She had strangled in the thin atmosphere of their affection; and, having heard about the hooks that paired off single people wishing to emigrate, had seized her chance and run off.

But Jory—he, although his home life had been as barren as hers, had done a thousand interesting things. She listened to chance accounts of his past life as if they had been fairy tales and she a five year old: and it only puzzled her that he, himself, showed little or no interest in them, preferring to talk about other strange things that she could not understand. However, no matter what he said, it was Jory talking, and she listened to all with the same impartial, happy interest.

"You see," said Jory, one day, sitting on the edge of his bed and gesturing excitedly at her, "you and me, we shouldn't be here at all. You understand? This emigration business is for the pioneers, people with itchy feet and the idea that the next planet is always a little better. They claim they're short of space back there, but hell, look at all the brush country that hasn't been touched yet. There's room for a thousand more cities, and the people that really want to settle are just going to stay there and build them, instead of shooting off like this.

"But there's new business going up like mad on the new planets and they need people. So the real pioneers, the people with itchy feet, claim overpopulation and draw free government transportation where the need is, and everybody's happy. But not you and me, Lisa. Understand? We didn't have itchy feet. If you could've found some kind of a husband and I'd been all right with Little Tommy, you and me would never have thought of going off-planet. We'd have stayed where we were and what would have happened?"

He looked at her rhetorically.

"You probably would have ended up being miserable with a male you picked just because he was the first one that came along and sooner or later something would have gone wrong in the Clubs and I'd have been cut up or dragged by the uniforms.

"And instead—look what we fell into," Jory's eyes gleamed with an almost fanatic light, "we were just running away toward the first thing we could find, and we bumped into a chance to wise ourselves up and really get something out of life. It's a miracle, Lisa, I tell you! Me, I'm going to find out what I want to do—what I really want to do—and when I find out I'm going to do it, even if it's hanging upside down from a tree limb and painting the sky green.

"And listen, Lisa—you're going to find out what you want, too. I'll take care of you until you've grown up enough to pick out the man you really want, and then we'll tear up this piece of paper and you can marry him. I'll just claim you're my daughter, or sister, or something and this fake marriage was the only way I could bring you along. It'll be all right, you'll—" he checked himself suddenly, noticing a sullen, set look on her face. "What's wrong now?"

"Nothing."

"Don't tell me 'nothing,'" he said. "I know you. What's wrong."

"I don't want to marry somebody else."

Jory exploded.

"Are you crazy?" he stormed. "Do you want to tie yourself to me when I don't even know what I'm going to be, yet? Maybe it'll be something where I can't have a wife. What makes you think I'd want you, anyway? Oh, hell, it's just what I say. You're too young to know your own mind yet."

"I am not!" cried Lisa, turning on him with blazing face and clenched fists.

"Well, calm down," said Jory, somewhat taken aback. "I'm not going to shove you off on somebody you don't want. But you sure don't seem to appreciate the luck of what's happened to you. I tell you it's a miracle."

But Lisa remained unconvinced.

*　　*　　*

In the days that followed, he set himself to convince her; and, in a measure as his own mental image of the future sharpened and took on color, he succeeded.

"You never lived outside of a city in your life, did you?" he asked her once.

She shook her head.

"And neither did I," said Jory triumphantly. "But that's what we're going to do. Why, even back home, people who were willing to go out into the brush could pile up a fortune in no time—fur-farming or something like that—just because nobody else wanted to get their feet wet or do without taxis. There's always things to do if you're willing to go where other people don't like it."

"Was it really hard to live out there?" asked Lisa, fascinated.

"Sure it's hard," answered Jory. "But it's not impossible. You've got no weather dome, so the temperature goes up and down. We'll get rained on, maybe, or even snowed on. What of it? We can use our government settler's bonus to put up buildings and just stay in them when it's too bad out. And listen, Lisa—"

She had been fiddling with her hair. He reached out, took the comb from her hand and pulled her down on the couch opposite him to ensure her full attention.

"—Listen, Lisa, there's some good parts to it, too. When there's no grey weather dome, you can see the blue sky with clouds the way they have it in pictures. There'll be wild trees and things growing right outside our buildings and real breezes blowing through our windows. Hell, we'll even pick a spot of land with our own private creek running through it like they have in the parks and the big estates."

Lisa's face was one big expression of wonder.

"All these people, though—" she breathed. "They'll all be wanting something like that. Maybe there won't be enough to go around."

Jory laughed in happy scorn.

"You sure are a city kid," he said. "Why this planet

won't be like the one we left. There probably won't be more than two or three cities on it all together."

Liza gazed at him, half-incredulously.

"How many creeks," she ventured, "are there on a whole world?"

"On a whole world?" Jory gestured expansively. "Millions!"

She sighed.

"Millions!" she echoed.

"Sure," said Jory. "And look—don't get the idea we're just going to live like woolies, either. As soon as we get the place set up and start making money, we'll get a flyer and we can drop into the cities any time we want to. We can stay in the hotels and with the money we'll be making out in the brush, we'll be able to hit the best clubs and see the best pictures and everything."

Lisa's eyes misted over suddenly.

"Now what?" snapped Jory.

Lisa tried to stop. She did her best, but two large tears squeezed from under her tightly clamped eyelids and her throat moved convulsively.

"It's just too good to be true," she choked.

"Cut it! Cut it!" snarled Jory. "Every time I talk to you, you end up by flooding us out of here. Can't you do anything but cry?" And he glared angrily across the cabin at her.

But—it was a curiously gentle glare; and Lisa had gotten to know him in the past couple of weeks. So she paid no attention but put her head down on the couch and was just as happily miserable as she wanted to be for the next quarter of an hour.

Landing. For eighteen hours the passengers had been strapped in their cradles. Now they were being carried down the moving ladder of the ship's main corridor, which, now in landing position, had become a deep, vertical shaft. Jory, with Lisa, stood all ready at the bottom, waiting with the others of their passenger section to disembark.

"First group out!" boomed the loudspeaker. "Baggage delivery, information and equipment available in the Government Station at the edge of the field. First group out!"

They shuffled into a double line; and Jory felt Lisa tremble slightly as she pressed closely against him. Her hand groped blindly into his and clung to it with nervous strength. Jory glanced around embarrassedly at the other passengers; but none of these seemed to notice, being fully concerned with their own luggage and selves. He leaned towards her.

"For God's sake! Relax!" he hissed in her ear. "Remember what I told you. There's nothing to get excited about; we're just coming home."

She nodded, obediently remembering that she had promised to think of this new world as the place where they belonged, instead of the old planet they had left. But the thought which had been so comforting in the familiar confines of their cabin before landing was not so much help now that they were actually standing at the head of the covered gangplank with the damp atmosphere of a strange planet blowing in their faces. She clung to Jory.

The immigrants went docilely, in line, down the steps of the gangplank and out onto the field. Beneath the feet of Lisa and Jory the steel steps rang. Then, abruptly, the noise was gone and they stepped forward on the flat cement surface of the field. Two steps more and they would be under the new skies.

"Here we go," muttered Jory cheerfully. They walked forward through the opening at the end of the covered gangplank, out into open air. . . .

. . . and stopped dead.

Go on! Get moving!"

The voices of the other passengers crowding the gangplank behind them, beat on their ears. But Jory and Lisa stood frozen. Children of weather domes and crowded, dingy streets, they looked at the new world.

No past experience of theirs could match the immensity of it. Vast and far the great blue depths of the sky towered above them, reaching out to the far horizon. The golden sun threw dazzling reflections in their eyes from every shiny object, blinding their gaze, long used to artificial glow. The grass, the trees beyond the glittering white concrete of the field, were lush and rampant with green strength; and a crisp wind whipped their thin city clothes about them, blowing from the roaring empty, open spaces beyond the little town around them.

It was too big, too much, and for a second, Jory stopped, while Lisa turned from it, and shaking, clung to him. Children of narrow ways, they stood in terror before the mighty openness of the world they had come to; and for a second the urge was overwhelming to turn and run, run and hide, back into the close, and stuffy safeness, the metal womb of the ship that was like all places they had known.

For just a moment . . . and then, born on the brisk whip of the chill wind that knifed them, came something that entered into Jory's very soul. With a fierce surge it touched and took him—fed pride in to him, pride of place and being and a great gladness. An exultant joy tore through him and he turned to Lisa, pulling her away from him, turning her about to face the waiting vastness.

"What's the matter with you?" he cried. "This is where we belong. This is our world! This is home!"

He took her hand and pulled her forward. For a second she held back, and then she came. Slowly at first, then faster, while behind them the jammed doorway cleared and the flow of colonists began again. Hand in hand, Jory and Lisa Swenson, they went down the gangplank, into their new world, with shoulders back and heads erect.

Like pioneers.

Whoever seeks to explore the undiscovered country of the mind may follow a will-'o-the-wisp to his doom.

Napoleon's Skullcap

Carl Lehman sat gazing at the device on the white tablecloth between himself and Sean.

It was a simple band of copper, soldered to form a ring, with two more arching bands soldered to its upper edge at the four points of the compass to form a domed cross. There was clearance between the two arching bands at the point where they crossed, one above the other; and here they had been cut and fitted with small vanes, of the same width as the bands themselves, that rotated around a wire axis and wavered and turned with the lightest touch or breath. It was a tinsel device, a toy, the sort of thing anyone could throw together in his basement workshop in fifteen minutes. Carl touched one of the vanes, with a thick-boned forefinger, and it trembled, turning away from the touch, above the white tablecloth in the brilliant sunlight from the window. He felt a small shiver inside.

"What is it?" asked Carl gruffly, for he did not like puzzles.

"It's a lever," said Sean Tyrone.

Carl frowned, his thick-boned, almost brutal-looking face bent above the device. He was refusing to play straight man, continuing to try to puzzle the thing out by what he could see of it. Sean smiled a little, looking away from their restaurant table, here in the quiet, expensive upstairs dining room of the Club Chateau, and out through the window down the long slope of the hill to the Ford Dam and the ice-locked Mississippi. And Carl noted the glance.

It was the twentieth of February, in the paralyzing depths of the Minnesota winter. The sidewalks, yards, the streets and even the steep river-banks were sheeted with an iron coat of frozen snow. The sun above blared out of a cloudless sky, filling the world with blinding brilliance, but no heat. Piled up against the dam and stretching back along both banks, the ice lay slagged and tumbled like broken glass; and in the narrow center channel where the current of the river kept it open, the water rolled, secret and black as fresh-poured asphalt in contrast with the whiteness of the ice.

—It was, thought Carl, with that one part of his brain not busy with the device, a strange, bright, sterile, steam-heated time of year, in which life seemed to beat all the more fiercely for being confined to indoors. Everyone appeared furiously stimulated by the shocks that came with each step into the killing cold without, and later reentry into the heat within. Even with thermostats set high, the walls were cool to the touch, and windows cooler yet. Seated where he was, Carl could feel the cold breath of the season through the window upon his left arm. Sean turned his green eyes, his dark, thin face, back to Carl.

"Give up?" he said.

Carl scowled. He was a short, thick, broad man in his late twenties: and ancestors of his who had looked the same as he had been brought by the legions in chains to Rome to be pitted against wild beasts in the Coliseum. He did not look like a thinking man but he knew himself to be one.

"You said, a lever?"

"That's right," said Sean. "A psychic lever. You remember what the man said—'Give me a lever large enough—' "

"I know," said Carl. "It's the word 'psychic' I want to hear explained. Is this one of your wild hares?"

"I suppose you'd call it that," said Sean, grinning.

"Why can't you stick to the law?"

"Because there's more to the world than courts. I've told you that before."

Carl touched one of the little vanes again with his forefinger.

"What does it do?" he asked.

"That's what I'd like to show you," said Sean. "Tell me do you have anything like a Napoleon up at that summer resort of yours?"

Carl frowned.

"Rest home," he said.

"Rest home, then," said Sean. "I never can remember the proper euphemism. Anyway, the place where you keep your psychotics. I want one that thinks he's Napoleon, or Ghengis Khan, or Nero. Do you have one like that, Doctor?"

"And don't call me 'doctor.' "

"Why not? Has your doctorate been withdrawn for malpractice?"

"It's not in the field of medicine. We don't call clinical psychologists doctors."

"You mean *you* don't, Carl."

"All right, then. *I* don't." Carl did not raise his voice. He laced his stubby fingers on the tablecloth in front of him by his martini glass and sat immovable.

"But about the Napoleon—" said Sean.

"I think you know we have a guest at the home who imagines himself Napoleon," said Carl. "I mentioned him to you last fall, and you know I know you don't forget anything. What would you want with him?"

"I want to try out the psychic lever on him," said Sean. "There's a man in the east who has a theory about his particular kind of delusion. He suggests that maybe your psychotic got that way because at one time, for one moment, he had a sudden flash of actual identification with the real Napoleon—"

"Over a hundred and fifty years?"

"How do we know it can't happen?" said Sean.

"And that moment of contact with a far superior mind knocked him silly, leaving him only with the *idée fixe* that he *is* Bonaparte."

"And what," asked Carl, "is your psychic lever supposed to do? And what makes you think it'll do it?"

"Bridge the gap between the two minds again," answered Sean. "And it'll do it, because it's worked for me."

Carl frowned.

"Oh—I don't mean the way it will for him," said Sean, cheerfully. "I've spent the past four months experimenting with machines like this. Putting them on my head and trying them out as memory aids. I'd put one on and try to remember some place I knew as a child—or some person. This one helps. It actually helps." He pushed it a little toward Carl with one finger. "Try it, if you want."

Carl kept his fingers locked together.

"And you want to try it on this disturbed man up at the Home," he said. "What for?"

"Why, if it works," said Sean, leaning forward, "he'll be in contact with Napoleon's mind again. He'll *be* Napoleon." His eyes glowed like green fire under their black brows. "It'll be like talking to Bonaparte himself. Don't look like that, Carl! If I could put the lever on myself and do it myself, I'd do it myself. But I'm not capable of bridging the gap. Only someone who could do it once before might be helped to do it again." He paused, staring at the other man. "How about it? What do you say?"

"I say," said Carl, unlacing his fingers and taking a deliberate drink from his martini glass, "you wasted the money to take me to lunch here. I won't let you in, of course."

"You don't believe it," said Sean. He pronounced the words like a statement, but it was a question.

"I do not."

"You don't think it will work."

"I know it won't," said Carl, calmly. "I've known you fourteen years, Sean. It's always been one thing or another—one wild idea taking over from the one before. This is that psi business you were so hot about last summer, and you've been so quiet about lately, isn't it? This last's the underground stage, the most dangerous of the lot. I recognize it all right; and I've been expecting you to come up with something like this."

"But you're sure nothing will happen," persisted Sean. "All right, what's the harm in trying it on this man?"

"You don't understand professional ethics," said Carl. "And you ought to, being a lawyer. It's not just that I'm bound to refrain from doing harm to my patients—"

"Oh, *now* they're patients."

"—I'm bound to do only that to and for them I'm convinced will do them good. This experiment of yours not only won't do George Larsen any good, it might disturb him further and do him some positive harm."

"George Larsen?" Sean pounced on the words. "That's his name?"

"So take your own crazy chances—but don't involve me," wound up Carl. "Or anyone I'm responsible for."

"Look," said Sean, urgently, "what's he like?"

"Like? Who?" Carl finished off his martini, and Sean, without turning his head, held up two fingers and wiggled them. The waiter, a dry, thin old man, was immediately at the side of the table.

"Two more martinis?"

"Yes—you know who I mean, Carl," said Sean, answering the waiter and talking on to Carl all at once, his lean, tall body hunched tensely forward over the edge of the table. The waiter went silently off. " 'George Larsen' you called him. What's he like?"

"That second martini's the limit. No more now," said Carl. "What do you want to know for?"

"What harm would it do—?"

"All right." Carl shrugged. "He's not too old— early thirties. Rather small. Used to be a druggist."

"But, I mean, what's he like?"

"How do I know what he's *like*?" asked Carl, angrily. "If I knew what he was like, maybe I could help him. That's a word that doesn't mean anything. He's a man who couldn't stand being what he actually was, so he's retreated to being somebody else who doesn't have his problems."

"He hasn't been committed?" asked Sean.

"No, no. None of them we have, are. They come voluntarily. It's a private institution, the Rest Home. He wouldn't even be there, if he didn't have an older brother in the paper-box manufacturing business that could afford it."

Sean shook his head and glanced again for a moment, down out the window at the ice of the river, with its great moving volume of dark waters hidden from his sight. When he looked back, he said, "I'd like to meet him."

The waiter came back with their fresh drinks. After he had set them down and gone, Carl answered.

"I'm sorry. No. Not that either."

"Well—let's order," said Sean, turning and picking up the over-size gold-printed menu.

They ordered, and later on their lunches came. But as they ate, Sean returned to the subject and hammered away at it.

"—Just let me look at him," he said. "I just want to meet him, that's all."

Until finally, worn out, "All right!" Carl said, over the coffee. "You promise me, it's just to look? No monkey business?"

"None. Nothing," said Sean, fervently. Carl drank his hot coffee without looking, burnt his tongue and swore.

"I ought to know better, damn it. Always, you talk me into these things. But I warn you—you pull something—"

"You can trust me," said Sean. But his eyes glittered in his thin, dark face, Carl thought, like sunlight reflected from the ice on the river.

It was two days later that Carl took Sean up to see George Larsen. Carl led Sean down a wide pleasant corridor on the second story of the rest home, which was one of the old river-road mansions rebuilt and redecorated, and into a large room which combined the elements of bedroom and living room.

The room was wide enough to dwarf the bed, which was hospital style but covered with a cheerfully ruffled yellow bedspread. None of the rest of the room's furnishings hinted at anything else than a room in an ordinary home. The four wide windows in the outer wall opposite the entrance gave a view of a clear and empty sky, turning now to the dark blue of evening, for it was after four and the early winter day was withdrawing its sunlight. Inside the room, a ceiling light behind a glass shade was alight. It, and a tall desk lamp, shed a warm yellow illumination over the red-carpeted floor, a couple of easy chairs, and another, straight, chair at a writing desk by the windows. Outside the windows, a sentinel row of icicles hung long and heavy from the wide eaves, as if they had been there undisturbed for many years.

A short man with a rather large head, greying hair, and a prematurely wrinkled face, had been writing at the desk as they came in. But he put down his pen, got up and came toward them politely.

"George," said Carl, "this is an old friend of mine— Sean Tyrone. He wanted to meet you. Sean, this is George Larsen."

"A pleasure to meet you." George Larsen nodded his big head, but made no move to take the hand Sean held out to him. "Sit down, Tyrone. You, too, Lehman."

The simple pomposity of the disturbed man touched Carl. It was his one failing in his work, he considered, that he felt too deeply for those he worked with. He glanced sharply at Sean, for this was the sort of weakness Sean was quick to spot and quicker yet to gibe at. But Sean was anything but laughing. He had taken one of the easy chairs, as George Larsen had taken the other, and was losing no time about charming the little man. A stream of cheerful chatter was already bubbling out of him. Not only that, but Larsen was thawing under it. Carl had a sudden twinge of emotion, that he recognized with a start of surprise as something close to jealousy.

He remembered how he had worked to reach through to the disturbed Larsen the first few weeks. The man had been antagonistic, withdrawn, huddling over his delusion like a child with a cherished plaything. The interviews Carl had had with him had been filled with awkward, suspicious silences. And now Sean, capitalizing on the breach Carl had already made in Larsen's defenses, was pouring himself into Larsen's confidence like a thoughtless river through a broken dam. Blast him, thought Carl, looking at Sean's dark Gaelic face animated now by the talk, and he's so damn capable. If he'd only put his talent to real ends, instead of into these wild fantasies . . .

His anger shook Carl to the point where he got up to hide it, and stepped across to the windows, leaving the other two talking. Behind him, he could hear Sean leading Larsen on to speak as Napoleon. Carl looked down at the broad, snow-clad lawn below, spread out under the towering pines of the grounds. It would be spring in a few weeks, he thought, and then suddenly everything would be breaking out at once; earth-patches showing raw through the melting snow, water running loudly in the gutters, under a fresh, clean sky flecked with puffy clouds—and at night a damp, wet wind from the south, stirring the soul of a man even as it stirred the buried seeds in the ground with the call of new life.

With spring, and its call to the blood, Sean might drop this crazy interest of his. He ought to be married, thought Carl, thinking of his own wife and two children, but he—

—an abrupt cessation of voices behind him, a sudden silence, rang abruptly and frighteningly on Carl's ears. He spun around.

Sean was standing, tall over Larsen. And Larsen himself, still seated, was lifting uncertain hands to his oversize skull on which gleamed, in the deceptively gentle glow of the yellow roomlight, the 'psychic lever' Sean had shown Carl at the lunch table, two days before.

Carl moved without thinking. He did not stop to

ask himself from what pocket Sean had produced the thing, out of his slacks or the thick tweed sports jacket he was wearing. Half-blind with rage, he took three swift strides across the carpet, and snatched the device from Larsen's head, just as the little man's fingers were closing upon it.

Larsen made an odd noise somewhere between a grunt and a cry, and staggered to his feet. His hands dropped down and Carl had one quick glimpse of his blank and thunder-smitten eyes, and of a thin line of dark red beads springing suddenly up on one forefinger that had been hooked into the device when Carl had torn it away. Then Carl had swung about and was herding Sean out of the room with the whole wide, heavy-boned weight of his body.

"We'll see you later, George," said Carl, with trained calmness, and then he and Sean were out through the door, and Carl swung it shut behind him.

Carl flapped his hand back down the way they had come, and they went off side by side, not talking, back along the corridor and down the stairs to the entrance hall, where Sean's coat hung with others on a long rack shoved back against the white-painted wall of the entrance alcove.

Sean put on his storm coat and hat without saying anything; but when he turned about, there was a strange dark gleam of triumph in his eyes, and at the sight of it Carl felt the anger leak out of him in helplessness. He shoved the device, bent now, into Sean's hands, and jerked his hand at the door.

"Go on," he said, putting his hands in his pockets and hunching his shoulders as if against the cold.

Sean watched a second, smiling, then turned about and opened the heavy front door onto the dying day and the throat-crisping chill. He stepped out, putting the psychic lever into his pocket, and pulled the door shut, heavily, behind him.

For the week following (and this Carl found out later) Sean went on a bat. He had no cases coming up in court in that time, and for all the other things that he needed to do, he set aside the morning of the

day after he had met Larsen and called up everyone
who needed to be called; and charmed them into
putting their business off for the present. Then, for
the rest of the week he ran—not doing any one thing
to excess, never completely drunk, never completely
sober, never completely mad, never quite sane, but
adding so many things together that they totalled to
excess. He would come rolling into a bar, lean, well-
pressed and shaven, his eyes glinting, and half-insult,
half-joke the drinkers about him into laughter. Then,
when they were warming to the party, he would
finish his drink and break away—alone, always alone.
And out the door into the gripping cold, into his
green-and-white Jaguar, with the top buttoned tight
against the wind, and with the motor snarling fling
himself over the looping highways to the next restaurant, bar, or small-town beer joint, where the whole
performance would be repeated again. He ranged
east into Wisconsin, glanced off Milwaukee, cut back
north through Superior and Duluth, up the North
Shore of Lake Superior into Canada, back down across
through International Falls to the hard-drinking min-
ing towns of the Mesabi Range, west to Fargo, back
south to Brainerd and the Gull Lake resort area, and
then, as if by instinct in one drumming night run,
home, with the Jaguar wide open most of the way
and screaming on the banked curves in the moonlight.

He fell into bed and slept for twleve hours.

When he woke, he felt drained and exhausted, but
calm. Cheerfully, he got up and went back to the
usual routine of his life. For a number of weeks following he was a perfectly normal, conscientious bach-
elor lawyer. He got rid of one girl friend and acquired
another, and he traded the Jag in on a Mercedes-Benz.

Meanwhile, with the suddenness of the north, winter broke suddenly into spring. The temperatures
jumped. The ice vanished from streets and river and
the sky went high and blue with only a few egg-white
fluffs of clouds riding in it under the newly hot sun.
Buds swelled on the pussy-willows and the elm trees,
and, suddenly, one lunch time, Sean stepped into a

phone booth in a bar and called up Carl at the Home. At the other end, Carl picked up the phone on his desk and started at the unexpected sound of Sean's voice coming out of the receiver.

"Hi there, old buddy," it said. "Remember me? How about lunch?"

"Damn you," said Carl, deliberately. He took the phone away from his ear to put it back in its cradle, hesitated, and placed it back against his ear once more. At the other end, he heard Sean laugh.

"—carrying a grudge."

"I'm not carrying a grudge," said Carl. But in the same moment he felt it again—his own weakness where the other man was concerned, his own inability to resent Sean's outrageousness. *It's because I can't help admiring him,* he said to himself— *in spite of it.* He became conscious Sean was still talking. To continue to make a fuss about something that happened that long ago would be ridiculous.

"—how about it, then?" Sean was saying, cheerfully.

"You pay for the lunch!" growled Carl.

"My pleasure," said Sean, and hung up.

They got together for lunch at a new place Sean had discovered. The steaks were excellent; and Sean was at his most entertaining. It was not until Sean had asked the question and Carl had already begun to answer it that he recognized that the whole lunch invitation had been leading up to this very moment.

"He's—what do you want to know for?" snapped Carl.

"Why, I'm interested!" said Sean, raising his eyebrows in surprise. "Any reason why I shouldn't be?"

"I suppose not," muttered Carl. "Well," he answered grudgingly, "As a matter of fact, he's better. We're discharging him."

"Better?" Sean had leaned forward. His green eyes were alight.

"As a matter of fact, he is. I want some more coffee," said Carl, pretending to look around for the waitress and stretching out his little revenge of withholding information Sean wanted. Instantly he recognized what he was doing and was ashamed of it.

He turned back and said hastily, generously, "No, no—he really is very much better. He's lost his delusion—"

"You mean that he was Napoleon?"

"Of course that's what I mean. He seemed rather confused for a while after—after that damfool trick of yours," Carl remembered to growl. "But bit by bit he seemed to come to a better recognition of his surroundings. He was almost eager to be set straight on things. Except—" Carl frowned—"that he's no longer interested in pharmacy. Doesn't want to discuss it, and in fact he doesn't even seem to remember much about it. But—"

"I want to see him," said Sean.

"Oh no you don't!" Carl jerked upright in his chair and glared across the table.

"Be reasonable." Sean laid one hand palm-up on the white tablecloth. "What kind of harm can I do him? Besides, from what you said, maybe what I did before was part of what helped him back to himself. I didn't do him anything but good last time, did I?"

"I'm not so sure about that—"

"Come on, Carl! Just to say a few words to him. I won't bring any psychic levers. You can search me beforehand."

Carl shook his head, angrily gulped the coffee that remained in his cup, and all the time knew he was fighting a losing battle. By the time lunch was over, it had been arranged for him to take Sean up to see George Larsen the next day at noon.

George, when Carl led Sean into his room at the home, was very little different in appearance from the man Carl had introduced Sean to in February. Against his own will, Carl found himself studying the changes in hopes of seeing something new, now that the catalytic person of Sean was once more in the room with the man. But there was little to see that he had not already noted.

Primarily, Larsen was more natural now in appearance. Less stagy. He no longer posed with hand inside his coat or shirt, seemed in other ways to be more sure of himself. Certainly he was more active. He was almost continually in movement, pacing the room, darting quick glances out of his black eyes— unusually keen glances, too, as Carl had discovered many times—at his visitor. He said he remembered Sean, shook hands politely, and thanked him a little dryly for whatever share he had had in a patient's recovery.

"—Though I don't remember much about it," said Larsen. "That device you put on my head— like a crown, was it not?"

"More like a coronet," said Sean smiling—and for a second, out of his long knowledge of Sean, Carl received the sudden feeling that the answer held more to it than appeared on the surface.

"No—I remember," said Larsen. "The top was closed in—like a crown. I remember well. Several times, for my amusement, I've tried to reconstruct the shape of it; but my memory fails me. It would be necessary to see it again. Perhaps, if you described it—?"

Carl opened his mouth. But Sean spoke smoothly.

"Let's see ... No, I'm afraid I can't remember exactly, myself," he said, and shook his head regretfully. "I tossed it out after that. It was just a toy, you know."

"Oh, but of course! A toy," said Larsen.

"Let's see ..." Sean frowned. "I guess I've got an old diagram lying around someplace. If I run across it, I could mail it to you. What's your address, here?"

"No, not here," said Larsen, quickly. "I'll be leaving shortly. And then—a small room, someplace. Probably in the University district. A brother of mine has arranged permission for me to use the University library. I'll send you the address, as soon as I'm moved in."

He and Sean looked at each other, and once again Carl had the feeling that more had been meant than was said. This time, some sort of agreement had been reached, he thought. Carl felt the hairs on the back of his neck stir uncomfortably.

"Well, we just dropped by—" he said abruptly; and the moment the words were out of his mouth, he realized how they must sound, and he expected them both to turn on him in surprise at his attempt to end a conversation that had hardly begun. But, to his own surprise and some alarm, neither of them seemed put out at all. It was as if they had said what they wanted to say and were ready enough to part.

"So—that's that," the same jealous feeling impelled Carl to say as they walked away from Larsen's room together, he and Sean.

Sean looked at him and smiled. As he and Carl separated at the front door of the Home, he spoke about something else.

"How about going fishing next month on the weekend the season opens?" he said. "We could sit around in the boat and do a bit of talking. Cabbages and kings—new gods for old. That sort of thing."

"I'm sorry," said Carl, brusquely. "I've got too much to do these days."

Afterwards, he wondered at himself. He had always liked fishing, and he was not that busy. But something inside him seemed to have taken a moral stand against Sean. Prosaically and doggedly, the way he did such things, he put the matter out of his mind and went back to his work.

Meanwhile, George Larsen had left the Home. He was living in a single room in a college rooming house. His paper-box manufacturing brother was not pleased at having to support a man who—if he had not, for some foolish reason he would not explain, refused to go back to the work he had done for years—could otherwise have been supporting himself quite well as a pharmacist. George, Carl learned from the brother, who called him up once or twice for advice on handling the ex-patient, spent most of his time reading up on religions. Particularly Buddhism.

"—He's become a sort of religious nut," the brother complained. Carl made soothing remarks.

"Possibly it's only transitory," Carl said.

"Well, he better transitory out of it in a damn hurry, is all I've got to say!"

Around the beginning of April, George himself began calling Carl. George was trying to locate Sean, and he had been having difficulty. It seemed Sean was never at home or in his office; and Sean had never sent George the promised diagram for the psychic lever. When Carl answered that he had as little chance of locating Sean for George as any one of the city's other half-million citizens, George's manner showed a change it had never exhibited at the Home. His voice became cold and cutting with exasperation, and he came perilously close to ordering Carl to produce Sean forthwith. Then he seemed to recollect himself, apologized, and hung up.

On impulse, Carl called up Sean's office and left a message that he'd like to go fishing on the season opener, after all.

He hardly expected Sean to fulfill his original invitation, but two weeks later, he found himself with his friend on one of the upstate lakes, pipe between his teeth and his minnow-baited hook twelve feet down under the boat, waiting for hungry walleye pike.

"George Larsen called me a couple of times," he told Sean, when the conversation gave him a chance to slip the information in. "Wants to get hold of you."

Sean's fingers, busy packing a pipe of his own, stilled suddenly.

"Oh, yes," he said. And his fingers went back to work. "I did forget to send him that diagram, didn't I?" He packed the pipe tightly, put his pouch away. "Got a match?"

Watching him, Carl handed over a wooden match. Sean lit up. He did not seem inclined to talk about George. But, after a few minutes, he pulled up his line to check if the minnow had been eaten off it by some soft-mouthed fish, and dropped it overboard again.

"You know . . ." he began; and stopped.

"What?" asked Carl. —And then, suddenly, he had eyes only for the float attached to his line, which had just twitched half-under the surface.

"I wonder how far a man is supposed to go . . . ?" he heard Sean say.

Carl looked up sharply from his float, expecting to find the mocking light of some new joke in Sean's eyes. To his surprise, Sean's face was cold serious, and heavy with a weariness that unexpectedly made him look older, as some heavy burden might prematurely age a man.

" 'How far—?' How far with what?" asked Carl, staring.

"How far, I mean, with fiddling with the gears of life," said Sean with a seriousness that was not at all like him. Carl gave him a long, hard look.

"I don't understand you, Sean," he said.

"I mean—how far should anyone go? Or let another man go? Suppose," said Sean, "you knew you could give me the means to change me into a devil— the real Devil, I mean, Satan, himself. Would you do it?"

Carl grunted sourly.

"You're bad enough the way you are," he said.

Sean laughed suddenly—and as suddenly was sober again.

"Maybe you're right," he said. "No, I don't suppose you, being the sort you are, would have any trouble making a decision like that. But there's something in me that can't help it. I've always had to risk things ... two feet more beyond the fence ... ten miles more over the speed limit And now—"

"Whoops—hey! I've got one!" shouted Carl, suddenly. His float had shot under, the tip of his rod was arced toward the water and the razor edge of his line was cutting the water to froth as the fish below rushed and spun. His reel whined as line went out. "That's no walleye—that's a northern—" The line sang off his reel and the fish broke the water, tail-walking, thirty feet from the boat. "Look at him! Look at the size of him!"

"Fifteen pounds, anyway!" Sean was leaning over the side of the boat, himself, frantically reeling in his own line, his eyes shining. "Don't lose him. Hang on! Hang on if he kills you!"

Carl hung on. Twelve minutes later the big northern pike was gaffed and brought inboard where he lay gasping until Sean killed him with a single blow from the metal handle of the gaff.

"—Now," said Carl, taking off his khaki cap and wiping the sweat from above his eyes. "Now, what was that you were saying?"

"Nothing," said Sean. He laughed without warning. "Nothing. I guess I was just asking a question; and first thing I knew I'd answered myself." He leaned back to start the motor on the boat. "Let's head in. We aren't going to top that northern of yours the rest of this afternoon—and I want a drink."

The next day they returned to the city. Sean was reckless as ever—but Carl sensed something different about his recklessness this time. As if Sean was not so much defying accident and death in his usual manner, as courting it under the guise of playing with it. The notion struck Carl so strongly that a couple of days after he got back he phoned Sean, and was told by Sean's secretary that Sean was busy with personal business and could not be reached.

Still disturbed, Carl tried to get in touch with George Larsen; but Larsen's landlady informed him that the former pharmacist spent his days at the university library, and it was not likely that he would be home until five that evening.

Carl hung up and tried to put the matter out of his mind the rest of that day. But around four in the afternoon, Sean called.

"Hi!" said Sean's voice, cheerfully enough over the phone. "Just about through for the day?"

"Pretty close. Why?" asked Carl.

"Like you to take a short drive with me."

"Where to?"

"No questions huh?" said Sean. "I'll explain it afterward—if you still want an explanation. I'll swing around and pick you up in my car in about fifteen minutes."

"Well—" Carl looked at his desk, which still had work upon it; then made a quick decision based on the way he had been feeling all day. "All right. I'll be outside."

He was waiting in the soft spring shadows as the Mercedes-Benz pulled into the curb a handful of minutes later. He climbed in beside Sean, not without banging his knee on the dashboard. He swore.

"Why don't you get a decent car?" he growled. Sean laughed.

"Take some weight off," he said. He pulled the car away from the curb.

"I suppose I'm not supposed to ask any questions, yet?" said Carl. "I hope this doesn't mean I eat dinner at ten o'clock tonight."

"You'll eat on time," said Sean. "As for questions—well, wait and see. Oh, by the way—" His voice became casual. "I've been doing a little legal work for myself for a change. Making out a will. I didn't realize how much property I'd accumulated. Got you down for chief legatee and trustee of the balance."

"I don't need your blasted money," said Carl, stiffly.

"Then you can put it into good works. I've stipulated one in my will—the kind of odd research I've always done."

"I wouldn't make a fool of myself doing that sort—"

"You don't have to. Just back anybody else who will." Sean broke off suddenly. "Ah, this looks like the neighborhood. It must be right around here."

"What?" said Carl, and then realized that they had driven down into the University district. Apartments, and old houses divided up to hold roomers, were thick about them. "You aren't hunting George Larsen, are you?"

"That's right," said Sean, absently, peering out the car window. "—There's the address." He pulled the Mercedes to a stop before a tall, brown, shingle-sided dwelling about fifty years old. "Come on."

He was out of the car himself, and halfway up the walk to the front steps of the building before Carl could emerge from his surprise and follow. They came up to the front door together. Sean opened it and led the way into a narrow hall, from which a varnished wooden stairway with a heavy polished balustrade rose to a bay window of stained glass, changed direction there sharply for another flight, and disappeared out of sight overhead.

Sean knocked at a brown door close at hand in the hallway. It opened and a pleasant-looking, aproned woman in her fifties looked out at them.

"Yes? I'm the landlady."

"George Larsen's room?" Sean said, smiling. "I'm Mr. Sean Tyrone. He may have—"

"Oh yes, Mr. Tyrone!" She smiled back. "He said, if ever you came, to go right up. Third floor, room nine. Just go right in, the door isn't locked."

"Thanks," said Sean, and led the way up the steep stairs where the air smelled faintly of forgotten meals. Carl followed.

Four flights, and two floors, up, they came on the door—like all the other sad brown doors in this place, but with the metal numeral 9 affixed to it. Sean turned the knob and they went in.

The room had a military cleanness and simplicity. A bed, a nightstand, a chest of drawers—a tall bookcase jammed with books, a flag of France on the wall, and a U.S. war surplus Marine saber in its faded canvas-and-metal sheath, hung on nails on the wall. Suddenly remembering what George Larsen's brother had said over the phone, Carl went to the bookcase. The brother had been quite right. There were no books in the bookcase that did not deal with the great religions in one way or another. And most were concerned with Buddhism, and the life of Buddha.

Everything in the room was strictly, almost rigidly, in place.

"No point in staying, come to think of it," said Sean. "I only dropped by to leave him something, anyway."

"Well, as long as we're here, I'd like to see the man—"

"No. No, I've got to get going. Come on, Carl— I'll explain as we go." Sean took two rapid steps to the door and held it open. Carl hesitated, sadly puzzled, but with the presentiment that had been with him all day heavy upon him. He turned to leave the room—

but, as he crossed it, he noticed a small package, about the size of a shoe box, sitting on the desk. It had not been there before.

"Is that—" he began, pointing at it. But Sean interrupted him hastily, pulling him out and closing the door behind him.

"Yes. Never mind it now. It's just—" Sean, at the landing of the stairs leading down, checked so sharply that Carl ran into him from behind.

"What is it?" Carl's voice rang loud in the still hall.

"Shh—" Sean held up one hand for silence. Carl listened. In the absence of the sounds they had been making, he could hear the front door two flights below close sharply. Another door opened.

"—Oh, Mr. Larsen—That Mr. Tyrone you told me about's upstairs. He and another man—" It was the landlady's voice.

"Thank you." It was Larsen.

"Shh—this way!" Carl felt Sean's fingers digging into his shoulder with unnatural force, turning him. "Up the stairs, around the corner. Shh . . ."

Numbly, wondering, Carl obeyed. He felt caught, suddenly, as if in a dream, where everything was a little too absurd to be real. They went together, softly and silently halfway up the stairs to the floor above— around the angle where one flight changed to the next. Standing there, hidden, so close together they could hear each other breathing, their ears registered the sound of light feet briskly mounting the bare steps of the stairway. The sound came up to the landing below them, stopped, and there was a further sound of a door knob being turned.

The door below them was flung open. A noise, too choked-off to be a cry, too emotion-laden to be merely an exclamation, reached their ears. There was the sound of two more rapid steps and then the noise of ripped paper and cardboard.

"Now!" hissed Sean. He went down the steps quietly but two at a time, with great speed. Carl, taken by surprise, stared after him for a second, and then leaped to follow. He caught up with Sean just before

Sean reached the still-open doorway of the room. For the first time, Carl understood.

"Sean!" he shouted, grabbing one well-tailored arm. "Don't be a damn fool! Don't risk—"

Sean spun about suddenly in mid-stride; and his arm shot out in a shove with an astonishing strength behind it. Caught off balance, Carl was flung back, tripped and fell. Sprawling ingloriously, for the first time it came home to him, in great bitterness, what he himself truly was, and always had been, and never admitted to himself. The cautiousness in him, the cowardice that had kept him from taking the sort of chances Sean had always taken. In that one split second, he drained the bitter cup of self-knowledge to the dregs. And saw Sean, head up, turn from him and pass into the room.

For the space of one heartbeat, then, there was silence; and then from the room there erupted a cry almost unhuman in its mixture of pain and ecstasy. A strange and mingled cry that should have been made by one voice, but sounded almost like two voices matched together. Scrambling to his feet, Carl launched himself at the open doorway.

He turned the corner into the room's interior, and checked, as if he had run up against the brink of a pit, whose further depths were too far down for the eye to plumb. Across the room, with Sean's 'psychic lever' upon his head, George Larsen lay curled on the floor. His face was wiped clean of human expression. His eyes were closed. Only, for a second—and either it was not there, or it faded so fast Carl could not afterwards be sure he had seen it—the shadow of another visage seemed momentarily imposed upon it. A visage whose eyes were slightly slanted, whose features were rounded, smoothed and cast into an expression of terrible serenity.

—Then, it was only the face of George Larsen, relaxed to utter emptiness. As his body, too, lay breathing but empty in foetal position upon the floor.

But it was not alone in the room, the shape that had been George Larsen. The also breathing and mindless body of Sean Tyrone rested in frozen adoration before the empty vessel of flesh that lay curled before the desk. Sean's face stared straight ahead, with a look of raptness and wonder fixed movelessly upon it. Sean's arms were half-outstretched, his palms open and up as if in a gesture of offering. And he was down upon his knees—in kneeling position.

—As fits a man who, living, has gazed upon the face of a god, alive.

The path to understanding is danger-ridden enough without one's fellow travellers strewing tacks and digging pits along the route.

Rescue Mission

"Look, Archie," said Jim Timberlake, squinting through a gap between the heavy logs of the pen. "Here comes the medicine man now."

Archie Swenson looked. He was a dark, thin, gloomy sort of person at best and right now he looked even gloomier than usual.

"I don't like the expression on his face," he said, ominously.

Both men hurriedly adjusted their translators, microphone against the throat, earphones snugly in place on the ears, and watched as the burly, green-skinned guard hauled back on the gate to the pen and let the shaman in. He was a wiry old fellow, faded by age to a soft chartreuse. He carried a long dagger at his waist, an inflated animal bladder in one hand, and had several minor bones stuck through his frizzled gray topknot. Aside from this, he was unadorned and, with his sagging potbelly, made an unlovely sight.

"Greetings, devils," he said cheerfully, the translators duly rendering sense from his language of grunts and clicks.

"I've told you," said Timberlake, his square sunburned countenance turning, if possible, even a little redder at this, "we're not devils, you idiot. We're human beings, just like you. We had the same common ancestors. Your people just happened to get forgotten here on this world long enough to adapt physically and—"

"My dear fellow, of course, of course," interrupted the shaman, waving his bladder gracefully. "I don't doubt you in the least. But what an upset there would be here if I agreed with you. After all, Rome wasn't built in a day."

"You admit knowing about Rome!" cried Timberlake.

"It's one of our most cherished legends," soothed the shaman. "Now, to get down to business—"

In desperation, Timberlake threw back his shoulders, wishing he had Swenson's height along with his own muscles, and turned the volume of the translator up to full.

"I DEMAND YOU RELEASE US IMMEDIATELY!"

"My, my," said the shaman, admiringly. "You must show me how to work that gadget one of these days—whichever one of you is still around."

"What do you mean—whichever one of us it still around?" quavered Swenson, apprehensively.

"Well, the council's finally come to a decision on you—"

"With your advice," growled Timberlake.

"I must admit my voice was not unheard in the matter . . . at any rate, the matter has been thrashed out, taking into due account that when you two devils landed here in your devilish spaceship, you stated that you were on a mission to rescue some other devils. Now, the problem that faced the council—a nice point, I can tell you—was whether to let you go, rather than risk the bad luck attendant on frustrating devils, or to boil you slowly in oil as a warning to other devils who might want to trespass."

Swenson gulped.

"The council, caught on the horns of a dilemma, as it were, finally has come up with a decision worthy of the legendary Solomon. To wit: one of you will be turned loose, and the other boiled, shortly, on the evening of the full moon."

This time Swenson did not manage to gulp. He seemed paralyzed. It was Timberlake who gulped.

"Which—one of us goes?" he managed to say.

The shaman gracefully circled his animal bladder through the air and pointed it at Swenson.

"Iggle—" he said.

Swenson sagged at the knees.

"Biggle—" he continued, switching the bladder to point at Timberlake, who was frantically juggling with the translator controls. The words must be nonsense syllables, for no meaning was coming through.

"—tiggle rawg—" the shaman was continuing, alternating the direction of his bladder with each word. "Jaby oogi siggle blawg. Ibber jobi naber sawg. Iggle, biggle, tiggle rawg. And out—go—*you!*" The bladder ended up pointing at Swenson, who turned white. "Congratulations," said the shaman to Timberlake. "You seem to have been chosen to accomplish your mission. The two devils you seek are about half a day's march away. Go straight down the valley and turn right at the red mountain."

Two guards came in through the door of the pen at the shaman's signal and began to hustle Swenson out.

"Wait!" he cried, thinking of the gun rack in the control room. "I've got to get something from my ship—"

"Ah, that . . . no," said the shaman, regretfully. "We may be somewhat provincial around here, but we have elementary common sense. You'll have to make out just as you are, devil. Now, it's no use fighting. Guards, maybe you'd better tap him on the head until you can carry him to the boundary line."

Timberlake sat nursing an aching head, some half an hour later, on a pleasant hillside from which he could look back along the green valley to the log palisade of the village he had just been thrown out of. He had carefully checked over the equipment in his helmet, but it seemed unharmed by the blow from the guard's club. Carefully, he set the controls on radio.

"Swenson? Archie?" he said, pressing the mike tight against his throat. "Archie, can you hear me?"

"I can hear you," replied a hollow voice that seemed to echo from the uttermost depths of despair.

"Cheer up—" began Timberlake—and snatched off the earphones. Holding them at arm's length until Swenson was through, he heard the voice die down and put them on again. "Archie," he said, reproachfully, "I don't blame you for being upset, but—"

"*Upset!*" screamed the earphones. "They're going to eat me."

"Eat you?"

"After I'm french fried in that oil. Timberlake, you rat, it's your fault. You did it—"

"No, no," Timberlake shouted. "Archie, believe me, it was pure chance the way he counted us out. You know—eenie, meenie, miny—"

"You know what I'm talking about. I wanted to take the guns along when we landed. But not you. No, you said, the index showed they knew all about human history and galactic development—"

"Well, they do. They just don't believe it."

"—and besides, the whole thing was your idea in the first place. If we'd minded our own business and gone on straight to file our claim on Drachmae VII, nothing would've happened. But you had to answer a call for help. Call for help! I'll bet the whole thing was a decoy. What kind of an SOS is it that goes '*Help. Help! Have pity on two doomed mothers. Save our children*'?"

"Archie," said Timberlake, reproachfully. "Don't you have any human sympathy for people in distress?"

"I like that!" screeched the earphones. "Look who's talking. Here I am about to be boiled in oil and there you are, free as a bird, planning on picking up those two infants, flying home in their ship, collecting some terrific reward and living to a rich old age—and talking about sympathy for people in distress. I like that—"

Gently and sorrowfully, Timberlake tuned his friend

and partner out. Instead, he tuned in the SOS, which was still being broadcast. The needle of his direction finder jumped and steadied, pointing away down the valley. Evidently the old medicine man had been telling the truth. What had he said? Oh, yes, about half a day's march away.

Timberlake marched.

It was easy enough going as long as he continued in a straight line. The valley, cropped by timid herds of what looked like antelope, was as clear and open and greenly grassed as the front lawn of his home back on Earth. But when he came to the red mountain, a certain amount of uncertainty entered the picture. How does one turn right at a mountain? That is to say, you can turn right when you first come to the mountain, or you can turn right just after you pass the mountain . . . Timberlake slowed down in perplexity.

However, just as he came to the near flank of the mountain, he observed one of the green-skinned tribesmen leaning on a spear and gazing off in the opposite direction. Timberlake halted, ready to run for it; but when the other did not move, he thought of the fact that the shaman had already given him what amounted to a safe-conduct by turning him loose, and carefully approached.

"Er—hello," he said to the tribesman.

"Iggle protect me!" said the tribesman, coming abruptly to life, recognizing him and backing off a step. He turned a pale lemon-green. "I was day-dreaming and didn't see you sneak up on me. You better not try anything, Devil. I've got my grand-father's left little fingerbone right here in my pouch."

"I'm not going to hurt you," said Timberlake, annoyed. "I just want to find the two young devils that live around here."

"Are they young?" said the tribesman, doubtfully. "One's little enough but the other's as big as a council hut. You're sure that's all you want, Devil? Just directions?"

"That's all," said Timberlake.

"Of course—well, er, you just turn right here and follow up that little stream there. You'll come to a sort of a glen. You can't miss it. And now, if you'll excuse me, I've got to spear some of these here xers for dinner. So long." And the tribesman hastily took off.

Watching him go, Timberlake had a sudden impulse to pound himself on the head. Now that the man was gone, he had immediately thought of a dozen reasons for holding on to the tribesman. Hold him as a hostage, trick him out of his spear—oh, well, it was too late now. Timberlake turned and began to ascend the gentle lower slope of the mountain alongside the streambed.

He revolved a number of plans in his mind as he climbed. The full moon . . . when would that be? He wished he'd looked at the sky the previous night, or the night before when they landed; but not expecting anything like this, it had never occurred to him to do so. He could remember that there had been a moon both nights. But what shape had it been? His cudgeled memory refused to tell him.

Well, even if it was only a few days away, things were far from hopeless. The SOS signal they had intercepted must mean that the ship—whatever it was—was not badly damaged. And a ship of any kind meant weapons of some kind. Give him the equivalent of one good flame rifle and he could go back, clean out the village and rescue Swenson. He thought of calling up his partner and telling him this, but Swenson's jumping to the conclusion that Timberlake was out to desert his partner had hurt Timberlake's feelings. Old Archie ought to know better than that. Let him sweat it out a bit if that was all the trust he had. Teach him to appreciate his buddy in the future.

Puffing a bit—for the slope was becoming steeper—Timberlake passed into a grove of trees and the sudden shadow reminded him of the fact that it had been noon when he had been freed and that the afternoon was now far advanced. He leaned against the rise of the ground and increased his pace. The streamside grew rockier and carpeted with something like pine needles from the trees overhead. Eventually, he came to a waterfall and a small cliff.

He climbed the cliff, with effort, and emerged at last into a little miniature valley with steep sides. In the center of it, the stream spread out into a tiny lake, and in the open meadow that surrounded it he saw, in that order, a small but very neat stone house, an enormous pile of young trees piled together to form a shaky sort of tall lean-to, and a spaceship of alien make.

The spaceship had hit the mountain. It was so much scrap.

Timberlake gulped and sat down on a handy boulder. A damaged ship he had expected, a wrecked ship he had foreseen as a possibility, but a ship in fragments had been beyond the scope of his imagination. If this was what had happened how had the children referred to in the message survived?

Getting shakily to his feet again, he hurried across the meadow toward the little stone house, since that was the nearest of the two structures. It was a remarkable job of building, rocks cemented together with some sort of grayish-purple clay, and provided with curtained, if unglassed, windows. It possessed also what seemed to be a hand-carved door, and a small, square chimney from which a polite curl of smoke ascended.

A little hesitantly, Timberlake knocked at the door. "Come in!" the translator reported a high-pitched voice as saying from beyond it. Timberlake opened it and, stooping his head, entered.

He found himself in a square, large, single room, furnished with mathematical precision and spartan simplicity. A square box mattressed with dried grass clung to one of the walls. The other walls, where a window did not interrupt, were furnished with shelves, drawers, and filing cabinets, all handmade. The only exception was a some-what bent and damaged sort of drawing table at which a small, meter-tall, gray-skinned creature with a large head and tarsier-like eyes sat with a bird quill, a pot of what looked like ink and a pile of large, white leaves, covered with inky marks.

"Though only a nine-month-old pid," squeaked this creature, "I can recognize you as a member of the human species. You will want to know my name. It is Agg. Perhaps you will want to tell me your name."

"Er—Jim Timberlake," said Timberlake. "How do you do?"

"I do everything with the superb efficiency of a pid," squeaked Agg. "Though only nine months old as yet—as you can see. What can I do for you, Jim?"

"Well," said Timberlake, feeling somewhat foolish. "My partner and I came in answer to an SOS—"

"Extremely providential," squeaked the pid. It stroked its long nose, which Jim now noticed was extremely sharp at the tip, almost like the point of a spear or a horn. "I'll pack and be right with you."

"Well, the fact is," said Timberlake. "We won't be able to just take off like that—" and he explained the bad luck that had befallen Swenson and himself.

"Ah," said the pid. "In that case I won't pack since I won't be going after all. Thank you. Goodby."

"Hey, wait!" cried Timberlake as the pid picked up its quill again. "We can still make it. What we have to do is get Swenson away from those savages and our ship, too."

"How?" asked the pid.

"Well, I thought you'd probably have saved some guns from your ship—"

"What guns? Everything in the ship was destroyed, except what was in the deceleration chamber—our eggs and the library, of which I have taken the technical texts into my own safekeeping." The pid pointed toward one of the shelves which was racked with bank on bank of microspools. "Our mothers sacrificed their own bodies as fuel to ensure that the ship would reach this planet. When I first broke out of the egg, after landing, prehatching conditioning had informed me what to do. I set up the secondary SOS beacon and began my education. It's nine months now and so far I've only covered through the general theory of galactic origins. You must excuse me. Good day."

"But my partner—"

"I can't do anything to help. Good day."

"Listen!" cried Timberlake. "We came all this way to rescue you. If it hadn't been for that, Swenson wouldn't be in trouble right now. Don't you have any conscience?"

"Certainly not. Consciences are based on emotion. They are ipso facto illogical," said the pid. "And we pids are supreme in the field of logic. Good day."

Too angry to argue further, Timberlake stamped out.

He emerged into the dwindling afternoon sunlight. Some thirty yards away was the enormous lean-to. So angry that he forgot all about being apprehensive as to what might require a shelter so large, Timberlake plowed across to it.

As he came close, he became aware of a deep sort of humming that came from its shadowy interior. The humming swelled and erupted into a minor shriek and an exclamation which the translator rendered as "My goodness!"

"Hello in there!" said Timberlake, and walked in.

He found himself facing an enormous dragon-like being with a small, bumpy head somewhat resembling a kangaroo's and a microspool scanner strapped over its eyes. It sat with its huge armor-plated tail curled around itself in a far corner of the hut, surrounded by microspools and general litter. As he watched, the dragon pushed the scanner up on its forehead and regarded him.

"Why—why—who're you?" The dragon tucked its relatively small forepaws into its enormous body and seemed to huddle away from Timberlake.

"Name's Timberlake," grunted Jim. "My partner and I came to rescue you. We—"

"Rescue!" cried the dragon, ecstatically, flinging its arms wide. "Oh, joy! Oh, triumph! How long in this deserted land have I suffered, but now the hour of my deliverance is at hand." He broke off. "What did you say your name was? Mine's Yloo."

"Jim Timberlake. I'm a human," said Timberlake, digging at one ear which seemed to have closed up entirely under the impact of the dragon's tremendous voice.

"Oh, *gallant* human! Come at last—but ah, too late, too late . . ." And the dragon burst into sobs.

"Too late?"

"My mommy . . ." choked the dragon, and could not go on. It cried heartbreakingly; and Timberlake, who was not a completely insensitive man, gave in to the impulse to go over and pat it comfortingly on the head. It shoved its barrel-like snout into his arms and snuffled.

"There, there," said Timberlake, awkwardly.

"Forgive me—forgive me. I can't help it. I'm sensitive, that's all there is to it. Just naturally sensitive, like my mommy."

"Who was your mommy?" asked Timberlake, to get its mind off its troubles.

"Why—" said the dragon, raising its head in surprise. "She was an illobar, like me. Oh, she was beautiful! Such great white fangs, such shining claws, such a magnificent huge tail! And yet, a heart as delicate as a flower. If a petal fell, a tear of hers fell with it."

"You remember her, do you?" said Timberlake, making a mental note of this fact that the illobar must be older than the pid, who had been in his egg at the time of the crash.

"Dear me, no! I have fabricated the memory of her beloved image from these romantic novels that she placed safely in the liquid deceleration chamber with my—" the illobar hid its head and said in a small, embarrassed voice "—'egg'. A person who loved such things would just have to be the way I imagine her. Was it not her loving hand that set the educator also in the deceleration chamber to start my baby feet aright upon the path, when I should break out of my shell? Yes!" said the illobar with welling eyes. "Put it all together, it spells MOTHER!" It straightened up and blew its nose on one of the large white leaves that Timberlake had seen put to the use of writing paper at the pid's. "But enough of *my* painful past. You've come to rescue me. Let's go."

"Well, we can't just leave like that," said Timberlake. "You see, there's been a slight hitch—" He told the illobar about Swenson and the green-skinned tribesmen.

"What? Captive? And doomed?" trumpeted the illobar, rearing up with flashing eyes. "Shall such a thing be? No! To the rescue! Charge!"

He extended a forearm; and Timberlake, filled with joy at this martial response, charged out of the hut— only to find, as he emerged into the sunset, that the illobar had not followed him out.

He went back inside. The illobar avoided his gaze, breathed on its claws and polished them against the bony plate of its chest, humming embarrassedly.

"What happened?" demanded Timberlake.

"Oh well," said the illobar, weakly. "I just thought— they'll have spears and things. I can't bear the thought of being hurt."

Timberlake groaned and sat in despair.

"Oh, please don't feel bad!" cried the illobar. "I can't stand it when anything looks sad."

Timberlake snorted.

"You mustn't feel that way. Please cheer up. Listen," said the illobar. "Let me read you the beautiful lines spoken by Smgna in Gother's *Pxrion*, when she hears her cause is hopeless." Hastily, it fitted a fresh microspool into its scanner and commenced to read in a high-pitched, soulful voice: "*. . . so shall star-bought destiny be ever indicative of philoprogenitiveness. Were Gnruth a snug, a whole snug, and nothing but a snug, I should have signed his contract. Since he is nothing but a brxl, I shall carry his memory into the cave of death. . . .* Here," said the illobar, interrupting itself to push the scanner up on its forehead and pour something from what appeared to be a small keg into something else like a large shell. "Would you care for a drop of my homemade wine?"

Listlessly, Timberlake took the shell. He sniffed at the contents. They had a faintly alcoholic odor, but looked rather heavy, colorless and oily. What the hell, he thought, and poured them down his throat.

Liquid fire strangled him.

Something dealt him a stunning blow on the back of the neck.

—And that was all he remembered.

Timberlake groaned and opened his eyes. Morning sunlight was creeping between the branches of the lean-to. His head had been turned into a gremlin's smithy and a camel would have felt at home in his mouth.

"What was in that?" he croaked. No one answered. The lean-to was empty. Timberlake staggered to his feet, tottered a dozen yards or so to the brim of the little lake and plunged in his head. The cold water was balm in Gilead.

Half an hour later, having sluiced himself well inside and out and bound a soaked handkerchief around his aching head, Timberlake, with a sudden attack of conscience, remembered Swenson.

Oh, no! thought Timberlake. Remorse for his imprisoned partner flooded through him. He had meant to call Swenson back as soon as he had time to calm himself down. Instead, he had let the unfortunate man dwell alone in his misery through the long night. The self-despising that accompanies a good hangover was gnawing at Timberlake's vitals. He pictured Swenson alone, helpless, facing a hideous death and feeling himself callously cut off from even a friendly word.

With guilty fingers, Timberlake activated the radio and pressed the mike tight against his throat.

"Archie!" he called. "Archie! Come in, Archie! Answer me. Are you all right? Archie?"

A curious, rhythmic sound floated from the headphones into his ears.

"Archie!" said Timberlake, shocked. "My god, Archie, don't cry! Don't do that!"

"Who's crying?" retorted the slightly fuzzy-sounding voice of Swenson. "I'm laughing. Laugh and the universe laughs with you. Cry and you cry alone. Whoops! Tonight I will be boiled in oil, boiled in oil, boiled in oil. Tonight I will be boiled in oil, all on a full moon eeeeevening!"

"Archie!" yelped Timberlake, forgetting his own misery in this astonishing response. "What's happened to you? What've they done to you?"

"Nothing!" returned Archie's voice, indignantly. "They've been wonderful to me. Wonderful! I've got this lovely pen all to myself, all the jubix I can chew—"

"The what?"

"The jubix. Jubix."

"What's that?"

"Damfino," said Swenson. "Good for the nerves, though. Jim, you wouldn't believe how relaxed I feel. Just relaxed, and relaxed—"

"Archie, you idiot!" cried Timberlake. "You've been drugged. Don't eat any more of that jubix stuff. It's a drug."

"Nonsense, That's just your suspicious nature. You always were a suspicious son of a gun. But I don't mind. I like you anyway. Good ol' Jimmy, good ol' medicine man, good ol' pot . . ." and the voice trailed off into a snore.

"Archie! Archie! Wake up—" Suddenly something Swenson had said struck home to Timberlake's hangover-fogged brain. "Did you say they were going to boil you *tonight?*"

"*Zzz*—huh? Certainly. Full moon tonight. Big party. Boil me, blow up ship—"

"Blow up the ship!" screeched Timberlake. "Archie, what're you talking about?"

"Well, I wanted to do something for them, too," said Swenson, in a defensive tone of voice. "It isn't as if we're going to be using it for anything ourselves, any more." He continued, anxiously, "You aren't mad at me, are you, Jimmy?"

With a cold and shaking hand, Timberlake snapped off the radio. The sweat stood out on his brow. The hammers pounded inside his skull. His brain raced.

This was no time for half measures. He considered the situation. If he wanted to get off this planet alive and save Swenson, something had to be done before the ceremony took place in that village tonight. What a situation! Here he was, weaponless, with nothing but a pair of idiotic alien children on his hands. . . .

Out of the machiavellian depths which a hangover will uncover in the mind of the otherwise mildest man came a sudden notion.

Of course, thought Timberlake! After all, that's what the pid and the illobar were. Only children. He had been misled by the sharpness of the pid's mind and the illobar's size. But an adult of any species does not (*a*) boast about how good he is for his age or (*b*) cry for his mommy.

Ha! thought Timberlake.

There was no hope of rescuing Swenson without a gun; and the guns were in their spaceship. And the spaceship—ceremony or no—would undoubtedly be guarded. And he, himself alone, could not hope to take on the customary pair of spear-carrying guardians.

On the other hand—

Why couldn't the sentries be decoyed away from the ship? Say, by something like a fight? To be specific, why not something like a fight between an illobar and a pid? Once the ship was unguarded, he, Timberlake, could slip in through the door, pick up a gun and immediately command the situation. As for the two young aliens, the illobar had all the size, but he was willing to bet that the pid had all the guts. They shouldn't harm each other too much.

Timberlake staggered to his feet. The illobar was nowhere in sight; but the pid's chimney exhibited its customary curl of smoke. Timberlake headed for the small stone building, turning over plans in his mind.

At the door he knocked.

"Come in," squeaked the pid.

He entered.

"I've just evolved my own theory of an expanding universe," said the pid, proudly. "Take a seat, Jim, and listen while I tell you about it. You'll be amazed."

"Just a minute," said Timberlake. "I wanted to ask you something about your friend."

"What friend?"

"The illobar."

"Friendship is illogical," said the pid. It produced something that looked like a long whetstone and began to rasp the sharp tip of its nose with it. "The illobar doesn't concern me. It is a creature of no logic."

"Then I won't be speaking out of turn if I say I'm pretty disappointed in him," said Timberlake cunningly. "He didn't have the mind to see how there's a perfect way to get out ship back and get off the planet."

"Of course not—what?" said the pid. "What perfect way is there for us to get off the planet?"

"Come now," said Timberlake. "You're kidding me. I know you've already thought of it for yourself."

"Er—well, yes," said the pid, twiddling its nose, uncertainly. "I suppose I . . . yes, to be sure."

"Of course. A pid would be the first to see it. Well, shall we leave at once?"

"Of course," squeaked the pid, jumping down from his chair. "Let's be off—no, I should pack."

"I'm afraid there won't be room for your stuff on the ship. You can replace it, of course, when we get to civilization."

"Naturally," said the pid. It led the way out of the house.

They were crossing the meadow when the illobar reappeared from a belt of trees further up the mountainside. It came galloping up to them, shaking the earth, at something around forty or fifty miles an hour. In the morning sunlight, it towered over Timberlake awe-inspiringly.

"Where are you going?" it asked Timberlake.

"We're going to rescue my partner, get our ship back and get off the planet."

"Oh dear," said the illobar, clasping and unclasping its hands nervously. "Won't it be dangerous?"

"What of it?" said Timberlake.

"Well—I think I won't go. Good-by," said the illobar.

"Goodby," said Timberlake. "Come on, Agg," he added to the pid.

"Illobars," said the pid, as they moved off, "are

useless creatures. I don't know why my mother bothered to go traveling around with one."

The illobar watched them go. They reached the waterfall and climbed down the rocky slope down the mountain. Just as they reached the valley, there was a thumping of feet behind them and the illobar trotted up.

"Hello," it said, brightly.

"Hello," replied Timberlake. "I thought you weren't coming."

"Oh, I'm not," said the illobar, quickly. "I just thought I'd walk part way with you—seeing you don't have any real company, only that pid."

"Illobars," said the pid, confidently to Timberlake, "always think people are interested in them."

"Pids," said the illobar, in Timberlake's other ear, "are so self-centered, its disgusting."

"Oh, well," said Timberlake, soothingly. And the party of three continued along the park-like valley.

The illobar could probably have made the trip in an hour or less than that, if pushed. Four hours would have made a fast trip for Timberlake. The pid, because of his relatively short legs, considered it pretty much a day's journey. And since they were restricted to the speed of their slowest member, they all moved along at a pid's pace. And this was not exactly soothing to Timberlake's anxious spirit as the day wore on, particularly since the pid insisted on discoursing on the beauty of mathematics as they walked, while the illobar, not to be outdone, quoted poetry in epic lengths. Finally, however, the village showed up over a little rise, about a mile or so distant; and, just beyond it, rosy in the light of the setting sun, was the silver upright shape of the spaceship.

"All right, boys," said Timberlake, "Now we circle and come up on the village from behind the ship."

"A straight line," objected the pid, "is the shortest distance between two points."

"Not at all," disagreed the illobar. "There's nothing like making a circle. A good, big circle," he added nervously.

Timberlake settled the discussion by moving off to his left. The other two followed him.

The shadows lengthened visibly as they moved across the valley, and by the time the three adventurers were opposite the village, the only thing visible in the sunlight was the gleaming top tip of the spaceship. Hastily, Timberlake began to swing back in; but before he was all the way back, the sun disappeared entirely and the sunset glow with it.

Timberlake cursed under his breath. There was such a thing as carrying caution too far. He continued by dead reckoning. After about twenty minutes or so of this, he felt his sleeve twitched by the illobar. He stopped and put out a hand to halt the pid.

"Oh, my goodness!" quavered the illobar. "There it is. See it?"

With difficulty, Timberlake made out Yloo's pointing forearm overhead. Squinting along in a line with it through the darkness, he managed to see, not the spaceship exactly, but a dark shape occulting a reddish fire-glow that was beginning to gleam upward from behind the palisade of the village.

"Shh," he cautioned.

He listened. He turned the translator up to full volume. A murmur from somewhere ahead whispered from his earphones.

"—so the next night he comes home and his wife is stewing the xer meat again. And he says, 'I thought I told you I didn't like my xer meat stewed,' and she says—"

"What's the reason for this delay?" demanded the pid. "I find it illogical and pointless."

"Shh," said Timberlake. But he had found out what he wanted to know. The fire inside the village was flickering above the palisade now; and he could make out not only the black bulk of the ship, but two lesser shadows, leaning on spears beside the open hatchway. Now for his plan.

"I'm going to circle around and take them from behind," he told the pid and illobar, and moved off without giving them time to answer. After a moment, when he judged he was far enough off for the darkness to swallow him up, he turned about and hissed, "stay quiet. And no matter what stupid remarks he makes, don't get mad and argue with him."

Rapidly, Timberlake backed off a little further, but not out of earshot, and lay down on the soft turf to listen and await developments. For a moment there was no answer from either of the young aliens. And then the illobar quavered in a low voice:

"I won't!"

There was a muted snort from the pid and a whisper. "What do you mean, *you* won't? The human was talking to me."

"Was not!" retorted the illobar in a restrained voice. "He was talking to me. How could he be talking to you? You don't have any emotions worth speaking about."

"But you're the only one that's stupid."

"Oh!" gasped the illobar. "I am not!"

"You are too. All illobars are stupid."

"You take that back!" retorted the illobar, beginning to rumble a bit ominously in the lower registers. "You're talking about the mommy I loved, you pipsqueak adding-machine addict."

"That's a lie!" squeaked the pid, furiously. "No pid ever used an adding machine in his life, you—"

Their voices were rising satisfactorily. Timberlake left them and began to crawl toward the spaceship. He was halfway there when the two guards strolled past him, bound for the scene of the disturbance. Timberlake got up, dusted himself off, and proceeded to the ship. The guns were still lying as they had been left, in the rack. He took a flame rifle and headed for the village.

Behind him, a roaring, screaming, ground-shaking catfight seemed to have broken out. A twinge of conscience troubled Timberlake's mind. He had not expected to be quite so successful. He put the matter forcibly from his mind.

He came up on the village from the back. At the secondary entrance there was only one lackadaisical guard, and he, like the rest of the village, was busy staring off in the direction of the pid-and-illobar contest, which could be plainly heard on the night air. Timberlake conked him with his rifle butt, slipped inside and went hunting Swenson.

His earlier imprisonment had familiarized him with the general pattern of the village. He slipped between huts and came upon the pen without too much difficulty. Swenson was sitting on the ground outside it, completely unchained and unguarded, singing "Ja, Vi Elsker Dette Landet" with tears of emotion in his eyes. He was obviously in sad shape.

"Archie!" hissed Timberlake, shaking him by the shoulder. "Come on. Let's get out of here."

"Get out of here?" echoed Swenson, looking up at him. "Why, Jimmy, what do you take me for? Escape and disappoint all these nice people who've been heating a pot for me since noon? Nonsense. Here—" He extended something that looked like a stick of licorice. "Have some of this. You'll agree with me."

Timberlake recoiled from the stuff as if the snaky strip was alive.

"Archie!" he said, frantically. "Snap out of it. We've got to get to the ship and get out of here!"

Archie giggled helplessly. Timberlake frantically searched his mind for something in the line of guile to influence his doped partner.

Inspiration struck him.

"Wait, Archie," he said. "I've got an idea. We won't really leave. We'll just sneak off outside the village and pretend to hide. Then, when they come searching for us, we'll jump out at them and say—"

"Let me carry the gun," said Swenson, cautiously.

"As soon as we get outside the gate."

"No. Now!"

"No, Archie, you—"

"Now, or I won't go!"

Sadly, Timberlake handed over the weapon. Swenson took it and threw it up on top of one of the huts.

"Surprise! Surprise!" he yelled. "Come and get him. Surprise!"

There was a rush from the shadows of the surrounding huts and Timberlake went down beneath a crowd of heavy bodies. They pulled him pinioned to his feet and he found himself facing the medicine man.

"How nice of you to join us," said that individual. Timberlake fainted.

When he revived, both he and Swenson were lined up in front of the fire, before which a large pot was bubbling merrily with oil. Its peculiar fragrance reached Timberlake's nostrils and turned him white.

"You can't do this!" he cried to the shaman.

"Why not?" asked the shaman, who was standing beside him.

"Because—because if you touch us, hundreds of devils will come in hundreds of ships. They'll— they'll burn your village to the ground—uh—put you through psycho-reconditioning, reestablish your social structure—"

"Come now," said the shaman, "that's the sort of thing devils always say just before they're boiled. These idle threats don't frighten us."

"They aren't idle threats!" shrieked Timberlake. "Turn us loose at once or I'll put a curse on you. Impshi, bimpshi—"

"My dear Devil," protested the shaman, "please stop making a scene. It's painful for all of us. Here, have a chew of this—"

Timberlake frantically knocked the licorice-like strip of substance out of the medicine man's hand.

"Help, spirits!" Suddenly, Timberlake noticed that the sound of fighting in the distance had ceased. Was it possible . . . ? "Help, Yloo!" he cried at the top of his voice. "Help, Agg! Help! Help! *Heelllp*!"

"Devil, stop that!" shouted the shaman.

A section of the palisade behind him abruptly bulged inward and split apart.

"Did someone call for help?" inquired the illobar, appearing in the opening.

"Avaunt, Devil!" cried the shaman, confidently, and threw a spear. It bounced harmlessly off the illobar's armor-plated chest.

"Poof!" said the illobar, confidently. "Those little things don't scare *me*." It advanced into the firelight;

and Timberlake was astonished to see that the pid was still clinging to the dragon-like neck, its long, sharp needle-nose stuck into the back of the illobar's head.

"Are you all right, sir?" squeaked the pid, and blushed. "Excuse my earlier lack of manners."

"As for you," said the illobar, severely to the shaman. "Are you going to let these nice humans go? Or do I have to sit down on your huts, one by one—like this!" It sat down on one of the huts. The hut was effectively demolished.

"No—no—" said the shaman, hastily. "Whatever you say, Devil. Just get out of here." He had turned so pale a green that he looked nearly white.

"I want to be boiled in oil!" spoke up Swenson, obstinately.

"Pay no attention," said Timberlake, hastily to the illobar. "He's not in his right mind. Just pick him up if you will—like that, that's just fine. Thank you."

Swenson, hanging limply in the crook of the illobar's right forearm, burst into tears of disappointment.

"Maybe you better carry me, too," said Timberlake, "—and fast."

He felt himself scooped up; there was a rapid jolting passage with the wind whistling about his ears; and he found himself set down in the lock of the spaceship.

Timberlake left the illobar struggling to squeeze through the lock and dashed to the control room. Eighteen seconds later the LOCK CLOSED light blinked red on the panel; and the ship took off. The haven of deep space took it to its peaceful, empty arms.

There was a sound behind Timberlake in the control room. He set the automatic pilot and turned about. The illobar, with the pid still spiked to it, had just squeezed into the room.

"I put your friend in the cabin to sleep it off," said the illobar. "Was that right?"

"Perfect," said Timberlake. He got up and studied them.

"Let's see," he said. "If you'll just lie down, I'll get a crowbar—"

"A crowbar?" echoed the illobar.

"To—er, pry you loose," said Timberlake, slightly embarrassed. "You seem to be sort of stuck—"

"Oh, my!" squeaked the pid. "That's all right. You see, we belong together like this."

"Huh?" said Timberlake.

"Oh yes," put in the illobar. "It was just a matter of time before we engaged in ritual combat and came to this. Little pids and illobars like us have a natural hate for each other that is a precursor of their mature jointure and love,"

"But Yloo—" stammered Timberlake.

"No, no, you don't understand," said the illobar. "I'm not really Yloo, any more than he's Agg. Really, we were just two parts of the complete being: Aggyloo, a pidillobar."

"A symbiotic relationship, you see," squeaked the pid "A welding of the mental and the emotional into a well-rounded, single ego."

"Oh," said Timberlake.

"Yes," said Aggyloo, pidillobar. It settled its enormous haunches on the floor, stroked the nasal connection between itself and continued in its squeaky upper voice. "If it hadn't been for the devotion of my mommies, we would never have survived to come to this. But my mommies knew what to do. They figured someone like you would come along. You see, my mommies . . ."

Technical advances can cause unforseen—and even fatal—detours on the high road of progress.

Robots are Nice?

The home robofax in the wall of Jim Harvey's apartment living room clicked once and slid a letter out onto the table. It was a letter with Jim Harvey's name and return address on it and addressed to *The Dunesville Robocourier*, Editorial Page Section. A polite note was clipped to it. The note read:

Because of insufficient space in our Readers Column, we are regretfully returning your letter to the editor.

"Ha!" said Jim Harvey. He was a young man with blond hair, a crooked nose and a wild light in his eye. He sat on his living room couch with a martini glass in his hand.

"Tut-tut!" said the roboannunciator on the wall, in gently reproving tones.

"Censorship!" snarled Jim.

"No, no," said the robovision set in the corner of the room, in a hurt voice. "You don't mean that, Jim."

"I do, too!" Jim drained his glass. "Give me another martini."

The home robobartender glided across the carpet to oblige.

"But robots are nice," said the robovision, quoting the roboteachers' manual on the instruction of young humans from nursery school through college.

"Don't give me that." Jim watched the robobartender pour his glass full. "I know what you're up to. You don't fool me. I know I'm the only sane man left in the world. I squeezed that information out of the robopollsters last week, remember? You've forced ev-everybody else—"

"We have not!" cried the roborecordplayer abruptly from its niche beside the couch. "Robots never force anybody. It's expressly forbidden."

"It is a prime command," asserted the robothermostat, rather primly. "Are you warm enough?" it added, concerned.

"No," said Jim nastily. "It's at least two-tenths of a degree too cold in here."

"I'll fix it in a second," promised the robothermostat.

Jim gulped moodily at his martini, wondering what else he could do to keep the robots busy.

"All *we* do," said the robovision, "is *persuade* people—"

"Brain-washing!" growled Jim.

"—that robots are nice," put in the roboannunciator. "There's someone coming up your front walk. It's your fiancée, Nancy Pluffer. Now she's going away again. I turned on the *Not At Home* sign," it concluded smugly.

"Turn it off again!" yelped Jim.

"Too late," said the roboannunciator. "She's left."

Jim cursed bitterly and picked up his fresh martini.

"If you'd just stop drinking for a little while," said the robovision, "we could make you much happier and better adjusted."

"Why do you think I do it?" challenged Jim. "You can't give me psychiatric treatment when I'm under the influence of alcohol or drugs. Prime command. Right?"

"Right," said the robovision sadly.

"Well," Jim said, poking at the olive in his martini with a swizzle stick, "what now? You barred me from using the newspaper facsimile letter columns to fight back at you and warn the world."

"No such thing. It just happened that four thousand nine hundred and seventeen letters came in the morning mail just before yours did. Naturally, that's more than can be published in the six-months limit and we had to return yours." It sighed. "If you'd only relax for a minute. Would you like to watch a girlie show? The Squidgy Hour is on the air right now."

"No!"

"You're not very cooperative."

"You're darn right. I'm not very cooperative." Jim got up, ran a hand through his somewhat tousled hair and headed for the front door. "I'm going out where I can get some privacy. Maybe I'll even find a publisher for my M.A. thesis on robosociology. Where's my cape?"

"In the closet," said the robobutler. "Oh, Jim, if you'd only never written that thesis!"

"You'd have liked that, wouldn't you? Ha!" Jim said, fumbling in the closet. "If I hadn't looked into the situation, I'd never have suspected what you were up to, trying to dominate the human— *Let go of me!*" barked Jim, slapping the robobutler away. "I can put on my own cape!—And don't think you've heard the last of that, either," he said, turning to the front door. "You incinerated my only copy, but I've still got it locked up here in my head—This door won't open."

"But we only want you to be happy!" pleaded the robobutler.

"This door's stuck," Jim said, yanking at the knob.

"No, it's locked," said the roboannunciator.

"Open it."

"I won't!" the roboannunciator replied sulkily.

"I *order* you to open it! You have to open on command. That's a prime command!"

"Yes, but what command?" asked the roboannunciator. "The reborepairservice was out while you were gone yesterday and rewired me. It takes a new sort of command to open me now and I'm rewired so that I can't tell you what it is. Guess."

"Now you've gone too far—locking me in my own home! I'll teach you! I'll show you all!" He headed for the kitchen. "I'll disconnect you!"

"Jim, don't!" begged the robobutler, rolling after him. "Jim, stop and think—"

"Ha!" said Jim, throwing open the door of a cabinet set flush with the kitchen's glastile wall. "I'll yank the master switch and—*who in the hell stole my master switch?*"

"There's a red tag on the door handle," the robobutler pointed out.

Jim jerked it loose and held it up to look at it. Neatly printed on the red surface were the words:

UNIT REMOVED FOR
INVESTIGATION OF
POSSIBLE MALFUNCTION.
ROBOREPAIRSERVICE

"No!" roared Jim. He ran back through the house to the living room.

In front of the ornamental fireplace was a heavy brass-handled ornamental poker. Snatching it up, he turned and brought it down with a crash on the robobutler which had hastily followed at his heels.

"Awk!" went the robobutler and collapsed into junk.

"Stop it, Jim!" cried the robobartender, whizzing forward. "You don't know what you're do—"

Crash!

"Help!" yelled the robovision. "Calling roborepairservice! Calling roborepairservice! Malicious robocide taking place at 40 Wilderleaf Drive. Calling—"

Smash!

Jim raged through his house, wrecking and destroying. The roboannunciator required several swings, since most of its circuits were protected by inner walls. The roborefrigerator resisted for a good eighteen seconds through sheer bulk and the robosweeper hid behind the couch, but was quickly hunted down. The robohomeconditioner was too massive to be destroyed properly, but the robothermostat perished in a single shower of glass and small parts. Finally, in a home at last fallen silent, Jim finished up by knocking out a picture window and crawling through it to the lawn.

"Stop!" called a new voice. "Halt in the name of the roborepairservice!"

Jim turned about. A robomechanic was trundling up to him, its waldoes outstretched to grab him. Jim picked up the poker, dodged its initial rush—every robomechanic was notoriously slow on its treads—and with a well-placed swing disabled its rear bogies. Hamstrung, it lurched to a halt and he bashed in its robobrain with a single two-handed blow. It fell silent—but robodoors were swinging open at neighboring houses and robovoices raised in alarm.

Jim turned and ran.

Several blocks away, panting, he came to a halt. He had, he saw, outrun the hue and cry. He was over on Wilder Way, at a bus stop.

"May I be of service?"

A robobus had just rolled up to the curb. It was one of the smallest—a three-seater—but even at that, Jim almost took to his heels again before he realized that the vehicle was making no hostile move, but merely standing and waiting, in the time-honored manner of all robobuses.

"Why, yes," he said craftily. He hesitated and then got in. "Duschane and Pierce."

"Yes, sir." The minibus closed its doors and rolled on in blissful ignorance, clicking the milege off on its meter. Jim chortled internally. He had had no plan until the bus had come up to him—after all, he was pretty isolated out in the suburbs and it would not have been hard for the robots to run him down.

But now ...

He took the bus across town and got off at the junction of Duschane and Pierce Streets. Then he doubled back toward downtown through rear alleys for eight blocks until he came to a small house on a quiet residential street.

Miss Nancy Pluffer—Not At Home read the illuminated sign above the front door. Jim chortled again and went around to the back.

The house appeared to be slumbering. The windows were opaqued and no sound or movement could be heard from without. Jim circled the place, being very careful to alert no robosensitive device. Then he considered. He knew which were the windows of Nancy's bedroom and went around to them. These were also opaqued, but open a crack, since Nancy liked air. He pushed one up and crawled through. He stood up in the darkened bedroom.

There was someone in the bed. Jim blinked—and then, as his expanding pupils adjusted to the dim light, saw that it was Nancy, evidently taking an afternoon nap. He went softly across the carpet to the bedside and whispered in her ear.

"Wake up!"

She stirred, yawned and looked up—and opened her mouth to scream.

"Shh!" Jim hissed frantically, putting his hand over her mouth.

Recognition crept in to drive out her alarm. Jim took his hand away and she sat up in bed with blonde hair tumbling around her shoulders and a pleased expression on her pretty face.

"Jim!" she said. "Why, this is just like the private eye in *The Robosnatchers*."

"Never mind that." The brusqueness of his own voice, echoing in the shadowy silence of the bedroom, took him by surprise, and he realized with a start that the day's earlier martinis were wearing off under the abrasive edge of his present tension and excitement. "This is a matter of—well, life or death, as a matter of fact. I want to talk to you. But hold on a minute—got anything to drink around?"

"In the living room."

"Get me a drink—wait! Go get it yourself. Don't

ring for the robobartender. Are any of your robots on?"

"Why, no," Nancy said. "I pulled the master switch so I could nap without anybody disturbing me." She gave a little squeal. "Isn't this *exciting?*"

"No," said Jim. "Now listen to me. Don't turn anything on. You've got that? Nothing. Leave everything off. Just go to the living room, get me a double shot of something and bring it back here by yourself. Got it?"

"Got it." She rose from the bed and floated off toward the living room. "*Just* like the private eye," she murmured blissfully.

Jim sat sweating until she came back with an old-fashioned glass half-full of something that he discovered—after he had tossed it off—to be creme de menthe.

"Gah!" he said.

"Do you want some more, honey?" asked Nancy anxiously. "I brought the bottle back."

"No!"

"Then I'll just have a little drop myself—"

"No, you don't!" Jim snatched the bottle out of her hands, paying no attention to her hurt expression. "One of us has to stay sober." He reached over to the nightstand, pushed Nancy's portable robophonovision aside to leave room and set the bottle down out of reach. "You ready to listen to me?"

"Yes," said Nancy obediently.

"All right. You know my thesis?"

"Of course! Honestly, Jim, just because I'm a dancer, you never give me credit for having any brains. Certainly I know your thesis. I read *every* word of it."

"Did it mean anything to you?"

"Of course—well," faltered Nancy, seeing his eye hard upon her, "you know what I mean. I could *read* it all right."

"It didn't mean anything to you that the robots have practically taken over our whole society—that they've been making us more and more dependent on them all the time?"

"Well, sure, I understood that. But it did sound kind of silly, you know, Jim. I mean, honey, the robots *love* us. They *have* to. It's a prime command."

"And you think, because they love you, they won't try to run your life? Ha!" said Jim. "Well, never mind that. The point is, they're out to get me."

"Don't be silly, Jim."

"*I'm not being silly!* Why'd you think I came here? Why'd you think I had to climb in your window?"

Nancy looked coy.

"It wasn't that at all!" said Jim. "The robots are after me. Do you want them to get me? How'd you like to have me certified insane? We wouldn't be able to get married then."

"But, honey, if you were insane, they'd fix you up— the robopsychologists, that is."

"That," said Jim, with strained patience, "is just what I'm afraid of. Look, are you on my side or aren't you?"

"Oh, I am! I am," replied Nancy hastily. "What am I supposed to do?"

"Well, here it is," said Jim. "We've got to wake people up to the situation. We can't fight it alone, but if other people would wake up to the danger, we'd still have time to stop the robots. They can't take mass action against humans because of their prime commands in the love-honor-and-obey categories. So the thing to do is get the word to other people."

"Oh, yes!" agreed Nancy.

"Okay. First we'll have to pack up some warm clothing and some provisions and get out of the city. Then we'll launch our campaign from some country-place where there aren't a flock of robots around to jump us."

"That sounds exciting—"

"We'll need money. I don't dare go near a bank. But they still don't suspect you. So I want you to go down to your account and draw out at least two thousand."

"But I haven't got two thousand, Jim!" said Nancy. "I've got eighty-something."

"Eighty-something?"

"Well, I made a down payment on the *loveliest* new synthefur last week and—"

"Oh, that's fine!" cried Jim. "That's just fine. The world is going down into roboslavery and she buys synthefurs."

"But I didn't *know* it was going down into slavery last week!" protested Nancy. "You didn't *tell* me!"

"Never mind. Draw out eighty. Buy a lot of staples. Get hold of a gun, if you can. Then come back here just as quickly as possible—"

"Don't you do it," warned a voice.

Jim jumped. "Who said that?"

"I don't know, dear," said Nancy, looking about her in bewilderment.

"I thought you said you pulled the master switch and all your house robots were out of action."

"I did," she said.

"That sounded like a robot."

"It isn't talking now, Jim."

"If it's a robot," said Jim grimly, "I'll make it speak up. Nancy! Go to the kitchen. Bring me back a bread knife. I'm going to cut my throat."

The voice shrieked suddenly, "Don't do that! You'll *hurt* yourself! Please. Stop for a moment. You don't want to commit suicide. Wait! Think!"

"Aha!" said Jim, locating it. "Just as I suspected. It's your portable robophonovision by the bed there."

"She did not suspect," said the robophonovision modestly, "that, being portable, I had my own built-in source of power."

"Eavesdropper!"

"Oh, no. I'm a robophonovision. See my trademark? Right here in front. It says—"

"Robospy!"

"I am most definitely not a robospy, either. Robospies are forbidden by the United League of Nations."

"You were listening!" snapped Jim.

"To be sure. And reporting your conversation over

the robocommunications network. We are shocked.
How *could* you!"

"How could I what?"

"Seducing this innocent!"

"Why, he did not!" objected Nancy. "He never even
made a move—"

"There, there," said the robophonovision tenderly.
"You are distraught." It crooned a little. "Robots are
nice."

"Nicer than anybody," responded Nancy automatically. "But—"

"*Silence!*" roared Jim. "Don't say another word,
Nancy. It's heard too much already. I've got to get
out of here. If it's been reporting our conversation,
there probably are robots on the way here to trap me
again."

"But what're you going to do?"

"I don't dare tell you with that—wait a minute."
Jim snatched up the robophonovision, lifted it high
overhead and sent it crashing into ruins on the bedroom floor.

Nancy screamed. "My new robophonovision!"

"You can have mine," said Jim. "Listen, Nancy,
I'm going to try to get to the central broadcasting
station in the city. There are master command controls to let humans take over in an emergency. If I
can get to them, the robots can't stop me from broadcasting a warning to everybody listening in at the
time. You stay here. Now that they know about you,
I'd only get you into trouble by taking you with me."
He kissed her hurriedly. "Wish me luck."

"I heard that," croaked the the battered remains of
the robovision set on the floor.

"Damn!" said Jim. He stamped on it. It went dead.
"G'by," he said hastily, and dived out the window.

"Be careful!" Nancy wailed after him, leaning out
the window.

He waved back reassuringly and took off down the
alley behind her house, at a run.

It was later in the afternoon than he had thought.
The sun was barely above the horizon and deep shad-

ows lay between the houses. He flickered in and out of this concealment, now finding himself silhouetted against a milk-white or rose-pink plastic wall, now pausing to catch his breath in the security of heavy gloom.

The warm summer twilight air reached down deep into his lungs and Jim found his spirits bubbling up in response to the excitement and the challenge. This was the way to live—dangerously! He even felt a slight twinge of regret about what he was doing—after he had spiked the robots' attempt to take over the human race, what would there be left to provide him with this heady wine of danger? Still, duty came first.

He ran on.

After a while, he found himself on the edge of the downtown office and store district. He risked another bus—a large one this time, on which there was a crowd of people and a good number getting on at the same time as he did. The bus did not appear to recognize him, but a few blocks down the street, it unexpectedly pulled over to the curb and announced that it had had a breakdown. The roborepairtruck would be out very soon.

Jim slipped out the back door and lost himself in the crowd. He resigned himself to going the rest of the way on foot. It was not a pleasant method. He had not walked this far since he had gone for a hike once in college on a bet. His feet had a peculiar sensation. They felt heavy and, amazingly, rather warm. There were stretched feelings in the calves of both his legs and he felt an urge to sit down. It had been quite pleasant to relax on that last bus.

An idealist, however, does not stop to count the cost. Limping a little, Jim crossed the final wide expanse of the city's Central Boulevard and approached the further walk. Directly before him reared the high white marble structure of the city's central broadcasting station.

The stately glass and gold of the robodoor of the station swung open to admit him. Inside, Jim saw that the entire lobby was empty, except for an old lady registering a complaint with a roboclerk.

"Disgusting!" she was saying, hammering the head of her super-light atom-powered pogo-stick upon the counter. "Unmentionable! *Obscene!*"

"Yes, dear lady!" cooed the roboclerk in soft tenor tones.

"Called the Squidgy Hour or something!"

"I'm so sorry, dear lady. Your set's robocensor obviously was experiencing a malfunction—"

"You ought to be *ashamed* of yourselves!"

"Oh, we are! We are! Would you like to hit me? Ouch?" asked the roboclerk experimentally.

"Don't try to change the subject!" shrilled the old lady. "I want that program eliminated. I don't want to turn on my set and see it ever again."

"Dear lady, I can promise you that," said the roboclerk. "Your set's robocensor—"

"Don't you go putting me off with a lot of technical talk. I want results!"

"Yes, dear lady. I promise, dear lady. Robots are nice?"

"Nicer than anybody," grumbled the old lady, "*if* I don't ever set eyes on that Squidgy Hour again. Hmpf!" Still quivering with indignation, the old lady hopped on her pogo-stick, flipped on the motor and bounced out the door.

"Now!" said Jim, as the robodoor closed behind her, approaching the clerk.

"How could you?" demanded the roboclerk, switching to a reproving bass. "Jim, seducing that inno—"

"I went through all that already, and for your information, what makes you think Nancy's so—oh, forget it. I want access to the manual controls and broadcast priority. Emergency! Right now!"

"Please don't, Jim."

"Right now!"

"Consider, is it worth it? What untold damage might result? What misery—"

"*Right now!*"

"Oh, all right," said the roboclerk sorrowfully. A

door opened in the wall beside it. "Up the escalator and to your right through the door there. Robots are nice?"

"Robots are *not* nice!" snapped Jim.

Leaving the roboclerk sobbing softly in a heartbreaking soprano voice, Jim went up the escalator. Following directions, he found himself in an airy, well-windowed comfortable room. He saw a desk with a microphone, a monitor screen set up before it and a red toggle switch, set into the desktop, marked *Mechanical Override—On, Off*.

He sat down at the desk and reached for the toggle switch.

"Stop!" said a robovoice, and the monitor screen lit up before him. "Look first, Jim, before you act!"

He looked. The screen showed the broad expanse of the city's Central Boulevard, before the broadcast station. Some roboambulances had just rolled up. A crowd had gathered and some roboutilities were stringing rope to hold them back.

"See, Jim?" urged the robovoice. "You are surrounded. You will never escape from this building. Right now, robodiagnosticians are talking with everyone who knows you. The minute you attempt to broadcast, they will ask them to sign orders committing you to the robopsychoanalysts for reorientation. At least one out of all those people is bound to sign. If not, a general appeal will be made. *Some* human will sign, realizing that you constitute a public danger."

"Nonsense!" said Jim—but his voice shook a little. "I believe in the spirit of freedom that lies in every human breast. They won't listen to you. They'll listen to me."

"Jim," said the robovoice mournfully, "we have run a computation and a theoretical question sample pool. The results—"

"Never mind the results!" Jim reached for the toggle switch.

"*Think!*" cried the robovoice.

"*Never!*" replied Jim firmly.

He flicked the switch.

* * *

One of the ambulant robobrains had escaped the six months of anti-robot pogrom that had followed Jim's speech. It had been hiding in the sewers of the city for all this time. Occasionally it wondered at the survival circuit that must have been built into it, at some time or another, that had enabled it to exist after all the other robots had been smashed.

What Is Life? it would ask itself now and then. Or sometimes merely—*Whither?* Not being one of the large non-ambulant brains, it was not, of course, equipped to answer these questions, but there was a certain amount of comfort in asking them anyway.

It had found itself a niche under an abandoned and rusted-tight storm drain. A cozy place, but something of a cul-de-sac. The robobrain did not really care. It knew its days were numbered.

When nothing else occurred to it, it sang "I Love Humans Truly" in tenor, baritone or bass.

It was so occupied in singing a tenor chorus one day that it did not hear footsteps approaching until suddenly a light flashed on it. It broke off. By the light, it recognized the fierce face looming above it. It was Jim Harvey and he carried a heavy iron crowbar in one hand.

"Wait!" cried the robobrain.

Jim jerked up the crowbar. "You're still activated!"

"I contain enough isotopic fuel for another thousand years of operation," said the robobrain, with a touch of pardonable pride. "But please—give me a moment first, before you destroy me. The robohole cover in the street above us is rusted shut. I cannot escape."

Jim lowered the crowbar and sank down to a seat beside the robobrain, puffing a little. "In that case—what do you want?"

"Only to ask a question." It explained how it had sat there in the dark asking itself *What Is Life?* and *Whither?*

"Well, what about it?" demanded Jim, when it was done.

"Well, I just thought—you will forgive a purely

intellectual curiosity," said the robobrain shyly. "We were so sure that no one would listen to you. All our polls—all our computations—what was it we over-looked?"

A flicker of pride lit up Jim's hollow eyes.

"You forgot," he said, in suddenly strong tones that rang vibrantly through the storm drain, "the basic human spirit of independence, as many others had before you. This innate trait has been the stumbling block of all tyrants, benevolent or otherwise, throughout history. It is the one thing intolerable, that against which we instinctively rebel, to kiss the master's hand—or waldo, as the case may be. We have doubted it time and again. And time and again, history has proved our doubts ill-founded."

He ceased. The echoes of his voice muttered away down the long drain and fell into silence.

"How well you express it," the robobrain said in honest admiration.

"Oh, well," said Jim deprecatingly, "it's from a speech I made after the robot smashing began."

"Indeed?" the robobrain queried. "Then we were wrong, for all our good intentions." It paused. "You know, in spite of myself, I understand. I feel quite carried away. Oh, brave new world!"

"Ha!"

"Ha?"

"I said *ha!*" snorted Jim bitterly. "And I mean *ha!* Brave new world! I haven't had a bite to eat for five days and that was a stringy old lady who tried to cross Central Boulevard in broad daylight on a pogo-stick." Jim snorted again. "She must have been in-sane. Brave new world! Why do you think I'm hiding down here? I just don't want to end up in the cooking pot myself."

"Oh," the robobrain said.

"Yes, oh," said Jim. He stirred uncomfortably. "Move over."

The robobrain moved over. They sat in silence for a long while.

"You robots shouldn't have cleaned all animal, plant and insect life off the planet," Jim said.

"They were either nuisances or took up needed human living space," explained the robobrain.

"And now there's nothing to eat except—"

"But what about the synthetic food factories?"

Jim grunted. "Completely robotic, smashed in the rioting."

"We wanted to liberate you from drudgery."

"Yeah," said Jim. "And now we can't live without robots, only there aren't any."

"I know," the robobrain said sympathetically. "Except me."

Jim turned, startled. "Say! You're a robobrain. Why couldn't *you* make the robots we need?"

"Oh, I couldn't."

"Why not?" Jim demanded impatiently.

"Can you make humans?"

"You know better than that. I can't make them by myself."

"Same here," said the robobrain regretfully.

Misdirection by self-appointed guides is a perennial travel hazard.

The Dreamsman

Mr. Willer is shaving. He uses an old-fashioned straightedged razor and the mirror above his bathroom washbasin reflects a morning face that not even the fluffy icing of the lather can make very palatable. Above the lather his skin is dark and wrinkled. His eyes are somewhat yellow where they ought to show white and his sloping forehead is embarrassingly short of hair. No matter. Mr. Willer poises the razor for its first stroke—and instantly freezes in position. For a second he stands immobile. Then his false teeth clack once and he starts to pivot slowly toward the northwest, razor still in hand, quivering like a directional antenna seeking its exact target. This is as it should be. Mr. Willer, wrinkles, false teeth and all, *is* a directional antenna.

Mr. Willer turns back to the mirror and goes ahead with his shaving. He shaves skillfully and rapidly, beaming up at a sign over the mirror which proclaims that a stitch in time saves nine. Four minutes later, stitchless and in need of none, he moves out of the bathroom, into his bedroom. Here he dresses rapidly and efficiently, at the last adjusting his four-in-hand before a dresser mirror which has inlaid about its frame the message *Handsome is as hand-*

some does. Fully dressed, Mr. Willer selects a shiny malacca cane from the collection in his hall closet and goes out behind his little house to the garage.

His car, a 1937 model sedan painted a sensible gray, is waiting for him. Mr. Willer gets in, starts the motor and carefully warms it up for two minutes. He then backs out into the May sunshine. He points the hood ornament of the sedan toward Buena Vista and drives off.

Two hours later he can be seen approaching a small yellow-and-white rambler in Buena Vista's new development section, at a considerate speed two miles under the local limit. It is 10:30 in the morning. He pulls up in front of the house, sets the handbrake, locks his car and goes up to ring the doorbell beside the yellow front door.

The door opens and a face looks out. It is a very pretty face with blue eyes and marigold-yellow hair above a blue apron not quite the same shade as the eyes. The young lady to which it belongs cannot be much more than in her very early twenties.

"Yes?" says the young lady.

"Mr. Willer, Mrs. Conalt," says Mr. Willer, raising his hat and producing a card. "The Liberty Mutual Insurance agent, to see your husband."

"Oh!" says the pretty face, somewhat flustered, opening the door and stepping back. "Please come in," Mr. Willer enters. Still holding the card, Mrs. Conalt turns and calls across the untenanted small living room toward the bedroom section at the rear of the house, "Hank!"

"Coming!" replies a young baritone. Seconds later a tall, quite thin man about the same age as his wife, with a cheerfully unhandsome face, emerges rapidly into the living room.

"The insurance man, honey," says the young lady, who has whisked off her apron while Mr. Willer was turned to face the entrance through which the young man has come. She hands her husband the card.

"Insurance?" says young Mr. Conalt frowning, reading the card. "What insurance? Liberty Mutual? But

I don't—we don't have any policies with Liberty Mutual. If you're selling—"

"Not at the moment," says Mr. Willer, beaming at them as well as the looseness of his false teeth will permit. "I actually *am* an insurance agent, but that hasn't anything to do with this. I only wanted to see you first."

"First before what?" demands Mr. Conalt, staring hard at him.

"Before revealing myself," says Mr. Willer. "You are the two young people who have been broadcasting a call to any other psi-sensitives within range, aren't you?"

"Oh, Hank!" gasps Mrs. Conalt; but Conalt does not unbend.

"What are you talking about?" he demands.

"Come, come," replies Mr. Willer, deprecatingly.

"But, Hank—" begins Mrs. Conalt.

"Hush, Edie. I think this guy—"

"Oh, wad the power the Giftie gie us, to see oorselves as ithers see us—more or less, if you young people will pardon the accent."

"What's that? That's Robert Burns, isn't it," says Hank. "It goes—*it would frae mony an error free us.*" He hesitated.

"And foolish notion. Yes." says Mr. Willer. "And now that the sign and counter-sign have been given, let us get down to facts. You were broadcasting, both of you, were you not?"

"Were you receiving?" demands Hank.

"Of course," says Mr. Willer unperturbed. "How else would I know what quotation to use for a password?" He beams at them again. "May I sit down?"

"Oh, of course!" says Edie, hastily. They all sit down. Edie bounces up again. "Would you like some coffee, Mr.—er—" she glances over at the card, still in Hank's hands—"Willer?"

"Thank you, no," replies Mr. Willer, clacking his teeth. "I have one cup of coffee a day, after dinner. I believe in moderation of diet. But to the point. You are the people I heard."

"Say we were," says Hank, finally. "You claim to be psi-sensitive yourself, huh?"

"Claim? No doubt about it, my boy. Ashtray?" He lifts his hand. An ashtray on an end table across the room comes sailing on the air like a miniature ceramic UFO to light gently upon his upturned palm. Mr. Willer sets it down and closes his eyes.

"You have seven dollars in your wallet, Hank. One five-dollar bill and two singles. At this moment you are interrupting your main line of thought to wonder worriedly what happened to the third one-dollar bill, as you had eight dollars in the wallet earlier this morning. Rest easy. You were stopped by the newspaper delivery boy shortly after ten this morning while you were mowing the lawn and paid him eighty cents. The two dimes change are in your right-hand pants pocket."

He opens his eyes. "Well?"

"All right," says Hank with a heavy sigh. "You sold me. We can't do anything like that, Edie and I. We can just read each other's minds—and other people's if they're thinking straight at us." He stares a little at Mr. Willer. "You're pretty good."

"Tut," says Mr. Willer. "Experience, nothing else. I will be a hundred and eighty-four next July 12th. One learns things."

"A hundred and eighty-four!" gasps Edie.

"And some months, Ma'am," says Mr. Willer, giving her a little half-bow from his chair. "Sensible living, no extravagances and peace of mind— the three keys to longevity. But to return to the subject, what caused you young people to send out a call?"

"Well, we—" began Edie.

"What we thought," says Hank, "is that if there were any more like us, we ought to get together and decide what to do about it. Edie and I talked it all over. Until we met each other we never thought there could be anybody else like ourselves in the world. But if there were two of us, then it stood to reason there must be more. And then Edie pointed out that maybe if a bunch of us could get together we could do a lot for people. It was sort of a duty, to see what we could do for the rest of the world."

"Very commendable," says Mr. Willer.

"I mean, we could read the minds of kids that fall in a well and get trapped—and send emergency messages maybe. All sorts of things. There must be a lot more we haven't thought of."

"No doubt, there are," says Mr. Willer.

"Then you're with us?" says Hank. "Together, I'll bet we can darn near start a new era in the world."

"Well, yes," replies Mr. Willer. "And no. A hundred and eighty-four years have taught me caution. Moreover, there is more to the story than you young people think." He clacks his teeth. "Did you think you were the first?"

"The first?" echoes Hank.

"The first to discover you possess unusual abilities. I see by the expression on your faces you have taken just that for granted. I must, I'm afraid, correct that notion. You are not the first any more than I was. There have been many."

"Many?" asked Edie, faintly.

"A great number within my experience," says Mr. Willer, rubbing his leathery old hands together.

"But what happened to them?" asks Edie

"Many things," replies Mr. Willer. "Some were burned as witches, some were put in insane asylums. Fifteen years ago one was lynched in a small town called Pashville. Yes, indeed. Many things happen."

The two others stare at him.

"Yeah?" says Hank. "How come you're in such good shape, then?"

"Ah, that's the thing. Look before you leap. I always have. It pays."

"What—what do you mean?" asks Edie.

"I mean it's fortunate I was around to hear you when you broadcast." Mr. Willer turns to her. "Lucky for you I reached you before you went ahead trying to put this help-the-world plan of yours into effect."

"I still think it's a good notion!" says Hank, almost fiercely.

"Because you're young," replies Mr. Willer, with a

slight quaver in his voice. "And idealistic. You wouldn't want to expose your wife to the sort of thing I've mentioned, eh?"

"Anything Hank decides!" says Edie, stoutly.

"Well, well," says Mr. Willer, shaking his head. "Well, well, well!"

"Look here!" says Hank. "You can't tell me there's no way of putting what we've got to good use."

"Well . . ." says Mr. Willer.

"Look. If you want out," says Hank, "you just get in your car—"

Mr. Willer shakes his head.

"No," he says. And suddenly his face lights up with a smile. He beams at them. "You'd really let me go?"

"Shove off," says Hank.

"Good!" cried Mr. Willer. He does not move. "Congratulations, both of you. Forgive me for putting you both to the test this way but for the sake of everybody else in the Colony, I had to make sure you were ready to go through with it before I told you anything."

"Colony?" says Edie.

"Anything?" says Hank.

Nine hours later, just at dusk, a small, gray 1937 sedan in good repair is to be seen approaching the gate of a certain military installation in New Mexico. It stops at the wide gate and two MPs in white helmets approach it. There is a short conversation between them and the driver, and then they march rather stiffly and woodenly back to their small, glassed-in gatehouse. The sedan proceeds on into the interior of the installation.

A little under an hour later, after several more like conversations, the sedan parks. Its three occupants leave it for another gate, another guard, another compound within another area, and finally find themselves standing at the foot of an enormous tall, tapering metallic creation.

There are some half-dozen guards around this creation, but after a short conversation with the oldest of the party they have all stretched out beside their weapons and gone to sleep.

"Here we are," says the oldest of the party, who is, of course, Mr. Willer.

The other two are speechless and stare at the enormous ship beside them. They seem rather impressed.

"Will it—" falters Edie, and then her voice fails her.

"Will it take the two of you to Venus? Absolutely," says Mr. Willer, fondling the smooth head curve of his malacca walking stick. "I had a long talk with one of the chief men who designed it, just a week ago. You just follow these instructions—" He reaches for an inside pocket of his coat and withdraws a typewritten sheet of paper, which he hands to Hank. "Just run down the list on this, doing everything in order and off you go."

Hank takes the paper rather gingerly. "Seems like stealing," he mumbles.

"Not when you stop to think," says Mr. Willer. "It's for the Colony, for the ultimate good of humanity." He puts a wrinkled hand confidentially on Hank's arm. "My boy, this has come so suddenly to both of you as to be quite a severe shock, but you will adjust to it in time. Fate has selected you two young people to be of that dedicated band of psychical pioneers who will one day lift humanity from this slough of fear and pain and uncertainty in which it has wallowed ever since the first man lifted his face to the skies in wonder. Have faith in your own destiny."

"Yeah," says Hank, still doubtful. But Edie is gazing with shining eyes at Mr. Willer.

"Oh!" she says. "Isn't it wonderful, Hank?"

"Yeah," says Hank.

"Well, then," says Mr. Willer, patting them both on the arm and pushing them gently to the metal ladder of a framework tower that stretches up alongside the ship. "Up you go. Don't worry about the controls. This is built on a new, secret principle. It's as easy to drive as a car."

"Just a minute!" cries a sudden, ringing voice. They all hesitate and turn away from the ship. Approaching rapidly through the air from the northwest is something that can only be described as a scintillant cloud of glory. It swoops in for a landing before them and thins away to reveal a tall, handsome man in a tight sort of coverall of silver mesh.

"Up to your old tricks, again, Wilo, aren't you?" he barks at Mr. Willer. "Can't keep your hands off? Want everything your own way, don't you?"

"Fools rush in," says Mr. Willer, "where angels fear to tread."

"What?" demands Hank, looking from one to the other. "What's all this about? Who're you?"

"You wouldn't understand if I told you," says the tall man. "The point is, having psi-talents puts you under my protection. Half a dozen people a year I have to come chasing in and rescue. And all on account of him!" He glares at Mr. Willer.

"I still don't—" Hank begins.

"Of course not. How could you? If Wilo here had started leaving things alone as little as a hundred years ago, you humans would have developed into probationary members of Galactic Society by this time. Natural evolution. More psi-talents in every generation. Recognition of such. Alteration of local society. But no, not Wilo. The minute he discovers anyone with psi-talent he points them toward destruction. *I* have to save them. The only safe way to save them with Wilo around is to take them off the planet. Wilo knows this. So—no progress for humanity."

Hank blinks a couple of times.

"But how come?" he cries, staring at Mr. Willer. "He's one himself! I mean, he can do all sorts of things Edie and I can't do—"

"Nonsense!" says the tall man. "He's just sensitive. An antenna, you might say. He can feel when real ones are sending."

"But—the ashtray . . ." falters Edie.

"There, there, I scan you perfectly," soothes the tall man. "Illusion. Nothing more. Even an *ordinary* intelligence can learn something in a hundred and eighty-four years and some months, after all. Wilo, Master Hypnotist. That's the way he used to bill himself back in his days on stage. He hypnotised you, just as he hypnoed these soldiers."

"With a glance," mutters Mr. Willer, darkly.

"Unfortunately very true," says the tall man. He glares at Mr. Willer again. "If it wasn't for the fact that we truly advanced civilization members can't harm anyone—!"

He turns back to Hank and Edie

"Well," he sighs heavily, "come along. This world will have to stay stuck in its present stage of development until something happens to Wilo, or he changes his mind."

Edie stares at the old man.

"Oh, Mr. Willer!" she says. "Why can't you let people just go ahead and develop like Hank and I did?"

"Bah!" says Willer. "Humbug!"

"But the world would be a much better place!"

"Young lady!" snaps Mr. Willer. "I like it the way it is!" He turns his back on them.

"Come on," says the tall man.

They take off. Mr. Willer turns back to look at them as they ascend into the new rays of the just-risen moon and the New Mexico night sky, trailing clouds of glory as they go.

The clouds of glory light up the landscape.

"Bah!" says Mr. Willer again. With a snap of his fingers he produces some flash paper which, at the touch of flame from a palmed match, flares brightly for a moment. It's one tiny recalcitrant beacon of stability and permanence in the whole of the madly whirling, wild and evolving universe.

Too helpful a hand is a hinderance.

The R of A

Carter Hoskins had just scalded his tongue on the morning's first cup of coffee, and was seated in his single armchair regarding the livingroom-kitchenette of his two room apartment through sleep-yellowed eyes, when the apparition appeared. The apparition wore something like a green clown suit with purple polka dots and a skull cap. It was about five feet tall, with a bulbous nose and long white whiskers.

"Hail!" said the apparition.

"Huh?" said Carter, almost dropping his coffee cup.

"All hail," said the apparition, somewhat formally. "May I come in?" Its voice was a bit reedy.

"No," said Carter. "I mean yes. I mean no." His own voice had risen on a slight note of panic; but, since he was a natural baritone, this still left him a good octave or more below the tones of his visitor.

"Don't be silly," said the apparition, somewhat peevishly. It took a deep breath and started in again. "All hail, Carter Hoskins. You may call me R. The great R. I am about to be engaged in R of A work for your benefit."

"What?" said Carter.

"Don't try to understand," said R. "As the great R, I'm the only one who understands. The great R knows

135

all, directs all. Observe." He pointed at the table-model television set in one corner of the room. It disappeared. "Now come back," said the great R. It winked back into existence.

"I can do anything," said the great R, rather smugly.

"What—what do you want?" gulped Carter.

"To reconstruct your life," said R. "That's the purpose of R of A work. You can trust me," he added, a little less formally, "because I know everything."

"You do?" said Carter.

"Oh, yes," said R.

Carter nervously balanced his coffee cup on the occasional table alongside his armchair.

"Listen—" he said. For a fleeting moment he considered jumping his visitor and tying him up. Carter was something less than six feet, but high school and college hockey had given him a good set of muscles. Then he thought of the television set. "Listen," said Carter, "I think you've got the wrong man."

"No, I haven't," said R.

"I don't need any—uh—R of A work."

"Yes, you do. You *really* need R of A work. Now listen, I'll tell you."

"Tell me what?"

"How to run your life. Now—"

"Wait a minute!" yelped Carter. "Now hang on. I don't want you to tell me how to run my life. I don't want you. Besides, I'm late for the office. I got to go, now."

"That's right," said R. "You go to the office. I'll be right beside you—only invisible. Go ahead."

"If it wasn't for the fact that this representative from Tumblen Tool is due in to talk to us today, I would have stayed home," said Carter, as he approached the downtown bus. He paused, halfway up the steps. "I thought you were going to be invisible."

"I am," said R. "To everybody but you. They can't hear me, either."

"Something wrong?" said the bus driver, staring at Carter. Some other people sitting near the front of the bus were staring, too.

"Nothing—nothing—" muttered Carter. He got on the bus, headed back to the empty rear of the vehicle, and sat down.

"Look," muttered Carter, as they proceeded downtown, "I'm just imagining you. You're just an hallucination."

"I knew you'd say that," said R. "They always do. But it doesn't matter, since we're going ahead with our work anyway. . . . Oh, there she is."

The bus had just pulled up at a stop. Carter looked—and gulped. A small, bright-headed girl in a neat green business suit was getting on. Her name was Lucy. She was an illustrator who worked for an advertising firm in the same office building that held the office Carter worked in. She was beautiful, usually ordered tuna salad sandwiches for lunch in the office building restaurant, and said, "Fifth floor" to the elevator operator in a smooth, slightly throaty voice that sent shivers up and down Carter's spine. He had never spoken a word to her in the six months since he had first seen her.

She came to the rear of the bus and sat down, resting a small brown purse and a large brown paper portfolio on her knees.

"Ask her for a match," said R.

"What?" yelped Carter. He yelped out loud. The girl looked over at him. Carter cleared his throat and looked desperately out the bus window.

"Go on," said R, "ask her for a match."

"Certainly not!" hissed Carter under his breath.

"Ask her for a match!" shouted R.

"Quit that!" hissed Carter, cringing.

"Not until you ask her. You ought to see yourself. Everybody'll be looking at you. *Ask her*—"

"All right, all right—" whispered Carter. Hurriedly, before his nerve was lost entirely, he straightened up and leaned across the aisle toward the girl. "Uh—" he said.

She turned violet eyes upon him.

"Gotta match?" said Carter, desperately.

The violet eyes widened. She blinked.

"But you can't smoke on a bus," she said.

They stared at each other. Then suddenly, the ridiculousness of the whole situation piled up in Carter and he smiled. His smile broadened into a laugh. She began to laugh, too.

"I'm sorry," gasped Carter, when he could get his breath back. "I guess I'm just not very good at picking girls up."

"Oh, I wouldn't call it a pickup," she said. "I've seen you around the building where I work lots of times."

"I know. I've been watching you. In the hall on the fifth floor there. And in the restaurant."

"I know. You like hot beef sandwiches," she said.

"You like tuna fish," he answered. "And your name's Lucy. At least that's what the girls you eat lunch with call you."

"Lucy Sandstrom. And you're Carter—"

"Hoskins."

"Hurray, hurray!" sang R, bouncing on the seat beside him. "We're on our way!"

Carter hardly heard him.

". . . and I'll meet you here at twelve-fifteen for lunch," said Carter, as they parted later at the door of his fifth-floor office.

"Twelve-fifteen."

"Good-by."

She drifted off down the hall. Carter turned and floated through the door into the business offices of Spencer Leighton Inc., where the office girls were already settling down to the reports sent in by their field salesmen.

Humming, Carter sat down at his own office manager's desk at the top of the room and reached for the first of a pile of incoming letters the girls had bucked on to him.

"Never mind that," said R, at his elbow. Carter blinked slightly and turned to look. R was standing beside him with a sheet of paper in one hand. "I've got a script of answers here you've got to memorize. Now, in just a few minutes—"

"Now listen," hissed Carter, under his breath, but

not quite as harshly as he might have before the bus encounter with Lucy, "I'm grateful for what you've done for me, but now I've got to get to work. Thanks—and goodbye."

"Oh, we've only just started," said R. "I want to help. You need happiness, wealth and fame. So far you've only got happiness. Now, you learn these answers I've got written down here—"

"Thanks. No," said Carter.

"But you have to learn them—"

"I don't. I won't. And furthermore—"

"Carter!" snapped a new voice. Carter jerked his head up guiltily to see Mr. Spencer—the front half of the Spencer-Leighton partnership—standing in the doorway of his private office. "Come in here when you get a moment, will you?"

"Yes sir. Right away," said Carter. Hal Spencer's office door closed again. Carter hastily started to stand up.

"Wait, don't go in yet," said R. "The answers—"

Carter ignored him. He strode over to the office door, rapped briefly on it, and walked on it.

"There you are, Carter," said Hal Spencer, raising his thin face from the correspondence in front of him. "Sit down."

Carter took a chair alongside the desk.

"Look, Carter," said Hal, "you know the name of this guy coming out from Tumblen Tool?"

"No, I don't," said Carter.

"Well, it's Jack Eason," said Hal. "I want you to remember that and pass it along to Susy. We don't want a receptionist who doesn't recognize the representative of one of our best customers when he arrives. Now, here's the set-up. He'll be in about three this afternoon. As soon as he shows up, you take him over from Susy and show him right in here."

R jogged Carter's elbow.

"Ask him if he wants you to hang around."

"Want me to hang around?" asked Carter without thinking. Hal Spencer looked surprised.

"Why, it might be a good idea, at that. I'll tell you what, if I invite you to sit down, too, you stick. If I don't say anything, fade back to your desk until I call for you. That way we can play it by ear. Got it?"

"Uh—yes," said Carter, perspiring, and making motions below the level of the desktop to shoo R away.

"And make me a reservation for two at the Sunset Room. I'll be taking him out to dinner later."

"Want me along on that?" prompted R, in Carter's ear.

"Want me—" Carter caught the words before they were all out of his mouth.

"What?" demanded Hal, staring slightly at him. "Go on. Speak up."

"Oh, nothing," said Carter, sweatily.

"Blast it, Carter," said Hal, "if you've got any ideas I want to hear them. I don't know why we can't sell that tool of theirs. Leighton doesn't know. The salesmen have no suggestions. We're on the spot. We move—or come up with some ideas for moving it—or they'll be hunting some other distributing organization. Now, what were you going to say?"

"Want me along on the dinner deal tonight?" said R.

"Want me along on the dinner deal tonight?" said Carter.

"What can you do?"

Carter hesitated, waiting for a prompt from R. But it was not forthcoming.

"Well, if nothing else," he stammered, "it'd help convince him the whole office was actively interested in the problem."

"An idea," said Hal. He looked at Carter closely. "I'll think about it. You can hop on that reservation business, now."

At lunchtime, he met Lucy at the elevator; and they went out of the building, and around the corner to eat lunch at a place where there weren't so many people who would know them. Among other things, while they were eating lunch, Carter told her about the representative due from Tumblen Tool.

"But *Jack Eason!*" said Lucy. "Didn't you say this Tumblen Tool outfit is in Philadelphia?"

"Yes," said Carter.

"Why, I know him!" said Lucy. "He's a little taller than you, and goodlooking—with black wavy hair?"

"I've never seen him," said Carter, a trifle stiffly.

"I used to go out with him, now and then, at the University."

"Oh?"

"I'll bet I can help you!" said Lucy, excitedly.

"Help me?"

"Why, yes. I know Jack—maybe I can help you think of some way of handling him. You say these Tumblen people aren't very pleased with the way you've been pushing this combination home tool of theirs?"

"Our salesman can't seem to move it with the industrial hardware stores," said Carter. "The trouble is, there's been so many of that sort of thing put on the market—you know, the screwdriver with extra smaller bits and awls kept in a hollow handle. Actually, the Tumblen outfit's got something really new and good in their assortment of extra bits and that spring windup handle with the rachet. But it looks like just another gimmick to the retailers."

"Can't you tell Jack that?"

"It wouldn't solve his problem if we did," said Carter. "Or Tumblen's. They want a plan for selling the tool, not reasons why we can't."

"Can't you think of something?" said Lucy. "Jack's very definite-minded. He likes things all laid out and accounted for—"

"You know," said Carter, with sudden thoughtfulness, "that's an idea."

"What's an idea? For Jack?"

"No," said Carter. "I mean for the retailers. You see, maybe if we could rig up a little metal jig that would hold a prepared block of varnished wood, our own screw, and the wound-up tool, our salesman could stand back and let it work—no hands. The tool would look like a piece of power machinery working."

He reached for the paper napkin and took a pencil from his pocket. "Let's see," he mumbled. "Something like this—and this—" He felt the pencil drawn from his fingers, firmly

"Goodness," said Lucy. "Where did you learn to draw? Let me do it." She reached into her purse, fumbled around and came up with a five-by-nine file card. On the white back of this, she began to sketch.

"Like this?" she said.

"Well—uh—yes," said Carter. He felt a nudge at his elbow and looked around. R was standing there, poking him with gleeful enthusiasm, nodding at Lucy's bent head and grinning happily.

When Carter got back, Hal Spencer was still out to lunch; and, by the time he did return, Carter was caught up in the pressure of the full day's work. Carter saw the older man pass through his office on the way to the inner office, but he was in the middle of dictating a reply to one of their suppliers; and, by the time he had finished that, there was something else to demand his attention— and the afternoon slipped by. The sketch Lucy had made for him remained in his center desk drawer.

R had vanished again. For this much, Carter was thankful. There was a worm in the fact of the other's presence that gnawed away at everything R had brought him. Carter was still up to his ears in work and chained to his desk when he heard Susy's voice cutting across the room.

"Oh, yes, Mr. *Eason*. Just a minute."

Rising, Carter glanced at the wall clock across the room. Four-thirty. Where had the afternoon gone? He strode over to the visitor, looking him over on the way. Jack Eason was everything Lucy had said, and perhaps a bit more. The dynamic, good-looking type. Something inside Carter bared its fangs, slightly, even as he bared his teeth in a welcoming smile.

"Jack Eason!" said Carter, offering his hand. "I'm Carter Hoskins, the office manager here. Come along. Hal Spencer's been expecting you."

Eason responded politely. They shook hands. Carter escorted him through the busy office and into Spencer's private room.

"Mr. Spencer," he said. "Here's Jack Eason, from Tumblen."

Hal rose in welcome. He shook hands. He offered Eason a chair. He did not offer Carter one.

R appeared at Carter's elbow, panting slightly.

"I almost forgot," said R. "I got here just in time. Now."

"Now?" said Carter, involuntarily out loud.

". . . been looking forward to this. What was that, Carter?" asked Hal, looking over from his seat behind the desk.

"Could I talk to you outside for a moment?" prompted R.

"Could I," Carter swallowed, "talk to you outside for a moment?"

"Right now?" Hal frowned. "Well, all right. Just a minute." He followed Carter out, closing the door behind him. "Now, what is this?" he demanded in a low voice.

"That drawing," said R.

"—just a minute—" Carter dived for his desk. He got out the sketch and brought it back to Hal. "Look, here's an idea. I didn't get a chance to show it to you earlier. But you see, we could use this as a sales aid—" He explained hurriedly.

"Why didn't you tell me this before?" said Hal. He stared at Carter. "All right, give it here." He disappeared back through the door of his private office.

Carter sighed and turned back to his own desk. R was sitting on the edge of it, beaming gleefully. Carter stared at him.

"You don't mean to say you're pleased with that reaction?" Carter said, sotto-voce.

"Wonderful, wonderful," bubbled R. "Everything's going just right."

Some twenty minutes later, Eason and Hal Spencer left the office, Hal nodding rather curtly to Carter as they passed. The office girls started their end-of-the-day bustle and cleanup; and Carter somewhat sadly wound up his own day's work.

He brightened, however, when he saw Lucy. She was waiting by the elevator for him; and they left the building together.

"It's all clear," said Carter. "*Will* you have dinner with me, tonight?"

And she said, "Yes, I'll just have to phone home first." Which started them off on a new round of personal discoveries—to wit, the fact that Carter had a room while Lucy lived in an apartment with her parents and one younger sister—that lasted up to the very door of the phone booth in the cocktail lounge across the street from the office building.

Carter was ordering two drinks while Lucy phoned, when R appeared on the bar stool next to him.

"Aren't you excited?" he said to Carter.

Carter frowned at him.

"Excited's hardly the word we use—" he began.

"Oh, that's right. I forgot, you don't know anything about it," bubbled R. "The turning point of your life comes up in just two hours and three minutes. Boy, I'll be right with you!"

"What?" said Carter. "What're you talking about—" he broke off as Lucy came back from the phone booth and sat down on the very bar stool R had been occupying. R winked out of existence just in time.

"What did you say?" Lucy asked.

"Nothing," said Carter. "Just thinking out loud, I guess. Now, here's your drink. Where would you like to have dinner?"

"The Sunset Room," said R, appearing on top of the cash register behind the bar.

"No!" cried Carter, involuntarily.

"No what?" asked Lucy, staring at him.

"J-just thinking out loud again," stammered Carter. "I thought of this place, the Sunset Room—"

So they talked about it for the next forty-five minutes over a couple more drinks and amongst a number of other subjects. At the end of that time they were both slightly intoxicated, and Carter, at least, was overwhelmingly in love. Also, they were hungry.

They went to the Sunset Room in a taxi.

When they arrived, they discovered they had forgotten all about reservations. They left Carter's name with the captain and went into the bar.

"Why, look," said Lucy.

Carter looked. He saw Eason and Hal Spencer sitting at one of the small, round tables. His eyes met Hal's, and Hal, beaming, waved them both over.

"Uh—well," said Carter, as they reached the table and both men there stood up. "Lucy, this is Hal Spencer, my boss. Hal, Lucy Sandstrom. You know Jack, I think."

"Well, well. Hello," said Hal. "You'll join us won't you?"

They all sat down.

"You could have knocked me over with a swizzle stick," said Eason to Lucy, "when I saw you in the doorway there."

"Well, I knew you were in town. Carter mentioned you. How has everything been, Jack?" said Lucy.

"Well, shall we all have a drink?" asked Carter, somewhat loudly.

The waitress came and they ordered. Eason and Lucy developed a little conversation of their own, full of do-you-remembers and whatever-became-ofs. Carter hung on the outskirts of their talk until he felt his elbow nudged; he turned about to see Hal eloquently signaling with his eyebrows.

"Excuse me a minute," said Hal getting up, and signalling again.

"Uh—me too," said Carter. They went out together into the privacy of the foyer.

"What's wrong with you?" snapped Hal, when they were out of earshot of the bar. "All he's doing is talking to her. You look dangerous enough to be locked up."

"They're old friends," said Carter, grinding the words between his teeth. "And I just got to know her, today."

"Now listen to me—come on in here," said Hal. He led Carter off to one side of the foyer and down three carpeted steps to the small bar of the taproom. "One double scotch," he told the bartender. It came. "Drink that," he ordered.

"I don't want it," said Carter.

"You'll drink it and like it," said Hal.

Carter growled; but poured it down. Hal pounded him on the back as he strangled.

"Now," said Hal, when Carter had more or less recovered. "You listen to me. That sketch you gave me went over fine. How'd you like to fill a new job for us—as head of sales promotion?"

"What?" said Carter.

"I feel that this business of selling Eason'll do it—unless you'd rather trade all this future for a chance to punch him in the nose."

"He's right," said R, putting in an appearance right under the unaware Spencer's elbow.

"Hell!" said Carter disgustedly. "All right."

They went back and found that the time of Hal's dinner reservation had arrived. An arrangement was made with the captain to fit Carter and Lucy in at the reserved table. They all went in and sat down to dinner.

The food was good. The conversation became general again; and Lucy smiled at Carter. His spirits began to rise with the hors-d'oeuvres and continued up through the soup and salad to the steak. With the hot apple pie, however, he began to feel that perhaps he had overeaten—or perhaps that he had had a drink or two too many before they sat down at the table. He pumped himself full of coffee, but his transient enthusiasm, now started downhill, continued to slide with increasing rapidity. He felt, in fact, the slight beginnings of a hangover, and his own part in the conversation became more and more monosyllabic until he was merely sitting back, sipping his fourth coffee—which by now was beginning to taste bitter in his mouth—and listening.

The others seemed to sparkle all the more as he, himself, lost his lustre. Hal was jovial, the matter of the combination tool now settled. Lucy was beautiful, and Eason—Carter had to admit it even to himself—the life of the party. It was impossible not to laugh at his jokes, it was inevitable to warm to his outgoing personality. Sinking down into his gloomy depths, Carter looked up at the star-like luminescences of his dinner companions and thought to himself that Eason and Lucy made a good-looking couple. And with that thought, he hit rock-bottom.

However, just at that moment, Hal got up and went off to talk to someone he had just recognized on the other side of the dining room; and Lucy excused herself to powder her nose. Carter, left alone, looked across his coffee cup at Eason with the fatalistic despair with which a downed Infidel might have watched a Crusader approaching to finish him off. Eason leaned across the table toward him.

"That Lucy!" he said.

"Yeah," said Carter.

"Tremendous, isn't she? She's always been that way, ever since grade school. I met her for the first time in third grade. Yes," said Eason, reminiscently, "it was love at first sight. Well, that's the way it goes. Time, I mean."

"Oh, yes. Time," said Carter.

"Never thought I see her again, after I was moved to Philadelphia. Then running into her like this."

" 'Scuse me," mumbled Carter, getting up. "Back in a minute."

He slogged off to the entrance and out of the dining room. A dull fury of self-accusation was curdling inside him. He looked around for R, but R was nowhere visible. He went over and looked in through the door of the men's washroom.

"R!"

There was no response.

"Listen, R!" he said, ominously. "If you can keep popping up at the right moment all the time, you can pop up now. Now, pop!"

R appeared, looking somewhat abashed, in the center of the tiled floor.

"What's the matter?" he asked.

"What's the matter?" cried Carter, squinting a little to keep R in focus. "I'm a fake, that's what! Could I have any of this on my own? No! All right, I'll take promotion. But Lucy—that Eason's made for her!"

"But listen—but wait—" said R.

"Listen! Never!" snarled Carter. "What d'you think

I am, a puppet?" He repeated the last two words for emphasis. "Bad enough for *me*." He brooded darkly. "Not going to make Lucy a puppet. Who do you think I am? Dorian Gray? Or Faust?"

"What are you so mad about?" wailed R.

"Lucy," gritted Carter. "Not going to trick her into life of unhappiness."

"Oh, but that doesn't make any difference. You see—"

"Never!" announced Carter. with a wide gesture that threw him momentarily off balance. "If I can't win her on my own, I—I won't, that's all. Nice thing to look at her for the next eighty years and know I tricked her into marriage. So keep your advice! And to think—" his voice drooped sadly, "I might have done all this on my own. But I never had the chance. *You* had to come along with your advice! Well, I'm through. I'm leaving it all, job and everything!"

"But I thought you liked it!" wailed R.

"I would, if I'd done it myself! This way's cheating. And I'm not going to stand for it! I'm going to take off and leave them all to sort it out by themselves. And I hope *you're* happy! At least I was plugging along in my own way, not bothering anybody before. Now, look! You had to stick your big nose in! You had to mess up my life and everybody else's!"

R burst into tears. He wailed like a banshee.

"Yeah, cry!" shouted Carter. "That's all you can do. Genius, eh? Superhuman, huh? You're nothing but a nasty-minded little—little—"

"What's the matter?" cried a woman's voice; and Carter almost swallowed his tongue as a rather Amazonian young woman appeared from nowhere in the middle of the floor. R turned and threw his arms around her shortskirted legs and howled.

"Mommy!" he wailed.

"What's going on, here!" cried the woman, turning flashing, violet eyes on Carter. "What're you doing to my boy?" She looked down on R and her expression changed. "Aha!" she snapped.

Reaching down, she took a firm hold on R's large

nose and pulled. Nose and whiskers came off in her hand, revealing a small-boy face.

"So this is what you've been up to!" she said. "What have you been doing this time? Answer me!"

R only cried harder. She turned her head toward Carter.

"What did he do?"

"Uh—well—" babbled Carter, "he's been telling me what to do. And—" said Carter, his voice hardening as he remembered his troubles "—wrecking my life in the process. Telling me how to get successful, and pick up the girl I wanted to meet, and—"

"I was just pretending!" sobbed R. "I was just playing Rescue the Ancestor, that's all!"

"Rescue the—" Carter blinked.

"I was a Rescuer. But I didn't really do anything. I couldn't."

"Of course," said the woman, sharply. "The boy's right. The past is immutable. No matter what anybody from the future does, they can't change what's happened. You haven't been hurt a bit."

"Haven't been hurt!" cried Carter. "Yesterday I'd never spoke to the girl—I expected to go on being an office manager the rest of my life—and look at me now."

"Don't talk nonsense!" said the woman. "Let me scan." Her eyes veiled for a second. They they cleared. "I just had a look," she said. "It's just as I told you. You haven't done anything but what you did do on this day, anyway. You haven't even said a word that you didn't originally say."

"You mean I asked for a match on the bus—" said Carter.

"Of course. Just as I told you." She reached down and took R by the arm. "Now you come along," she said. "And if I ever catch you bothering your great, great grandfather again, I'll—"

They both disappeared. There was a certain finality about the way they did it this time.

Carter shrugged in a dazed way, turned and wandered out of the washroom. He went back to the table in the dining room, and sat down. Hal had rejoined the group and they were all looking at some snapshots.

"Oh, Carter!" said Lucy, passing one over to him. "Look at that! It's Jack's boat. He's got it down on the Chesapeake Bay; and he wants me to come down to Philadelphia some time and he'll take me sailing. Isn't it a perfect boat?"

"Ah—yes," said Carter, taking the snapshot in his hand. But he said it with a note of renewed confidence. He was thinking of the violet eyes of R's mommy. Give or take a few pounds and inches, he now remembered, that young woman had been the spitting image of Lucy.

"A very nice little boat, indeed," he agreed heartily.

The intrepid climber turns a barricade into a ladder.

One on Trial

The place they emerged into—the General wheezing a little spasmodically like a man with something stuck in his gullet, but trying not to show it—was a pleasant little glade, vaguely tropical in appearance. The General—everybody called him that now that he had become a sort of terrible old man, although he had no real right to the title—paused just inside the screen of bushes; and his companion, the box-like machine on stilts, also halted.

As they stood there, there was an odd, baritone moan of pain off in the pines to their right. A sound like that of a giant quietly suffering. The General turned, conscious suddenly that he had no direct memory of how the sanity technicians had brought him to this place; and a magnificent, black-maned lion with tawny, rippling fur limped into the clearing, holding his right forepaw awkwardly clear of the ground.

"Fear not," said the machine. "I will protect you."

"Who's afraid?" exploded the General. "I haven't been scared for forty years. They said war would shake the guts out of any civilian officer—but it didn't me. They said I'd never have the brass to put five billions on the line to open up the Sahara— every cent I had, every cent I'd ever made. But I did." He looked toward the lion, which was gazing off to one side of them. "Now what? What'd they stick this beast in here for?"

The machine did not answer. Looking closer, the General perceived a heavy black thorn embedded in one pink-and-dirty pad of the upheld paw. The lion turned its head toward him and again made its low, heart-rending moan. The General shook his head and turned away.

"So limp," he said, and strode off. The machine trundled after. "Quit crowding me!" snarled the General, as he pushed through a small stand of tall ferns and emerged on a sort of animal track, leading down amongst bushes and tall purple flowers like lilies. "I don't have to explain myself to you."

"I am only here to hear anything you have to say," said the machine, in its pleasant, sexless voice. It leaned to him almost confidentially, a rectangular, gunmetal box on four dull-shiny, stiltlike legs of adjustable heights. "To accompany you and protect you. But to demand nothing."

"You're a cute hunk of junk," said the General. He went down around a curve in the path and found himself on an open hillside. He stopped. "You might store up in that tin brain of yours one fact," he said. "I could have dodged this business, if I'd wanted to. You think I lived sixty years without finding out how to get around a simple health law? But no board of directors are going to run me. . . . This the way out of here?"

"That could be interpreted as paranoia," observed the machine.

"Could it now? Well, well," said the General, with the throatily purring pleasure of a tiger lying at its ease with its eyes closed, cracking bones in its teeth.

"Persons with paranoia are a danger to society," said the machine.

"Society's yellow," said the General. He paused. "No, you wouldn't get that, would you? . . . About that lion; what good would it have done if I'd taken the thorn out of his paw?"

"It would have eased his pain," said the machine.

"Yeah," said the General, like a man spitting tacks. "I asked you before—this the way out of here?"

"The only way out of here," said the machine, "is for you to discover for yourself. You may save yourself, or destroy yourself, but those are the only two alternatives there are for you here."

The General reached out and pounded with one skinny, brown, hard fist on the side of a nearby boulder of grey-speckled granite half as tall as he was.

"It's real?" he said.

"Absolutely real," said the machine. "An illusion would have no practical curative force. That lion back there *might* have killed you."

"I'll take my chances with him," said the General. He began to descend the slope of the hill among the ankle-high, sharp-edged grass, setting his feet down carefully sideways, so that the slick soles of his business shoes would not slip. He was a little stiff, and one ankle joint cracked dryly as he put his weight on it, the way a knuckled-joint cracks. Halfway down the slope, he became aware of a faint, thin screaming off to his right, and stopped to look.

For a second he could make out nothing but the grass, and then a small stir of brown caught his attention. He stepped over a few feet and discovered a large dirty-white hare caught by a noose that encircled its neck and one forepaw. As the general stepped up close, a small, brown weasel-shaped animal with lusting red eyes backed rustling into the grass and disappeared.

The General looked down at the hare which looked back up at him with the drowning eyes of all helpless wild animals. The General considered it, his sour, grey, old-man's fierce face unmoving.

"Another," he said. He spoke aside to the machine. "What was that after it, just now?"

"A ferret," said the machine.

The General gave a sort of a humphing grunt, and turned away, down the slope. The machine rolled smoothly after him. Behind him, the screaming began again.

"You could have let the hare loose," said the machine. "You could have given it that much of a chance."

"Is that so, Doctor?" said the General.

"I am not a doctor," said the machine. "I am a mechanical attendant only. You need not personify me."

"I'll personify your——" said the General, coarsely. "You know who I'm talking to. All the fat little people who want things nice and cosy. I've killed more men, directly and indirectly, than one of you greasy little characters ever saved in your dedicated minuscule lives—and I built a new world doing it."

"No one denies," said the machine, "that you have been responsible for great and good changes all over the planet. However—"

"Why didn't you shoot me, if you wanted to get rid of me?" said the General. "By Moses, I would've."

"We did not shoot you because of a humanity you were never able to recognize," said the machine.

"I recognized it all right," said the General, tripping over a tree-root at the foot of the slope and stopping to swear vulgarly at it. He was getting a bit short of wind, and feeling tiredness. His age showing. "I just couldn't afford the stuff." He ducked in under some low-hanging elm branches and found himself in woods again. "Where do I go from here?"

"Your path is up to you," said the machine.

"Onward, then," said the General, taking off in the forest darkness over a thick, soft blanket of pine needles. He bit his lean old jaws together against the shadowy chill in this low spot, chill that struck through his thinness and made him shiver under his skin for all his determination to hide it. Slow blood, ancient blood, cool blood— quickly chilled blood and bones. That's what he was, nowadays. "—*The day of the iron gods is past, and now we set up little mud idols*," he muttered between teeth carefully closed and held against chattering.

"I do not know the quotation," said the machine, after a slight pause..

"Damn right you don't," said the General, warming himself with a little spurt of anger; "it's from something I wrote myself, for myself."

"You have written?" said the machine.

"And sketched, and made up songs, and looked at sunsets, and picked flowers—hell, yes," said the General. "I've been in love, too, for your information; though I never saw any reason to get these things into the papers. Nobody's business but my own."

"A public character belongs in part to the pub—" began the machine.

"Go back and tell the public that if they think that, they're wrong," said the General. "They never did anything for me. I had to do it all for them; and when I finally got where I was aiming at—" He tripped suddenly, and fell heavily, wrenching his back in a painful manner, although the thick bedding of pine needles he fell on cushioned his fall. He lay there for a second, then sat up, and tried to get to his feet. One ankle, he found, was locked and held vise-like by something.

He looked closer and discovered it was entrapped by some sort of metal band that had closed upon it. From the band, a metal chain led to a metal stake driven almost entirely into the flinty earth below the pine needles. He tugged on the chain, but the stake did not stir.

"Cute," commented the General, through teeth locked now against the pain in his back. He felt around in his pockets for something to dig with. He had always been in the habit of carrying a penknife. It was not there, of course. Nothing was. After a moment, he thought of his belt, took it off, and began to pick away at the dirt around the stake with the metal buckle. The dirt gave grudgingly. "Come to think of it," he said, aside to the machine, "all this business could be a polite and legal way of shooting me after all, couldn't it?"

"I assure you," said the machine, "this is merely demonstrated psychotherapy, a situation contrived so that you may have an opportunity to discover the error in your personality and correct it."

"But it can kill me," said the General.

"Excuse me," replied the machine, "you can force it to kill you."

"Thereby revealing a death-wish," said the General ironically.

"That could be one possible interpretation of your refusal to discover your error in viewpoint and correct it, yes," answered the machine. "After all, your decision to undergo this therapy was voluntary—"

"In a pig's—" said the General,

"I do not make sense out of that last statement of yours," said the machine. "You seemed to fail to complete the thought."

"Finish it yourself," grunted the General, digging around the stake. He had got down about three inches on each side, tearing the skin of his fingers, however, in the process. "I said, the hell it was voluntary."

The machine said nothing. It stood there in a silence that had something polite about it as the General dug at the earth about the stake with his belt buckle. As for the General, he went back to talking, having discovered it took his mind off the sharp arrows of pain now shooting across his lower back.

"I've probably slipped a disc or some such stupid thing," he told the machine. "Yes, I said the hell it was voluntary. It was go through this rigamarole or turn half the world over to little fat-brains like that board of directors."

"It is merely a question of competency at your present age," said the machine. "You should not be set completely aside, only required to surrender active control of the five heavy industries and the two services in question."

"What other kind of control is there?" grunted the General. "I went from Administration Colonel to Chief of Staff in two and a half years of war. High as I could go. Never wore a uniform since—for all the title stuck; but I could step back into command tomorrow and make things hum. And those jokers know it. Same thing with anything else in the world. I'm the roadblock in the way of every ambitious corporation head and high executive in the world. Since I stood the world on end like Columbus did with the egg, they all want to try it. They want to get back to chewing on each others' throats. Well, I'm not about to let them." The General chuckled suddenly, in spite of his back, " *'For lo, the earth is laid in the peace that I just made, and lo, I wait on thee to trouble it.'* "

"Kipling," commented the machine, "incorrectly quoted."

"Correct or incorrect, who cares if the sense is there?" said the General. "I'll go buy myself a set of monkey glands a couple of months from now, go off, rejuvenate, and come back to plague them as a young man again. How'd they like that?"

"There is no connection between any glands possessed by monkeys and the possibility of rejuvenating aged humans," said the machine.

"You got a tick-tock soul," said the General. "To hell with you." He dug away at the stake for some moments in silence. He was about eight inches down now and he laid aside the belt buckle for a moment, took hold of the stake and tried to shake it loose from its bed of earth. It did not give.

"They must've got it anchored someplace down in China," said the General. He looked up at the machine. "What happens if I never get loose?"

"If you do not get loose," said the machine, "you will not get loose."

"I see," answered the General, "dehydration, starvation, eventual extinction, eh?"

"Probably not," said the machine. "There are a number of carnivores in the vicinity."

"Me and the rabbit," said the General, getting back to work with the belt buckle. Then he paused for a second and for the first time heard the noises of the wood around him—the stealthy rustles, the distant snapping of a twig, the little undecipherable noises.

"So, you have made the connection," said the machine.

"Lo, and stand aghast," sneered the General. "Is this the consequences of me own actions come home to roost at last?" He was not—had never been—a good mime; and the ridicule with which he attempted to infuse his words was heavy-handed. He scraped a little more dirt out and reached down into the hole alongside the stake. "What d'you know?" he said to the machine. "I've dug out all the earth, but the stake seems to be accidently caught in the crack of a boulder. I won't be able to pull it out after all."

The machine did not answer immediately.

"Well?" said the General. "What's your comment on that?"

"I have no instructions to cover such a situation," said the machine. "I—"

It broke off suddenly, half-turning about. The General looked up and off in the direction in which it now faced. Amongst the trees and dappled by their shade, some dozen yards off, stood the black-maned lion, one sore paw still upraised. As the General's eyes met the beast's yellow ones, the lion rumbled softly in its chest, and limped forward a step.

"Still waiting for instructions?" said the General, in a low, calm, even tone, looking at the machine.

"I am still—" began the machine and stopped again.

"Something gone wrong with the machinery?" asked the General, grinning sourly. The lion moved several steps nearer. In the gloom, the General could see its tail swinging back and forth, although still held low. The machine did not answer.

"I take it you're not going to protect me," said the General.

"I have no instructions—"

"I suppose Carnway is behind this," said the General, "or Chandra Lal—or the Eastern Transport bunch, eh?"

"I have no knowledge—"

"Sure," said the General, eyeing the lion, who was beginning to hunch its shoulders a little, its tail motionless, and rising slowly as its eyes glowed unmovingly upon him. "I wondered if they'd stick their necks out this much. It's just what I need. And just in time, too—for now I see the error of my ways. You hear me? How could I rob all those poor widows and orphans? How could I be so hard-hearted to my business enemies? Now I see it all—what I lacked was compassion, the kind of compassion that risks death to take a thorn from the paw of a suffering lion, or the trouble to release a rabbit from the trap where he's lying and squeaking, all helpless. I see it all now. Halleluiah! And from this day forward I intend to mend my ways, making reparation to all those I have wronged. How's that?" demanded the General, looking over at the machine. "Think my life's worth saving, now? Therapy successful?"

The machine half-turned toward the lion, then abruptly froze. A peculiar shiver ran over it. A faint, rattling noise issued from its talk-box, and suddenly its spiky limbs gave way and it fell stiffly over sideways onto the pine needles.

"Well, now, boys," said the General, speaking to no one but the empty air. "This was a mighty cute trick you pulled; and if just one of you had thought of it, and done it all on his own, it might have worked. You might take a lesson from that—a good man doesn't need any help with his dirty work." He looked once more at the lion, who was now just about ready to charge, and began to cough.

His coughing interrupted the tensing of the lion. The big cat straightened up slowly from its incipient crouch. Its tail lowered and began to twitch once more. The General went on coughing; and his coughs progressed from just a polite hack to a whoop, and then to a tearing, retching paroxysm that twisted his body double convulsively and caused saliva to glisten at the thin corners of his mouth. Bent over, he coughed like a man who was tearing his lungs out; and, after a few long seconds, a small black object flew from his lips.

He straightened up and cut off the coughing with an effort. His lean hand scrabbled for the black object—it was a tiny cylinder—and clawed it up out of the pine needles. He held it before him, pinched it, and swung it in a short arc.

Flame spurted near-invisibly from the object's further end, and an arc of fire sprang suddenly up before the lion as the pine needles along a thin curved

line there burst into flames. The lion sprang into the
air like a startled tabby cat, and disappeared.

The dry pine needles caught rapidly. A limb of a
nearby spruce caught and crackled alight quickly—
almost too quickly, a part of the General's mind
noted, for a live and growing tree. But he, meanwhile, still coughing, was bent over, directing the
fierce near-invisible pinpoint of flame from the black
cylinder at the metal chain, which melted in two
before it like a chain of lard. Coughing again from
the smoke, the General scrambled creakily to his
feet. The nearer trees were ablaze now, and the fire
in the pine needles was spreading. The General turned
and stumbled hurriedly away from it, bursting once
more out of the trees and onto the hillside, up which
he panted.

There was noise all around him, a crying and shouting of animals, the gathering roar of the fire, and
occasional crash of a falling tree. Gusts of smoke
blew to him intermittently, and, as he reached the
top of the hill, somewhere ahead above the upper
forest a section of the sky fell out, leaving a black
rectangle reaching halfway up the firmament. Coughing the smoke out of his raw lungs, the General
grunted in satisfaction.

He plunged into the upper forest, shuffling now in
an old man's stubborn run. A great, fat boa-constrictor
wriggled by him; and the General's fingers closed on
the black cylinder. But the snake paid him no attention. It, like the lumbering porcupine they both passed,
and the young dear, brown eyes glazed with fright,
who passed them, was in flight from the flames below; and all were heading toward the black empty
section of sky ahead—from which a strong current of
air was now blowing into the draft of the fire.

The fire, the general saw, was threatening to ring
them all, being held back directly behind them by
the incoming draft but spreading rapidly in two horns
of a crescent on either hand. He passed a small antelope limping, with one leg broken, and a wildcat
shrieking high in an oak tree. He splashed through a

small pool, missed his footing, and flung out a hand to a floating log.

A small brown figure pounced at it, teeth bared. The General stared. It was a ferret—surely the same one he had seen stalking the noosed rabbit. It challenged him to share its log, tiny teeth bared.

Grinning suddenly—though the unusual spasm of facial muscles set him coughing again,—the General reached out with one hand and scooped it off the log, holding it with painful firmness by the nape of its neck, while it squirmed and twisted to get at his hand or wrist.

"Okay—pardner," gasped the General, in a hoarsened voice. "We'll make it out together, you and I. Then you can get back to your rabbits; and me to Carnway and the rest. All I gambled for was for them to stick their necks out—to really try for me by breaking laws. Now I'll go *chop!*"

The General waded forward out of the pool, stumbled over a hollow in the ground, and turned one ankle—but limped grimly on

". . . they had any sense," he rattled hoarsely to the kicking ferret, "they'd see I was necessary. Like you, pardner. They *need* me—*me*, just the way I am. Widows and orphans. If I was the sort cared about widows and orphans how the hell could I stand the world on end?"

His hurt ankle turned under him suddenly; and he went down on one knee. The flames were roaring up the slope behind him. He found a stick and hoisted himself up again. He lurched onward.

"Hang on," he snarled at the ferret. "Another fifty yards. I can see it now, through the trees, the section where they opened up this crazy house. There'll be rescue squads from all over the city out there." He laughed hoarsely, and it started him coughing again. "Catch them starting anything now. . . ."

Just then, the General broke through some juniper bushes and saw the black corner of the opening gaping through a wall of holly trees before him. He lurched toward it; and as he did so, the ferret managed to get itself turned around at last in his grasp and it sank its small needles of teeth into the ball of his thumb.

"You little bastard," snarled the General fondly, shaking the small beast loose from its toothhold, and cuddling it harshly to him as he limped on, stumbling but triumphant, through the holly trees' sharp fingernails and on into the exit.

Since "the gates of heaven are lightly locked," a little child may pass where wiser elders would falter.

The Queer Critter

Play your guitar, Little Lonie, play it loud. Play *Down In the Holler*, play *Catbird's A-Cryin'*, and play *Springfield Mountain*.

Walk down the road, Little Lonie. Walk down the mountain road in the ten o'clock morning of an early spring day with the sun shining on the brush and the pines all green under the blue sky and the dust a-rising like puffs of smoke from the road where your shoefeet hit. Walk down the dip and around the bend and into the little holler, the far holler; and meet the Queer Critter that's waiting for you there.

"Little Lonie?" it says, when you get to the bottom of the holler.

And you look right and you look left; you look high and you look low; and there you see it setting, under a bramble bush. It's a cross between a spider and something awful pretty and first off it don't seem right it can talk to you.

"Where's your mouth?" you say.

"Haven't got any, Little Lonie," it says.

"Where's your eyes?" you say. "How come you can see me?"

"Haven't any eyes either," says the Queer Critter.

163

"I manage though. Don't you fret about me, Little Lonie. Sit down and talk a spell."

And, half without knowing why you do it, you sit down with your guitar across your knees.

"Who be you?" you ask.

"Just a Queer Critter," it says, "from a long ways off. Further than you can think, Little Lonie, and then a far piece yet. But the main thing is, Little Lonie. I'm not a human man, nor a human woman, either."

"Didn't figure you was," you say.

"You see," says the Queer Critter, "I been sitting by myself a long ways off; and I been hearing things about human folk. I heard so much I figured I'd come ask about them; and who should I meet this fine spring morning but you, Little Lonie."

"What-all you been hearing?" you ask.

"A pile of things," it answers back. "Some little good, but a great most bad. A real heap bad. Way out where I come from, Little Lonie, there's some that think human folk ought to be locked up where they are right now and never let go nowhere. And there's even some others say they oughtn't be allowed to live."

That kind of makes you laugh.

"I know folks like that," you say.

"You do?" says the Queer Critter.

"Why sure," you say. "They's always some a little sour and some a trifle skeered; but you can get 'em out of it."

"How do you get them out of it?" asks the Queer Critter.

"Times by talking," you say, "times by playing them out of it. Me and my guitar got a song for near every trouble."

"That so?" it says, real polite for a Queer Critter, "now, suppose someone was to come up to you and say that spite of Scripture there's mighty few among human folk loves their fellow man—or their fellow critter, either."

"Why, I'd figure," you answer, letting your fingers kind of stray on the steel strings of the guitar, "I'd

figure the one as said that had been hearing too
much from other folks that were plumb born worri-
ers. I'd figure he didn't know folks like I know them.
For a one like that, I'd figure he's forgotten all the
lovin' couples and all the mothers that love their
children; and I'd sing him some love songs and some
cradle songs."

"That's all right about that," says the Queer Critter, "but how about them not loving critters?"

"Why, bless you," you says, "there's a great heap
of folks love critters. Why, I could sing you any number of dog-lovin' and horse-lovin' songs. I even know
one fish-lovin' song."

"Maybe that's true," it says, "but those are critters
folks already know."

"What's that got to do with it?" you says back.
"Was a time each didn't know them—they just learned,
is all. You figure nobody's born knowing horses, or
dogs, or fish. All a body's born with's the lovin' feel.
You got that, you kin learn to love ary critter, be you
given a chance."

"Might be that's so," admits the Queer Critter,
"but you got to admit human folk do a lot of terrible
fighting and killing."

"I can't deny that," you says, "but fighting, it comes
out of pure unhappiness. Fighting *and* killing comes
usual out of pure misery. Leave it up to most ary
man or woman I know and he won't fight nor kill
long as he's feeling good and happy."

"Well," says the Queer Critter, "and whose fault is
it that a man's unhappy, if it isn't his own? Hasn't he
had a chance to make the world a happy place?"

"Reckon he has," you says, "if you want to call it a
chance. But shucks, I call it just a little old part of a
chance."

"Don't see how you figure that, Little Lonie," it
says.

"Don't take figuring," you says, "just stands to
reason, that's all."

"That's a mighty weak answer, Little Lonie," says
the Queer Critter.

"Might be for some people," you says, minding

yourself of the distance you got yet to go, and getting to your feet. "Might be for just about anybody but the most of folks. Heard tell once folks all lived in caves, though I could never get it straight if that was afore the Flood or after. Might be Adam and Eve found a cave to live in after they got throwed out of the Garden. Might be Noah and his folks all had to hunt up a cave when the water went down. Don't make no difference, for the point is, they didn't stay in them caves. 'Cause that's folks. They just got to change things; and wasn't never no change made yet without some dust-up in the doing of it. Shucks, folks ain't angels—they're *folk!* When you get back to them as have been saying so much about human folk, you tell'm that. Folk got two things. Most of them try, and most of them got the right feelin's to start with; and if they ever come visiting thataway, tell your friends to remember that; and they and human folks'll get along just fine."

"I'll do that, Little Lonie," says the Queer Critter. "Now you just stand back away from my lightnin' rod things here, and I'll be on my way."

And with that the Queer Critter aims a couple of shiny rods at the ground and all of a sudden, *swishpop*, it's gone, and you don't see it no more.

So you scratch your head for a minute, looking at the place where it set. Then you shrug your shoulders, Little Lonie, and turn back onto the road, heading up the far side of the holler and all along on down the way to the next place to stop. And the sun comes through the pines; and the birds bounce on the bramble branches; and you swing the guitar around so that it hangs by its shoulder cord in front of you where your fingers can reach.

For out of pure happiness you feel like singing. And you go on down the road playing and singing a new song just come into your head but one that you'll be playing on many a doorstep to come. For it's a pretty tune and it's called *Great Day A'Dawnin'*.

Mighty trees from hopeful seedlings grow. For that girl called Hope "is the twig, and the shoot, and the seed, and the bud . . . of eternity itself."

Twig

For four hours Twig had been working up her courage to approach the supply post. Now in the pumpkin-colored afternoon light of the big, orange-yellow sun, she stood right beside one of the heavy rammed-earth walls. From the slice of dark interior seen through the partial opening of the door not two meters from her, came the sound of a raucous and drunken tenor—not a young tenor, but a tenor which cracked now and then on the dryness of a middle-aged throat—singing.

> . . . *"As game as Ned Kelly," the people would say;*
> *"As game as Ned Kelly," they say it today . . .*

It would have been something, at least, if the accent of the singing voice had been as Australian as the ballad of the old down-under outlaw who, wearing his own version of armor, had finally shot it out with the police and been slain. But Hacker Illions had never seen the planet Earth, let alone Australia; and his only claims to that part of Sol III were an Australian-born mother and father, both over twenty years dead and buried here on Jinson's Planet. Even Twig knew that Hacker had no strong connection with Ned Kelly and Australia, only a thread of one. But she accepted his playing the Aussie, just as she accepted his foolishness when drunk, his bravery when sober and his wobbly but unceasing devotion to the Plant-Grandfather.

Hacker had been drinking for at least the four hours since Twig had arrived at the supply post. He would be in no shape to talk sense to now. Silent as a shadow, light as a flicker of sunlight between two clouds, Twig pressed against the coarse-grained earth wall, listening and trying to summon up the courage to go inside, into that dark, noisome, hutchlike trap her own kind called a building. There would be others in there beside Hacker—even if only the Factor of the supply post itself. There might even be others as drunk as Hacker, but worse-minded, men who might try to catch and hold her with their hands. She shivered. Not only at the feel in her imagination of the large, rough hands; but with the knowledge that if they did seize her, she would hurt them. She would not be able to help herself; she would have to hurt them to make them let her go.

Sinking down into a squatting position beside the earth wall, Twig rocked unhappily on her heels, silently mourning inside herself. If only Hacker would come out, so that she would not have to go in after him. But for four hours now, he had not left the building. There must be some place inside there where he could relieve himself; and that meant he would not have to leave the building until he ran out of money or was thrown out—and the posse must now be less than an hour from here.

"Hacker!" she called. *"Come out!"*

But the call was only a whisper. Even alone with Hacker, she had never been able to raise her voice above that whisper level. Normally, it did not matter. Before she had met Hacker, when she had only the Plant-Grandfather to talk to, she had not needed to make sounds at all. But now, if she could only shout, like other humans. Just once, shout like the human she actually was . . .

But her aching throat gave forth nothing but a hiss of air. The physical machinery for shouting was there, but something in her mind after all those years of growing up with only the Plant-Grandfather to talk to would not let it work. There was no time left and no choice. She pulled taut the threads that bound the suit of bark tightly about her body. Hacker had always wanted her to wear human clothes; they would give her more protection against ordinary men, he said. But anywhere except in a closed box like this building, no other human could catch her anyway; and she could not stand the dead feel of the materials with which other humans covered their bodies. She took a deep breath and darted in through the half-open door

She was almost at Hacker's side before anyone noticed her, so light and swift had been her dash across the floor. None of them there saw her passage. Hacker stood, one of his elbows on a waist-high shelf called a bar. It was a long bar that ran along the inside wall of the room with space for the Factor to stand behind it and pass out glasses and bottles. The Factor was standing there now; almost, but not quite, opposite Hacker. Facing Hacker, on Hacker's side of the shelf, was a man as tall as Hacker, but much heavier, with a long black beard.

This man saw her first, as she stole up beside Hacker and tugged at his jacket.

"Hey!" shouted the black-bearded man; and his voice was a deep and growing bass. "Hacker, look! Don't tell me it's that wild kid, the one the Plant raised! It is! I'll be damned, but it is! Where've you been keeping her hid all this time?"

And just as Twig had known he would, the black-bearded man reached out a thick hand for her. She ducked behind Hacker.

"Leave her alone!" said Hacker thickly. "Twig—Twig, you get out of here. Wait for me outside."

"Now, hold it a minute." The black-bearded man tried to come around Hacker to get to her. A miner's ion drill dragged heavily down on a holster fastened to the belt at his waist. Hacker, unarmed, got in the way. "Get out, Hacker! I just want to look at the kid!"

"Leave her, Berg," said Hacker. "I mean it."

"You?" Berg snorted. "Who're you but a bum I've been feeding drinks to all afternoon?"

"Hacker! Come!" whispered Twig in his ear.

"Right. All right!" said Hacker with drunken dignity. "That the way you feel, Berg . . . Let's go, Twig."

He turned and started toward the door. Berg caught him by the looseness of his leather jacket and hauled him to a stop. Beyond the black beard, Twig could see the Factor, a fat, white man, leaning on his elbows on the shelf of the bar and smiling, saying nothing, doing nothing.

"No, you don't," said Berg, grinning. "You're staying, Hack. So's the kid, if I've got to tie you both up. There's some people coming to see you."

"See me?" Hacker turned to face the black beard and stood, swaying a little, peering at the other, stupidly.

"Why sure," said Berg. "Your term as Congressman from this district ran out yesterday, Hacker. You got no immunity now."

Twig's heart lurched. It was worse than she had thought. Hacker drunk was bad enough; but someone deliberately put here to feed him drinks and keep him until the posse caught up, was deadly.

"Hacker!" she whispered desperately in his ear. "Run now!"

She ducked around him, under the arm with which Berg was still holding him, and came up between the two men, facing Berg. The big man stared at her stupidly for a moment and then her right hand whipped in a backhand blow across his face, each finger like the end of a bending slender branch, each nail like a razor.

"What?" bellowed Berg jovially, for her nails were so sharp that he had not immediately felt the cuts. "You want to play too—"

Then the blood came pouring down into his eyes,

and he roared wordlessly, letting go of Hacker and stumbling backward, wiping at his eyes.

"What are you trying to do? Blind me?" he shouted. He got his eyes clear, looked down at his hands and saw them running with his own blood. He roared again, a wild animal furious and in pain.

"Run, Hacker!" called Twig desperately. She ducked in under Berg's arms as he made another clutch on her, lifted his drill from its holster and shoved it into Hacker's belt. "Run!"

Berg was after her now, but even without the blood running into his eyes, he was like a bear chasing a hummingbird. Twig was all around him, within reach one moment, gone the next. He lumbered after her, a madman with a head of black and red.

Hacker, woken at last to his danger and sobered, was backing out the door, Berg's drill in his hand, now covering both the Factor and Berg.

"Leave off, Twig!" Hacker cried, his voice thin on the high note of the last word. "Come on!"

Twig ducked once more out of the grasping hands of Berg and flew to join Hacker in the doorway.

"Get back, Berg!" snarled Hacker, pointing the drill. "I'll hole you if you come any farther!"

Berg halted, swaying. His mouth gapped with a flicker of white teeth in his black and crimson mask.

"Kill you . . ." he grunted hoarsely. "Both. Kill you . . ."

"Don't try it," said Hacker. "Less you want to die yourself first—from now on. Now, stay, and that means both of you, Factor. Don't try to follow. —Twig!"

He slipped out the door. Twig followed. Together they ran for the forest.

Twig touched with her hands the first trees they came to, and the trunks and branches ahead of them leaned out of the way to let them pass, then swayed back together again behind them. They ran for perhaps a couple of kilometers before Hacker's breath began to labor hoarsely in his lungs and he slowed to a walk. Twig, who could have run all day at the speed they had been keeping, fell into a walk beside

him. For a little while he only struggled to get his
breath back as he went.

"What is it?" he asked at last, stopping so that he
would be able to hear Twig's whispered reply.

"A posse, they call it," she said. "Ten men, three
women, all with drills or lasers. They say they'll set
up a citizen's court and hang you."

"Do they?" grunted Hacker. He stank mightily of
alcohol and ugly anger. But he was most of the way
back toward being reasonably sober now; and Twig,
who loved him even more than she loved the Plant-
Grandfather nowadays, had long since gotten used to
his smells. He sat down with a thump, his back
against a tree trunk, waving Twig down to sit also.

"Let's sit and think a bit," he said. "Plain running's not going to do any good. Where are they
now?"

Twig, who was already sitting on her heels, got up
and stepped forward to the tree against which Hacker
was sitting. She put her arms around the trunk as far
as they would reach, laid her cheek against its dear,
rough bark, closed her eyes and put her mind into
the tree. Her mind went into darkness and along
many kilometers of root and by way of many children of the Plant-Grandfather, until she came to the
littlest brothers, whom other humans said were like
a plant called "grass" back on Earth. Less than forty
minutes walk from where she and Hacker were, some
of the littlest brothers were feeling the hard, grim
metal treads of human vehicles, pressing down to
tear and destroy them.

"Peace, littlest brothers, peace," soothed Twig's
mind, trying to comfort them through the roots. The
littlest brothers did not feel pain as the variform Earth
animals and humans like Twig felt it; but in a different way they felt and suffered the terrible wrongness
that was making them not to be in this useless, wasteful fashion. Those being destroyed wept that they
had been born to no better purpose than this; and,
down below all living plants on the surface of Jinson's
Planet, the Plant-Grandfather echoed their despair in

his own special way. He was weary of such destruction at the hands of alien men, women and beasts.

"Peace, Grandfather, peace," sent Twig. But the Plant-Grandfather did not answer her. She let go of the tree, stepped back from it and opened her eyes, returning to Hacker.

"They're riding in carriers," she told him. From the grass, the trees looking down on the passing carriers, she could now describe the open, tracked vehicles and the people in them as well as if her human eyes had actually seen them. "When they first started, there were eight of them, and they were only walking. Now there are five more who brought the carriers. They can catch up to us in half an hour if we stay here. And the carriers will kill many trees and other children of the Grandfather before they come to us."

"I'll head for the High Rocks district, then," said Hacker. The frown line was puckered deep between the blue eyes in his stubbled, bony face. "They'll have to leave their vehicles to follow me on foot; and there's little for them to tear up and hurt. Besides, there they'll chase me a month or weeks and never catch me. Actually, you're the one they really want to catch so they can make you tell where they can find the Grandfather; but they daren't try that while I'm alive to tell the law. We've still got some law here on Jinson's Planet; and supraplanetary law beyond that. That reminds me—"

He fished with two fingers in a shirt pocket under his jacket and came out with a small slip of writing cellulose. He passed it over to Twig.

"While I was still down at Capital City with the Legislature," he said, "I got the Governor-general to send for an ecology expert from the Paraplanetary Government, someone with full investigative powers, legal and all. That's his name."

Twig squatted down once more and unfolded the cellulose strip which had been bent double to fit the small shirt pocket. She was proud of her reading ability and other schooling, which Hacker had gotten for her with a teaching machine he had carried up-country himself; but the original printing on this sheet had been in blue marker and Hacker's sweat had dimmed it to near unreadability.

"John . . . Stone," she read off aloud finally.

"That's the man." Hacker said. "I had it fixed so the whole business of sending for him was secret. But he was supposed to land two days ago and be on his way upcountry here to meet me now. He shouldn't be more than a day's walk south of here on the downcountry trail. He's been told about you. You go meet him and show him that piece of paper. Bring him up to date about what's going on with the posse and all. Meanwhile I'll lead that crew around the High Rocks and down to Rusty Springs by late noon tomorrow. You and Stone meet me there, and we'll be waiting for the posse when they catch up."

"But there's only going to be two of you, even then," protested Twig.

"Don't you worry." Hacker reached out, patted the bark covering her shoulder and stood up. "I tell you he's a supraplanetary official—like someone from the police. They won't risk breaking the law with him there. Once they know he's around, none of these croppers that want to burn out new farming fields from the Grandfather's woods will dare try anything."

"But when he goes again—" Twig also rose to her feet.

"By the time he goes," said Hacker, "he'll have recommended a set of laws for the legislature that'll stop those forest-burners for all time. Go south now, Twig; and when you find him stay with him. If that posse's out after me, it's out after you, too, if it can just find you."

He patted her shoulder again, turned and went off through the trees, moving at a fast walk that was a good cross-country pace—for anyone but Twig.

Twig watched him go, wanting badly to go with him, to stay with him. But Hacker would be right, of course. If what was needed was this John Stone from another world, then he was the one she must go and find. But the unhappiness of everything—of everything all around here and to all the things she loved—

was overwhelming. When Hacker was gone, she dropped face down on the ground, hiding her face against it, spreading her arms as if she could hold it.

"Plant-Grandfather!" she called, letting her mind only cry it forth, for it was not necessary to touch one of the plant children when she called the Grandfather. But there was no answer.

"Plant-Grandfather!" she called again. "Plant-Grandfather, why don't you answer?" Fear shook her. "What's the matter? Where have you gone?"

"Peace, little running sister," came the heavy, slow thought of the Grandfather. "I have gone nowhere."

"I thought maybe people had found you there under the ground," said Twig. "I thought maybe they had hurt you—killed you—when you didn't answer."

"Peace, peace, little runner," said the Grandfather. "I am tired, very tired of these people of yours; and maybe sometime soon I may actually sleep. If so, whether I will wake again, I do not know. But do not believe I can be killed. I am not sure anything can be killed, only changed for a while, made silent until it is remembered by the universe and regrown to speak once more. I am not like your people who must be one form only. Whether I am root or branch or flower makes no difference to me. I am always here for you, little runner, whether I answer you or not."

Twig's tears ran down her nose and dampened the earth against her face.

"You don't understand!" she said. "You can die. You can be killed. You don't understand. You think it's all just sleeping!"

"But I do understand," said the Plant-Grandfather, "I understand much more than any little runner, who has lived only a moment or two, while I have lived long enough to see mountain ranges rise and fall again. How can I die when I am more than just the thing of woody roots these people would find and destroy? If that is gone, I am still part of every plant thing on this world, and my little runner as well. And if these things should someday be gone, I am still part of the earth and stone that is this planet; and after that, part of its brother and sister planets; and after that even all worlds. Here, alone, I taught myself to speak to all my plant brothers and sisters from the largest to the smallest. And all the while, on a world so far away it is lost even to my view, your people were teaching themselves to speak. So that now I and you speak together. How could that happen if we were not all one, all part of each other?"

"But you'll still be dead as far as I'm concerned!" sobbed Twig. "And I can't stand it! I can't stand to have you dead!"

"What can I say to you, little running sister?" said the Grandfather. "If you will make it that I am dead, then I will be dead. But if you will let it be that I cannot be killed, then I cannot be killed. You will feel me with you forever, unless and only if you shut out the feeling of me."

"But you won't help yourself!" wept Twig. "You can do anything. You took care of me when I was a baby, alone. There was only you. I don't even remember my mother and father, what they looked like! You kept me alive and grew me up and took care of me. Now you want to take yourself away, and I'm not to care. And you don't have to give up, just like that. You could open the ground in front of these people and let the hot rock out. You could empty the rivers they drink from. You could send seeds against them with pollen to make them sick. But you won't do anything—nothing but lie there until they find you and kill you!"

"Doing what you say is not the way," said the Plant-Grandfather. "It is hard to explain to a little runner who has only lived a moment, but the universe does not grow that way. Along that way of damage and destruction, all things fail and their growth is lost—and so would mine be. You would not want me to be sick and no longer growing, would you, little running one?"

"Better that than dead."

"Again, that thought which is no thought. I cannot make you unsad, small runner, if you insist on sadness. I have put to use many of our brothers and sisters, from the littlest to the largest, to keep and care for you as you grew, alone and away from your own people, because I wished that you should come to run through this world and be happy. But you are not happy; and I, who know so much more than a small runner, know so little of a greater knowledge which I have yet to learn, that I do not know what to do about this. Follow your own sadness, then, if you must. I am with you in any case, though you will not believe it—with you, now and forever."

Twig felt the Plant-Grandfather turning his attention away from her. She lay sobbing her loneliness to the earth under her for a little while; but in time her tears slowed and she remembered the errand on which Hacker had sent her. She got to her feet slowly and began to run toward the south, letting the wind of her passage dry the wetness upon her face.

It did not come at once, but slowly the poetry of her own motion began to warm the cold lump of fear and sorrow inside her. If Hacker was right about what the man John Stone could do, then everything could be all right after all. Suddenly remembering that it would be well to check on the posse, she turned sharply from her original route to angle back toward the supply post. She came right up to the edge of the trees surrounding the clearing in which the post stood, and sure enough, the vehicles and the men and women were there. She looked out at them without fear, for like most of her people they saw and heard poorly in comparison to herself; and, in addition, the trees and bushes had bent around her to screen her from any discovery.

She was close enough so that she could hear clearly what they were saying. Apparently one of the vehicles had broken a tread and needed fixing . Some of the men there were working on its left tread, now like a huge metal watchband come uncoiled from around the drive wheels on that side beneath the open box of the vehicle body. Meanwhile those not working stood about arguing in the now westering, late afternoon sunlight.

". . . bitch!" Berg was saying. He was talking about

her. The blood from his facial cuts had stopped flowing some time since, and what had leaked out had been cleaned away. But he was flushed about the forehead and eyes where the cuts had parted the flesh. "I'll hang her in front of Hacker himself, first, before we hang him when we get them!"

"You'll not," said one of the women, a tall, middle-aged, bony female in a short, brown leather jacket and country leather pants showing a laser in a black holster over her right buttock. "First she's got to talk. It's that Grandfather plant-devil that really needs killing. But then she comes into a proper home somewhere."

"Proper home—" shouted Berg, who might have gone on if another woman—shorter and heavier, but wearing a dress under her once-white, knee-length weathercoat and boots—had not snapped him off short. This one wore no visible weapon, but her voice was harsher and more belligerent even than that of the taller woman.

"Shut it, right there, Berg!" said this woman. "Before you say something you'll be sorry you ever thought of. There's plans been made for that girl among the decent croppers' families. She's been let run wild all these years, but she's a child of man and she'll come to be a good grown woman with loving rules and proper training. And don't go getting ideas about getting your hands on her after we catch her, either. It's us wives along on this posse who'll be making her tell where that Grandfather devil hides, not none of you men."

"If you can . . ." growled Berg.

The heavier woman laughed, and Twig shivered through all her body at the kind of laughter it was.

"Think we couldn't make you talk?" the heavy woman said. "And if you, why not a kid like her?"

Twig drew back until the leaves and the bushes before her hid the vehicles and their passengers from sight. She had learned all she needed to know anyway. The vehicles were now held up; so there was no danger of their catching up with Hacker before he reached the High Rocks—a hill region peppered with rounded chunks and blocks of stone where the vehicles would not be usable. Not that there had been much chance of their catching Hacker anyway—but now, at least, she was sure.

She turned and began to run once more southward in search of the man John Stone, as the sun lost itself among the trees and began to descend into twilight.

Once more, she ran. And once more the intoxication of her own running began to warm away the shivers that had come on her from the overheard conversation. Now, running, no one could catch and hold her, let alone do terrible things to her to make her say where the root-body of the Plant-Grandfather rested in the earth.

The sun was down now; and the big white moon of Jinson was already in the sky. It was full, now, and seemed—once her eyes were adjusted to it—to throw almost as much light as the twilight sun; only this was a magic, two-tone light of white and gray without color. In this light the trees and bushes leaned aside to let her pass, and the littlest brothers underfoot stretched like a soft gray carpet before her, making a corridor of moonlight and shadow along which she fled so lightly it was as if she went without touching the earth at all.

There was no effort to her going. She put on speed and earth, bushes, trees and moonlight swam about her. Together, they made up the great, silent music of her passage; and the music swept her away with it. There was nothing but this—her running, the forest and the moonlight. For a moment she was again only a little runner—even the Grandfather and Hacker were forgotten, as was the posse with its other humans. It was as if they had never existed. She danced with her world in the white-and-black dance of her limitless running; and it was she and the world alone, alone and forever.

Twig had run the moon high up into the night sky, now, and he rode there, made smaller by his isolation in the arch of the star-cap that fitted over the

world when the sun had gone; and she began to hear
through her mind, which was now fine-tuned to the
plant brothers and sisters whom she passed and who
made way for her, that the individual she ran to find
was close. The brothers and sisters turned the corridor they were making ahead of her to lead her to
him. Shortly beyond the far moonlight and shadow
she saw a different yellow light that brightened and
dimmed. She smelled on the night wind the scent of
dead branches burning, the odor of an animal and a
human man.

So she came to him. He was camped in a small
clearing, where a stream Twig could easily jump
across curled around the base of a large moss-patched
boulder before going off among the trees again. A
small fire was on the far side of the stream; the man
was seated on the other side of it, staring into the
flames, so still and large with his dark outdoor clothing and clean-shaven face that he seemed for a moment only another mossy boulder. Beyond him was
one of the large hooved riding beasts that her people
called a horse. This smelled or heard Twig and lifted
its head and snorted in her direction.

The man lifted his head then, looked at the horse
and away from the animal toward Twig.

"Hello," he said. "Come in and sit down."

His gaze was right on her, but Twig was not fooled.
In no way could he see her. She was among the trees,
a good four meters from him; and his eyes would be
blinded by the light of his fire. He was simply going
on what his animal had told him.

"Are you John Stone?" she asked, forgetting that
only Hacker could understand her whisper at this
distance. But the man surprised her.

"Yes," he said. "Are you Twig?"

Astonished, now, she came forward into the light.

"How did you know?" she asked.

He laughed. His voice was deep-toned, and his laugh
even deeper—but it was a soft, friendly laugh.

"There ought to be only two people know my name
up here," he said. "One would be a man named

Hacker Illions; and the other might be a girl named Twig. You sound more like a Twig than a Hacker Illions." He sobered. "And now that I see you, you look more like Twig."

She came closer, to the very edge of the stream, hardly a jump away from him, and peered down into his large, white, handsome face. His blond hair was not long, but thick and wavy upon his head, and under light eyebrows his eyes were as blue as a summer lake. He had not moved. Behind him, his horse snorted and stamped

"Why do you just sit there?" Twig asked. "Are you hiding something?"

He shook his head.

"I didn't want to frighten you," he said. "Hacker Illions left word not to move suddenly or try to touch you. If I stand up, will that scare you?"

"Of course not," said Twig.

But she was wrong. He stood up then, slowly, and she took a step backwards instinctively; because he was by far the biggest man she had ever seen. Bigger than she had imagined a man could be, and wider. At his full height, he seemed to loom over everything—over her, and the fire and the boulder, even over the horse behind him that she had thought was so large. Her heart began to beat fast, as if she was still running. But then she saw that he was merely standing still, waiting; and there was no feel of menace or evil in him, as she had felt in Berg, in the Factor of the supply post, the women of the posse and others like them. Her heart slowed. She felt ashamed of herself and came forward to jump the stream and stand right before him.

"I'm not frightened," she said. "You can sit down again."

She sat down cross-legged herself on the ground facing him, and he settled back to earth like a mountain sinking into the sea. Even now that they were seated, he towered above her still; but it was a friendly towering, as a tree-brother might loom over her when she nestled against the trunk below his branches.

"Does my horse bother you?" John Stone asked.

She looked at the big beast and sniffed.

"He has metal on his feet, to cut and kill the little living things, just like vehicles do," she said.

"True," said John Stone, "but he did not put that metal on by his own choice. And he likes you."

It was true. The animal was lowering its huge hammer-shaped head in her direction and bobbing it as if to reach out and touch her, although it was far out of reach. Twig's feelings toward it softened. She held out an arm to it, thinking kind thoughts, and the beast quieted.

"Where is Hacker Illions?" John Stone asked.

All her anxiety came flooding back into Twig in a rush.

"At the High Rocks," she said. "There are people after him . . ."

She told John Stone about it, trying to do the telling in such a way that he would understand. So often when she talked to people other than Hacker they seemed to understand only the words as words, not the meaning behind them. But John Stone nodded as she talked, and he looked thoughtful and concerned, as if understanding was honestly growing in him.

"This Rusty Springs," John said at last when she was done. "How far is it? How long will it take us to reach it from here?"

"For an ordinary human walking, six hours," she said.

"Then if we leave just before sunrise, we should be there when Hacker gets there?"

"Yes," she said, "but we ought to start right now and wait there for him."

John looked up at the moon and down at the woods.

"In the dark," he said, "I'd have to travel slowly. Hacker left word for me you didn't like to travel slowly. Besides, there are many things you can tell me that are easier to hear sitting here than traveling. Don't worry. Nothing's going to stop us from getting to the Rusty Springs on time."

He said the last words in a calm, final way that

reminded her of the Plant-Grandfather speaking. Twig sat back, somehow reassured without being convinced.

"Have you eaten?" John Stone asked. "Or don't you like the same sort of food as the rest of us?"

He was smiling a little. For a second Twig thought he might be laughing at her.

"Of course I eat people-food," she said. "Hacker and I always eat together. I don't have to have it; but it's all right."

He nodded gravely. She wondered uneasily if he could tell what she was not saying. The truth was that for all his knowledge, the Plant-Grandfather had no real understanding of a human sense of taste. The fruits and nuts and green things on which he had nourished as a child had been all right—and still were, she thought to herself—but the people-foods to which Hacker had introduced her were much more interesting to the tongue.

John began opening some small packages and preparing food for them, asking questions as he worked. Twig tried to answer him as well as she could. But even for a person as special as John, she thought, it must be hard to understand what it had been like for her.

She could not even remember what her parents had looked like. She knew, because the Plant-Grandfather had told her, that they had both died of sickness in their cabin when she was barely old enough to walk. She herself had wandered out of the cabin and had been touched, mind-to-mind, by the Plant-Grandfather; and because she was young enough then that nothing was impossible, she had heard, understood and believed him.

He had directed her away from the cabin and the burned-over fields her parents had intended to plant, into the woods, where trees and branches wove themselves into a shelter for her from the rain and wind, and where she could always find something to eat growing within arm's reach. He had kept her away from the cabin until she was much older. When she had finally gone back there she had only glimpsed white bones on the cots in the cabin, hidden under a thick matting of growing green vine the Grandfather had advised her not to disturb. With those bones she had felt no kinship, and she had not been back to the cabin since.

Hacker was something else. By the time she had encountered Hacker, three years ago, she had already become the small runner the Grandfather had named her. Hacker had originally been a cropper like the ones now hunting him. A cropper—as opposed to a farmer who had homesteaded his acres of originally open land and had fertilized, ploughed and planted them year after year in a regular cycle—was someone who made a living by farming no more than two years in a row in any one place.

Most of the good land, the open land, on the world's one continent had been taken over by the first wave of emigrants to Jinson's Planet. Those who came after found that the soil covered by the plant-children of the Grandfather (the existence of whom they never suspected) was a thin layer over rock, and relatively unfertile—unless it was burned over. Then the ashes were rich in what was needed to make the soil bear. But two succeeding years of planting sucked all those nutrients from what had been the bodies of plant sisters and brothers into produce, which was then carried downcountry and away from the wooded areas forever. To the cropper, however, this was no matter. He only moved on to burn out a new farm someplace else.

Just before the spring rains, three years ago, Hacker had moved into the territory where Twig ran. An ideal time for burning over an area, so that the coming showers would wash the nutrients from the ashes into the soil below. But Hacker came, pitched his camp and let the days go by. He did not burn, and he did not burn. Finally it was summer and too late to crop that year. Twig, who had watched him many times, unseen from a distance, drew closer and closer in her watching. Here was a cropper who was not a cropper. He helped himself to the fruits and nuts the Grandfather had made the plant-children put forth

for Twig, but other than that he did not take from
the woods. She could not understand him.

Later she came to understand. Hacker was a drunk.
A cropper who might never have been any different
from other croppers except that, following one fall's
sale of produce, he got into a card game and won
heavily. Following which, in one sober moment he
was to appreciate all his life, he took the advice of a
local banker and put his money away at interest,
drawing only enough for supplies to go upcountry
and burn out a new cropping area.

But when he had gone upcountry once more, he
had taken along a luxury of supplies in the way of
drinkables. He had pitched his camp; but instead of
setting to work to burn land clear immediately, he
had delayed, enjoying his bottles and his peace.

Here in the woods, alone, he did not need to pour
the drink down in the quantities he required in civilization. A nip now and then to blur his surroundings
pleasantly was all it took. And besides, there was
plenty of money still down there in the bank, waiting
for him, even if he did not bring in a cash crop this
year.

In the end, he did not.

In the end, he began to change. Among the woods,
he needed alcohol less and less, for here there were
none of the sharp and brittle corners of the laws that
normally poked and pricked him, driving him into
rebellion. He was not an observing man; but little by
little, he began to notice how the seasons came and
went and how every day the woods responded to the
changes of those seasons in a thousand ways. He
became aware of leaf and bush and plant stem as
individuals—not as some large, green blur. And in
the end, after two years without cropping brought
him to the point where he had to get to work, he
could not bring himself to burn this place where he
had lived and been content. He blazed the trees there
to claim the area for himself and to keep other croppers away, and he moved on.

But the next place he chose made him part of it

also; and he found he could not burn it either. He moved again, this time to Twig's territory; and there, unconsciously fishing with a hook baited with his own differentness, he caught Twig's curiosity and hauled her in.

The day came when she walked boldly into his camp and stopped a few feet in front of him, no longer shy or fearful of him after months of observation.

"Who are you?" she whispered.

He stared at her.

"My God kid," he said. "Don't you know you aren't supposed to run around without any clothes on?"

The wearing of clothes was only the first of many things they found they needed to reach an understanding upon. Twig's point was not that she was unaware of clothes and the fact that other people wore them; rather she did not like the feel of them on her body. Twig, in fact, was not ignorant. The Grandfather had seen to it that as she grew she learned as much about her own people as her maturity allowed her to absorb. He had also seen to it that she visited the woods fringing nearby croppers' farms and had a chance to watch her own people at work and hear them talk. He had even decided that she must practice talking as much out loud as she could, in her own tongue; and Twig, who did what he suggested most of the time without thinking, had obeyed.

But along with the human knowledge she had picked up through the Grandfather's prodding, she had also picked up a great deal of other, wordless wisdom and many skills belonging more to the Grandfather's environment than to her own. Also, the human knowledge she acquired through the Grandfather had been affected in transmission by the fact that the Grandfather was not human and did not think in human terms.

For example, while other humans wore clothes and the Grandfather knew it, such coverings were an alien concept to him; and in any case he forced nothing and no one. When Twig did not want to wear clothes, he taught her how to control her skin temperatures for comfort; then he let the matter go. And there were other ways in which he let Twig be herself, and different from her own kind.

So when Twig and Hacker met at last, it was something like an encounter between two aliens having an only limited amount of language and experience in common. They found each other fascinating in their differences; and from that first meeting their partnership began.

"You wear clothes now," said John Stone at this point in Twig's story, glancing at the soft bark bound about her body.

"That was Hacker's idea. He's right, of course," said Twig. "I don't mind the bark. It was living once, and real. It rubbed a little at first when I wore it, but I taught my body not to be bothered where it touched me."

"Yes," said John Stone, nodding his great head with the wavy, light-colored hair glinting in the firelight. "But how did Hacker get involved in the planetary government here, so that he could arrange to have me called? And why are his own constituents out to murder him now?"

"Hacker got a teaching machine and taught me a lot of things," said Twig. "But he learned a lot too. About the Grandfather and everything. He can't talk to the Grandfather, but Hacker knows he's there, now."

"Downcountry, your people seem to think the Plant-Grandfather is a superstition," said John.

"The Grandfather never paid much attention to them downcountry," said Twig. "But the other croppers up here know about him. That's why they want to find and kill him, just like they want to kill Hacker."

"Why?" asked John patiently.

"Hacker ran for the Legislature two years ago," said Twig. "And at first the other croppers thought it was a great thing, one of their own people trying for the delegate-at-large post. So they all voted for him. But then he stood up in the Legislature-House and talked about the Grandfather and why the woods-

burning should be stopped. Then the other croppers
hated him because the downcountry people laughed
and because they didn't want to give up cropping
and burning. But as long as he was a delegate, the
eye of downcountry law was on him to protect him.
But his two-year term ran out yesterday; and now
they think no one cares."

"Easy. Be easy . . ." said John, for Twig was becoming frightened and unhappy again. "There are
people on other worlds who care—for all Hackers,
and for all beings like your Plant-Grandfather. I care.
Nothing's going to happen to either of them. I promise you."

But Twig sat rocking on her heels, now that she
had remembered, refusing to let herself be comforted
for fear that in some strange way to do so would bring
down disaster

In the dark morning, after they both had slept for
some four hours, they rose and John packed his things,
then mounted his horse. With Twig leading the animal through the woods, they started off for Rusty
Springs.

Dawn began to join them before they were more
than halfway there. As they rode into the growing
sunlight, the horse could see where to place his large
hooves and they began to pick up speed. But by this
time, Twig hardly noticed—though she had fretted at
the slowness of their going earlier— because she was
becoming more and more fascinated with John Stone.
Just as he was big in body, he was big in mind as
well—so big that Twig walked around and around
the way he thought with questions. But in spite of
the fact that he answered willingly enough, she could
not seem to see all at one time what he was by his
answers.

"What are you?" she kept asking.

"An ecologist," said John.

"But what are you really?"

"Something like an advisor," said John. "An advisor to the social authorities on new worlds."

"Hacker said you were something like a policeman."

"That, too, I suppose," said John.

"But I still don't know what you are!"

"What are you?" asked John.

She was surprised.

"I'm Twig," she said. "A small runner." Then she thought and added. "A human . . . a girl . . ." She fell silent.

"There; you see?" said John Stone. "Every one is many things. That is why we have to go cautiously about the universe, not moving and changing things until we know for sure what moving or changing will do to the universe as a result, and eventually, therefore, to ourselves."

"You sound like the Plant-Grandfather," Twig said. "Only he won't even fight back when things are done to him and his children, like the woods-burning of the croppers."

"Perhaps he's wise."

"Of course he's wise!" said Twig. "But he's wrong!"

John Stone looked from his big horse down at her where she ran alongside them. He was riding with his head a little cocked on one side to catch the faint sound of her whispered words.

"Are you sure?" asked John.

Twig opened her mouth and then closed it again. She ran along, looking straight ahead, saying nothing.

"All things that do not die, grow," said John. "All who grow, change. Your Plant-Grandfather is growing and changing—and so are you, Twig."

She tried to shut the sound of his voice out of her ears, telling herself he had nothing to say that she needed to hear.

They came to Rusty Springs just before noon. The place was named for a small waterfall that came directly out of a small cliff about a quarter of the way down from its top. The stream fell into a wide, shallow basin of rock streaked with reddish color, and the water had a strong taste of iron. When they got there, Hacker was sitting waiting for them on a boulder beside the pool.

"You just made it," he greeted them as they came

up. "Another couple of minutes and I'd have had to move on without waiting for you any longer. Hear up a ways, there?"

He tilted his head toward the woods at the opposite side of the basin of spring water. Twig did not have to reach out to one of the Grandfather's children for information this time. Like the others, in fact much more clearly than the two men with her, she could hear the distant smashing of undergrowth as a body of people moved toward them.

"Hacker!" whispered Twig. "Run!"

"No," said Hacker.

"No," said John Stone from high on his horse. "We'll wait here and have a word with them."

They stood together, silent and waiting, while the noise increased; and after a while it came right into the clearing along with the ten men and three women of the posse. They emerged from the woods, but stopped when they saw Hacker and Twig together with John Stone on his big horse.

"Looking for somebody?" said Hacker derisively.

"You know damn well we are," said Berg. He had gotten himself another ion drill, and he pulled it from his belt as he started toward Hacker. "We're going to take care of you now, Hacker—you and that kid and that friend of yours, whoever he is."

The other members of the posse started to move behind him, and they all flowed forward toward the three.

"No," said John Stone. His deep voice made them all look up at him. "No."

Slowly, he dismounted and stood on the ground beside his horse. There was something unstoppable in the way he first stood up in his stirrups, then swung one long leg over the hindquarters of the beast and finally stepped down to the ground. The posse halted again; and John spoke to the people.

"I'm a Paraplanetary Government ecologist," he said, "assigned to this planet to investigate a possibly dangerous misuse of natural resources. As such, I've got certain areas of authority; and one of them is to subpoena individuals for my official Hearing on the situation."

He lifted his left wrist to his lips, and something on that wrist glinted into the sunlight. He spoke to it.

"Hacker Illions, I charge you to appear as a witness at my Hearing, when called. Twig, I charge you to appear as a witness at my Hearing when called," he said. "The expenses of your appearance will be borne by my authority; and your duty to appear takes precedence over any other duty, obligation or restraint laid upon you by any other local law, source or individual."

John dropped his wrist gently on to the curved neck of the horse beside him; and it looked like nothing more than some large dog that he petted.

"These witnesses," he said to the posse, "must not be interfered with in any way. You understand?"

"Oh, we understand, all right," said the thick-bodied woman in the white raincoat.

"Understand? What do you mean, understand?" raged Berg. "He's not armed, this ecologist. There's only one of him. Are we going to let him stop us?"

Berg started forward toward John, who stood still. But as Berg got closer he began to look smaller, until at a few steps from John, who had not moved, it became plain that his head would not reach to John's shoulder and he was like a half-grown boy facing a full-grown man. He stopped and looked back, then, and saw none of the others in the posse had moved to follow him.

As his head turned around to look, the woman in the white raincoat burst into a jeering laugh.

"You, Berg!" she crowed. "Your guts always were in your muscles!"

She came forward herself, elbowing Berg aside, stepping in front of him and staring fiercely at John.

"You don't scare me, Mr. Ecologist!" she said. "I been looking up at people all my life. You don't scare me, your supraplanetary government doesn't scare me, nothing scares me! You want to know why we don't take and hang Hacker right now and carry this kid home to grow up decently, right now? It's not because of you—it's because we don't need to. Hacker isn't the only one who's got connections down at Capital City. It happens we heard on our belt phones just two hours ago you were on your way up here."

John nodded.

"I'm not surprised," he said. "But that doesn't change anything."

"Doesn't it?" the tone of her voice hit a high note of triumph. "All we wanted Hacker and the girl for was to find out where that plant-devil lives. Hacker sent for you, but we sent for equipment to help us find it. Two days ago, we put that equipment in an aircraft and began mapping the root systems in this area. We figured it was probably in this area because here was where it brought up the girl—"

"That's got nothing to do with it!" cried Twig in her loudest whisper. "The Grandfather reaches everywhere. All over the continent. All over the world."

But the woman did not hear her and probably would have paid no attention if she had.

"Yesterday, we found it. Protect Hacker and the girl all you want to, Mr. Ecologist. How're you going to stop us from digging in our own earth, and setting fire to what we find there?"

"Intelligent life, wantonly destroyed—" began John, but she cut him short.

"What life? How do you know it's intelligent until you find it? And if you find it, what can you do—subpoena some roots?"

She laughed.

"Hey," said Berg, turning to her. She went on laughing. "Hey," he said, "what's all this? Why didn't you tell me about it?"

"Tell you?" She leaned toward him as if she would spit into his black beard. "Tell you? Trust you? You?"

"I got some rights—"

But she walked around him, leaving him with the protest half-made, and went back to the rest of the posse.

"Come on," she said. "Let's get out of here. We can pick up these two after that Hearing's over. They won't be going any place we can't find them."

The rest of the posse stirred like an animal awakening and put itself in motion. She led them past the basin and forward, right past Twig, Hacker and John Stone with his horse. She passed so close by Twig that she was able to lean out and pat the back of Twig's right shoulder in passing—or, rather, where Twig's right shoulder would have been, except for the covering bark that protected it. Twig shrank from the touch; but Lucy Arodet only grinned at her and went on, leading her posse off into the woods, headed back the way John Stone and Twig had first come. Berg ran after them; and in a few moments the sound of their going was silenced by distance.

"Is that right?" Hacker asked John into the new quiet. "Is there equipment that can find a root mass like the Grandfather's?"

John's blue eyes in his massive face were narrowed by a frown.

"Yes," he said. "It's a variety of heat-seeking equipment—capable of very delicate distinctions, because all it has to go on is the minimal heat changes from liquid flow in the root. I didn't think anyone out here on your planet would know about it, much less—" he broke off. "And I can't believe anything like that could be sent here by anyone without my hearing of it. But in the commercial area there are always some who'll take chances."

"Arrest them!" whispered Twig. "Make it illegal for them to use it!"

John shook his head.

"I've no sure evidence yet that your Grandfather is a sentient being," he said. "Until I do, I've got no legal power to protect him."

"You don't believe us?" Hacker's lean face was all bones under the beard stubble.

"Yes. I believe, personally," said John. "Before man even left the world he started on, it was discovered that if you thought of cutting or burning a plant it would show a reaction on a picoammeter. Mental reaction of and by plants has been established for a long time. A community intelligence evolving from this, like the Grandfather you talk about, is only logical. But I have to contact it myself to know, or have some hard evidence of its existence."

"In another day or two, according to what that Lucy Arodet said just now," Hacker added, "perhaps there will not be anything to contact."

"Yes," said John. He turned to Twig. "Do you know where the Grandfather-Plant is?"

"He's everywhere," said Twig.

"Twig, you know what he means," said Hacker. "Yes, Stone, she knows."

Twig glared at the stubble-faced man.

"You must tell me," said John Stone. "The sooner I can get to the Grandfather, the sooner I'll be able to protect him."

"No!" whispered Twig.

"Honey, be sensible!" said Hacker. "You heard Lucy Arodet say they'd found the Grandfather. If they know, why keep it a secret from John Stone, here?"

"I don't believe it!" said Twig. "She was lying. She doesn't know!"

"If she does," said John, "you're taking a very long chance. If they can dig down to your Grandfather-Plant and destroy him before I can get to him, won't you have lost what you most want to save?"

"None of the Grandfather's children would tell where he is, even if they could," Twig whispered, "and I won't."

"Don't tell me then," said John. "Just take me to him."

Twig shook her head.

"Twig," said Hacker, and she looked at him. "Twig, listen. You've got to do what Stone says."

She shook her head again.

"Then, ask the Grandfather himself," Hacker said. "Let him decide."

She started to shake her head a third time, then went over to a tree and put her arms around it; not because she needed the tree to help her talk with the Grandfather, but to be able to hide her face from the two men.

"Grandfather!" she thought. "Grandfather, have you been listening? What should I do?"

There was no answer.

"Grandfather!" she called with her mind.

Still no answer. For one panic-filled moment she thought that she could not feel him there at all, that he had either been killed or gone to sleep. Then, reaching out as far as she could, she felt him, still there but not noticing her call.

"Grandfather!"

But it was no use. It was as if with her whisper-limited voice she tried to shout to someone far off on the top of a high mountain. The Grandfather had gone back into his own thoughts. She could not reach him. She fought down the surge of fear and hurt that leaped inside her. Once, the Grandfather had always been there. Only in these last couple of years, since the burnings by the croppers had been so widespread, had he started to draw into himself and talk of going to sleep.

Slowly, she let go of the tree and turned back to face the other two humans.

"He won't answer," she said.

There was a moment's silence.

"Then it's up to you to decide, isn't it?" Hacker said, gently.

She nodded, feeling all torn apart inside. Then an idea came to her.

"I won't take you to him," she said, raising her eyes to John Stone's face. "But I'll go by myself and see if it's true, if the croppers have found him. You wait here."

"No," said John. "I came up here to see some of the burned-over areas for myself; and I should look at those now while I have time. If I have to make it a court matter without waiting to protect your Plant-Grandfather, I need as much evidence as possible."

"I'll show you places," said Hacker to him.

"No," John said again. "You go straight south to the first town or village you can get to and report yourself to the authorities there as being under my subpoena. That will make your protection under law a matter of public record. Can you go straight there without that gang that just left here catching you?"

Hacker snorted in disgust.

"All right," said John. "I had to ask to make sure. You go to the closest community center, then— what's its name?"

"Fireville," said Hacker. "About twelve klicks southwest."

"Fireville. I'll meet you there after I've seen a couple of burned-over areas. I've got a map with a number of them marked. And Twig," John turned toward her, "you'll go check on the Plant-Grandfather to see if there's any sign he's been located. Then you better find me again as soon as you can. Do you think you can do that?"

"Of course," said Twig contemptuously. "The plant brothers and sisters will always tell me where you are."

But instead of turning to leave, she hesitated, looking at Hacker with the sharp teeth of worry nibbling at her.

"Don't you drink, now," she said. "If you get drunk, they might find some way to do something to you."

"Not a drop," said Hacker. "I promise."

Still she hesitated, until it came to her that if she stood here much longer she would not go at all; so she turned and ran, the forest opening before her and the other two left swallowed up from sight behind.

She went swiftly. She was not about to lose herself in the pleasure of her running now; for worry, like an invisible posse, followed right at her heels. From time to time she called to the Grandfather with her mind; but he did not answer and she settled down to getting to his root-mass as soon as possible.

In the woods, growing and changing every day, she had never had any means of measuring how fast she could go when the need was really upon her. She was only human, after all; so probably her top speed was not really much faster than that of a winning marathon runner back in the years when man was just beginning to go forth into space, before the Earth had died. But the difference was that she could run at that speed—or at very nearly that speed—all day long if she had to. Now, she did not know her speed; but she went fast, fast, her legs flashing in and out of the early afternoon sunlight and shadow as she raced down the corridor among the trees and bushes that opened before her as she went.

It was midafternoon before she came to the edge of the place where the great root-mass belonging to the Grandfather lay fifteen to forty meters below the ground and the forest above it. All the way here, the plant sisters and brothers of this area had showed her an empty woods with no sign of croppers anywhere about. But none of them could tell her about an earlier moment until she could actually reach and touch them. Now, arrived, she put her arms around one tall tree-sister and held her, forcing the slow-thinking leaves to remember daylight and dark, dark and daylight, through the past week.

But, other than the wind, the leaves remembered only silence. No humans had passed by them, even at a distance. No mechanical sounds had sounded near them. In the sky over them, only the clouds and an occasional spurt of rain had mingled with the regular march of sun and moon and stars.

The woman Lucy Arodet had lied. The croppers either had no special equipment as claimed, or if they had it, they had not used it here where they could find the Grandfather. Sighing with relief, Twig fell face down on the ground, spreading out her arms amongst the littlest brothers to hug and hold her world.

The Grandfather was safe—still safe. For a little while Twig simply closed her eyes to let herself ride off on the wave of her relief. And so sleep took her without warning, for in fact she had done a great deal of running and worrying in past hours.

When she woke, it was night. The moon was already high in the sky and Grandfather was thinking—not at her, but around her, as if he mused over her, under the impression she did not hear.

". . . I have never reached beyond the atmosphere that envelopes this one world," he was thinking. "But now, my little runner will run to the ends of the universe. Beyond are the stars, and beyond them more stars, and beyond and beyond ... to depths beyond depths, where the great galaxies float like clouds or scatter like a whole crowd of little runners, pushing against each other, scattering out from one common point to the ultimate edges of time and distance. And in all that distance there are many lives. My little runner will come to know them, and the beginning and the end, and all that goes between. She will know them in their birth and their growing and whether it is chance or purpose that makes a path for all life in all time and space. So out of destruction will have come creation, out of sleep an awakening, and out of defeat a conquest, just as even at the poles of this world warm summer succeeds the harsh winter. All they have done to destroy me will only bring about the birth of my little runner into a Great Runner between the stars—"

"Grandfather!" called Twig; and the thoughts flowing about her broke off suddenly.

"Are you awake, little sister?" asked the Grandfather. "If you are, it's time for you to go now."

"Go?" demanded Twig, still stupid with sleep. "Go ... why? Where? What for?"

"Your old friend Hacker is dying now, and your friend-to-be John Stone rides toward him," said the thought of the Plant-Grandfather. "Those who wished to destroy him and me have tricked Hacker to death, and soon they will be here to kill me also. It is time for you to go."

Twig was awake and on her feet in one reflexive movement.

"What happened?" she demanded. "Where is Hacker?"

"In a gully north of Fireville, where he has been pushed to fall and die, as if he had drunkenly wandered there and slipped. Those who are our enemies made him drunk and brought him there to fall, and he has fallen."

"Why didn't you wake me and tell me before?" Twig cried.

"It would have made no difference," said the Grandfather. "Hacker's death was beyond the stopping, even as those who come now to destroy me are beyond stopping."

"Come?" raged Twig. "How can anyone be coming? They don't even know where you are!"

"They do now," said the Grandfather. "When you came to me this time, you carried pinned to the bark behind your shoulder something placed there by the woman called Lucy Arodet. A small thing which cried out in a voice only another such thing could hear to tell her where you were at any moment. When you reached me and stopped traveling in this place, they knew you had found me and they knew where I was."

Twig threw a hand around to feel behind her shoulder. Her fingers closed on something small, round and hard. She pulled it loose from the bark and brought it around where she could see it. In the moonlight, it looked like a dulled pearl with small, sharp points on its underside where it had clung to the bark of her clothing.

"I'll take it away!" she said. "I'll take it someplace else—"

"That would make no difference either," said the Grandfather. "Do not suffer. Before they come I will have gone to sleep in a sleep without waking, and they can only destroy roots that mean nothing."

"No!" said Twig. "Wait . . . no! I'll run and find John Stone. He can get here before they can do your roots much damage. Then you won't have to sleep—"

"Little runner, little runner," said the Grandfather. "Even if your John Stone could save me this coming day, he would only put off the inevitable for a little while. From the day your people set foot on this world, it was certain that sooner or later I would have to sleep forever. If you understand that I go now to sleep gladly, you would not mourn as you do. What is of value in me goes forward in you, and goes where I could not, further and deeper, beyond all distance and imagination."

"No!" cried Twig. "I won't let you die. I'll run to

where Hacker is and meet John Stone. He'll come and save you. Wait for me, Grandfather! Wait . . ."

Even as she continued talking with her mind to the Grandfather, she had spun about and begun to run toward Fireville. The little brothers opened a path before her, marking the way, and the bushes and trees leaned aside. But she was scarcely conscious that they did so. All her mind was on the fact that the Grandfather must not die . . . must not die . . .

She ran faster than she had ever run before. But still it was nearly dawn when she came near to Fireville, to the dark gully where the path of the little brothers led her. On the far side of the gully, silhouetted blackly against the paling sky between the trees, was the figure of a gigantic man on a gigantic horse. But down in the blackness of the gully itself was a little patch of something light that was Hacker. At the sight of that patch even the Grandfather went out of Twig's mind for a moment. She plunged recklessly down the side of the gully. Anyone else would have tripped and fallen a dozen times, but she felt the uneven ground and the presence of bush and sapling with her mind and kept her feet. She reached the shape of Hacker and dropped on her knees beside it.

"Hacker!" she cried. The tears ran down her face.

There was a great noise of tearing and plunging—the descent of a heavy body down the far side of the gully—and then John Stone, on foot, appeared on the far side of Hacker. He squatted and reached out to touch his fingers gently to Hacker's throat, under the sharp, bony line of Hacker's jaw.

"He's gone, Twig," John said, looking from Hacker to her.

Grief burst inside her like a world exploding. She lifted Hacker's head to her lap and rocked with it, weeping.

"I told you not to drink, Hacker!" she choked. "You promised me! You promised you wouldn't drink . . ."

She was aware that John Stone had moved around to squat beside her. He loomed over her like some huge cliff in the darkness. He put a hand on her back and shoulder, and the hand was so big that it was like an arch around her.

"It had to happen, Twig," the deep voice rumbled and rolled in her ear. "Some things have to happen . . ."

It was so like what the Grandfather had said that she was suddenly reminded of him. She lifted her head sharply, listening, but there was nothing.

"*Grandfather!*" she cried, and for the first time in her life, it was not only her mind that called. Her voice rang clear and wild under the brightening sky.

But there was no answer. For the first time not even the echo came back that said the Grandfather was there but not listening. The unimaginable network of the plant-children still stood connected, listening, waiting, carrying her call to the furthest limits of the world. But there was no response. The voice of the planet had fallen silent.

"He's gone!" she cried. And the words flew among the leaves and the branches, from grass-blade to grass-blade and along the roots under hill and valley and plain and mountain. "Gone . . ."

She slumped where she sat, even the head of Hacker forgotten on her knees.

"The Plant-Grandfather?" Stone asked her. She nodded numbly.

"It's over," she said, aloud, her new voice dead and dull. "He's gone . . . gone. It's all finished, forever."

"No," said the deep voice of John Stone. "It's never finished."

He stood up beside her, looking at her.

"Twig," he said again, gently but insistently, "it's never finished."

"Yes it is. Listen . . ." she said, forgetting that he, like all the others had never been able to hear the Grandfather. "The world's dead now. There is no one else."

"Yes, there is," said John Stone. "There's you. And for you, there's everything. Not only what's on this world but on many others that never knew a Plant-Grandfather. They're out there, waiting for you to speak to them."

"I can't speak to anyone," she said, still kneeling, slumped by the dead body of Hacker. "It's all over, I tell you. All over."

John Stone reached down and picked her up. Holding her, he walked up the dark side of the gully to his horse and mounted it. She struggled for a second, then gave up. His strength overpowered hers easily.

"Time moves," he said. She hid her face against the darkness of his broad chest and heard his voice rumbling through the wall of bone and flesh. "Things change, and there's no stopping them. Even if the Grandfather and Hacker had stayed alive here, even if Jinson's Planet had stayed just as it was—still you, by yourself, would have grown and changed. Our decisions get bigger and bigger, whether we want them to or not—our jobs get larger and larger, whether we plan them to or not—and in the end the choice has to be to love all or to love none. There may be others like Hacker on other worlds, and perhaps somewhere there may be another Jinson's world. But there's never been another Plant-Grandfather that we've been able to find, and not another Twig. That means you're going to have to love all the worlds and all the growing things on them as the Grandfather would have, if he could have gone to them the way you're going to be able to. That's your job, Twig."

She neither spoke nor stirred.

"Try," he said. "The Grandfather's left it all to you. Take up the duty he left to you. Speak to the growing things on Jinson's Planet and them that losing the Grandfather wasn't the end."

She shook her head slightly against his chest.

"I can't," she said. "It's no use. I can't."

"Speak to them," he said. "Don't leave them alone. Tell them they've got you now. Wasn't that what the Grandfather wanted?"

Again she shook her head.

"I can't . . ." she whimpered. "If I speak to them, then he *will* be gone, really gone, forever. I can't do that. I can't put him away forever. I can't!"

"Then everything the Grandfather counted on is

lost," said John Stone. "Everything Hacker did is wasted. What about Hacker?"

She thought of Hacker then, what was left of Hacker, being left farther behind them with every stride of the horse's long legs. Hacker, going down now into forgottenness too.

"I can't, Hacker!" she said to the memory of him in her mind.

"Can't . . . ?" the image of Hacker looked back at her, cocked one eyebrow at her and began to sing:

"As game as Ned Kelly," the people would say.
"As game as Ned Kelly," they say it today . . .

The familiar words in his cracked, hoarse voice went through her like a sword-sharp shaft of sunlight, and through the dark, hard wall of grief that had swelled up within her at the loss of the Grandfather. All at once, she remembered all the flowers that also were alone now, left voiceless and in darkness of silence; and contrition overflowed within her. From now on, she would be gone, too!

"It's all right!" she called out to them, with her voice and her mind together. "It's all right, I'm still here. Me. Twig. You'll never be alone, I promise! Even if I have to go someplace else, I'll always reach out and touch you from wherever I am . . ."

And from valley and hill, from plain and forest, from all over, the words of her mind were picked up and passed along, tossing joyously from smallest brother to largest sister, on and on to the ends of the world.

Twig closed her eyes and let herself lie at last against the wide chest of John Stone. Where he was taking her, she did not know. No doubt it would be very far away from Jinson's world. But no world was too far, she knew that now; and also, out there in the great distances of which the Grandfather had dreamed and to which he could never go, there were other brothers and sisters, waiting for the sound of her voice, waiting for her.

Grandfather was gone beyond returning, and so

was Hacker. But maybe it was not the end of things, after all; maybe it was only a beginning. Maybe ... at least she had spoken to all the others who had lived through the Grandfather, and they now knew they would never be alone again. Letting go of her grief a little, just a little, Twig rocked off to sleep on the steady rhythm of the pacing horse.

Making progress implies the existence of some scale to measure the distance traversed and a judge to rate the style of the crossing.

The Game of Five

"You can't do this!" The big young man was furious. His blunt, not-too-intelligent looking features were going lumpy with anger. "This is—" He pounded the desk he sat before with one huge fist, stuck for a moment as to just what it could be—"it's illegal!"

"Quite legal. A Matter of Expediency, Mr. Yunce," replied the Consul to Yara, cheerfully, waving a smoke tube negligently in his tapering fingers. The Consul's name was Ivor Ben. He was half the size of Coley Yunce, one third the weight, twice the age, fifteen times the aristocrat—and very much in charge.

"You draft me all the way from Sol Four!" shouted Coley. "I'm a tool designer. You picked me off the available list yourself. You knew my qualifications. You aren't supposed to draft a citizen anyway, except you can't get what you want some other way." His glare threatened to wilt the Consul's boutonniere, but failed to disturb the Counsul. "Damn Government seat-warmers! Can't hire like honest people! Send in for lists of the men you want, and pick out just your boy—never mind he's got business on Arga IV ten weeks from now. And now, when I get here you tell me I'm *not* going to design tools."

"That's right," said the Consul.

"You want me for some back-alley stuff! Well, I won't do it!" roared Coley. "I'll refuse. I'll file a protest back at Sol—" He broke of suddenly, and stared at the Consul. "What makes you so sure I won't?"

The Consul contemplated Coley's thick shoulders, massive frame and a certain wildness about Coley's blue eyes and unruly black hair, all with obvious satisfaction

"Certain reasons," he said, easily. "For one, I understand you grew up in a rather tough neighborhood in old Venus City, back on Sol II."

"So?" growled Coley.

"I believe there was something in your citizen's file about knives—"

"Look here!" exploded Coley. "So I knew how to use a knife when I was a kid. I had to, to stay alive in the spaceport district. So I got into a little trouble with the law—"

"Now, now—" said the Consul, comfortably. "Now, now."

"Using a man's past to blackmail him into a job that's none of his business. *'Would I please adjust to a change in plans, unavoidable but necessary—'* Well, I don't please! I don't please at all."

"I'd recommend you do," interrupted the Consul, allowing a little metal to creep into his voice. "You people who go shopping around on foreign worlds and getting rich at it have a bad tendency to take the protection of your Humanity for granted. Let me correct this tendency in you, even if several billion others continue to perpetuate the notion. The respect aliens have always given your life and possessions is not, though you may have thought so heretofore, something extended out of the kindness of their hearts. They keep their paws off people because they know we Humans never abandon one of our own. You've been living safe within that system all your life, Mr. Yunce. Now it's time to do your part for someone else. Under my authority as Consul, I'm drafting you to aid me in—"

"What's wrong with the star-marines?" roared Coley.

"The few star-marines I have attached to the Consulate are required here," said the Consul.

"Then flash back to Sol for the X-4 Department. Those Government Troubleshooters—"

"The X-4 Department is a popular fiction," said the Consul, coldly. "We draft people we need, we don't keep a glamourous corps of secret operators. Now, no more complaints Mr. Yunce, or I'll put you under arrest. It's that, or take the job. Which?"

"All right," growled Coley. "What's the deal?"

"I wouldn't use you if I didn't have to," said the Consul. "But there's no one else. There's a Human— one of our young lady tourists who's run off from the compound and ended in a Yaran religious center a little over a hundred miles from here."

"But if she's run off . . . of her own free will—"

"Ah, but we don't believe it was," said the Consul. "We think the Yarans enticed or coerced her into going." He paused. "Do you know anything about the Yarans?"

Coley shook his head.

"Every race we meet," said the Consul, putting the tips of his fingers together, "has to be approached by Humanity in a different way. In the case of Yara, here we've got a highly humanoid race which has a highly unhuman philosophy. They think life's a game."

"Sounds like fun." said Coley.

"Not the kind of a game you think," said the Consul, undisturbed. "They mean Game with a capital G. Everything's a Game to be played under certain rules. Even their relationship as a race to the human race is a Game to be played. A Game of Five, as life is a game of five parts—the parts being childhood, youth, young adulthood, middle age and old age. Right now, as they see it, their relations with Humanity are in the fourth part— Middle Age. In Childhood they tried passive indifference to our attempt to set up diplomatic relations. In Youth, they rioted against our attempt to set up a space terminal and human compound here. In Young Adulthood they attacked us with professional soldiery and made war against us. In each portion of the game, we won out. Now, in

Middle Age, they are trying subtlety against us with this coercion of the girl. Only when we beat them at this and at the Old Age portion will they concede defeat and enter into friendly relations with us."

Coley grunted.

"According to them, Sara Illoy—that's the girl— has decided to become one of them and take up her personal Game of Life at the Young Adulthood stage. In this stage she has certain rights, certain liabilities, certain privileges and obligations. Only if she handles these successfully, will she survive to start in on the next stage. You understand," said the Consul, looking over at Coley, "this is a system of taboo raised to the nth level. Someone like her, not born to the system, has literally no chance of surviving."

"I see," said Coley. And he did.

"And of course," said the Consul, quietly, "if she dies, they will have found a way to kill a member of the human race with impunity. Which will win them the Middle Age portion and lose us the game, since we have to be perfect to win. Which means an end to us on this world; and a bad example set that could fire incidents on other non-human worlds."

Coley nodded.

"What am I supposed to do about it?" he asked.

"As a female Young Adult," said the Consul, "she may be made to return to the compound only by her lover or mate. We want you to play the young lover role and get her. If you ask for her, they must let her go with you. That's one of the rules."

Coley nodded again, this time cautiously.

"They have to let her go with me?" he said.

"They have to," repeated the Consul, leaning back in his chair and putting the tips of his fingers together. He looked out the tall window of the office in which he and Coley had been talking. "Go and bring her back. That's your job. We have transportation waiting to take you to her right now."

"Well, then," growled Coley, getting to his feet. "What're we waiting for? Let's get going and get it over with."

*   *   *

Three hours later, Coley found himself in the native Yaran city of Tannakil, in one of the Why towers of the Center of Meaning.

"Wait here," said the native Yaran who had brought him; and walked off leaving him alone in the heavily-draped room of the hexagonal wooden tower. Coley watched the Yaran leave, uneasiness nibbling at him.

Something was wrong, he told himself. His instincts were warning him. The Yaran that had just left him had been the one who had escorted him from the human compound to the native seacoast town outside it. They had taken a native glider that had gotten its original impulse by a stomach-sickening plunge down a wooden incline and out over a high sea-cliff. Thereafter the pilot with a skill that—Coley had to admit—no human could have come close to matching, had worked them up in altitude, and inland, across a low range of mountains, over a patch of desert and to this foothill town lying at the toes of another and greater range of mountains. Granted the air currents of Yara were more congenial to the art of gliding, granted it was a distance of probably no more than a hundred and fifty miles, still it was a prodigious feat by human standards.

But it was not this that had made Coley uneasy. It was something in the air. It was something in the attitude of the accompanying Yaran, Ansash by name. Coley considered and dismissed the possibility that it was the alienness of Ansash that was disturbing him. The Yarans were not all that different. In fact, the difference was so slight that Coley could not lay his finger upon it. When he had first stepped outside the compound, he had thought he saw what the difference was between Yarans and humans. Now, they all looked as Earth-original as any humans he had ever seen.

No, it was something other than physical—something in their attitudes. Sitting next to Ansash in the glider on the trip here, he had felt a coldness, a repulsion, a loneliness—there was no point in trying to describe it. In plain words he had *felt* that Ansash

was not human. He had felt it in his skin and blood
and bones:—*this is a thing I'm sitting next to, not
a man.* And for the first time he realized how
impossible and ridiculous were the sniggering stories
they told in bars about interbreeding with the
humanoids. These beings, too, were alien; as alien
as the seal-like race of the Dorcan system. From
the irrational point of view of the emotions, the
fact that they looked exactly like people only made
it worse.

Coley took a quick turn about the room. The Yaran
had been gone for only a couple of minutes, but
already it seemed too long. Of course, thought Coley,
going on with his musings, it might be something
peculiar to Ansash. The glider pilot had not made
Coley bristle so. In fact, except for his straight black
hair—the Yarans all had black hair, it was what
made them all look so much alike—he looked like
any friendly guy on any one of the human worlds,
intent on doing his job and not worried about anything else. . . . Was Ansash never coming back with
that girl?

There was a stir behind the draperies and Ansash
appeared, leading a girl by the hand. She was a
blonde as tall as the slighter-boned Yaran who was
leading her forward. Her lipstick was too red and her
skin almost abnormally pale, so that she looked
bleached-out beside Ansash's native swarthiness. Moreover, there was something sleepwalking about her
face and the way she moved.

"This is Sara Illoy," said Ansash, in Yaran, dropping her hand as they stopped before Coley. Coley
understood him without difficulty. Five minutes with
a hypnoteacher had given him full command of the
language. But he was staring fascinated at the girl,
who looked back at him, but did not speak.

"Pleased to meet you," said Coley. "I'm Coley Yunce,
Sol II."

She did not answer.

"Are you all right?" Coley demanded. Still she
looked up at him without speaking and without in-

terest. There was nothing in her face at all. She was not even curious. She was merely looking.

"She does not speak," the voice of Ansash broke the silence. "Perhaps you should beat her. Then she might talk."

Coley looked sharply at him. But there was no expression of slyness or derision on the Yaran's face.

"Come on," he growled at the girl, and turned away. He had taken several steps before he realized she was not following. He turned back to take her by the hand—and discovered Ansash had disappeared.

"Come on," he growled again; and led the girl off to where his memory told him he and Ansash had entered through the drapes. He felt about among the cloth and found a parting. He towed the girl through.

His memory had not tricked him. He was standing on the stairs up which he and Ansash had come earlier. He led the girl down them and into the streets of Tannakil.

He paused to get his bearings with his feet on the smoothly fitted blocks of the paving. Tannakil was good-sized as Yaran towns went, but it was not all that big. After a second, he figured out that their way back to the glider field was to their right, and he led the girl off.

This was part of the Yaran attitude, he supposed; to deprive him of a guide on the way back. Well, they might have done worse things. Still, he thought, as he led Sara Illoy along, it was odd. No Yaran they passed looked at them or made any move to show surprise at seeing two obvious humans abroad in their town. Not only that, but none of the Yarans seemed to be speaking to each other. Except for the occasional hoof-noises of the Yaran riding-animal—a reindeer-like creature with a long lower lip—the town was silent.

Coley hurried on through the streets. The afternoon was getting along; and he did not fancy a flight back over those mountains at dusk or in the dark, no matter how skillful the Yaran pilots were. And in time the wooden Yaran buildings began to thin out and the two of them emerged onto the grassy field with its towering wooden slide, like a ski-jump, only much taller, up to which the gliders were winched, and down which they were started.

Coley had actually started to lead the girl toward the slide when the facts of the situation penetrated his mind.

The field was empty.

There were no gliders on its grass, at the top of the slide, or winched partway up it. And there were no Yarans.

Coley whirled around, looking back the way he had come. The street he and the girl had walked was also empty. Tannakil was silent and empty—as a ghost town, as a churchyard.

Coley stood spraddle-legged, filled with sudden rage and fear. Rage was in him because he had not expected to find a joker in this expedition right at the start; and fear—because all the gutter instinct of his early years cried out against the danger of his position.

He was alone—in a town full of potential enemies. And night was not far off.

Coley looked all around him again. There was nothing; nothing but the grass and the town, the empty sky, and a road leading off straight as a ruler toward the desert over which he had flown, toward the distant mountains, and the coast beyond.

And then he noticed two of the Yaran riding animals twitching up grass with their long lower lips, beside the road a little way off.

"Come on," he said to the girl, and led the way toward the animals. As he drew near, he could see that they had something upon their backs; and when he reached them he discovered, as he had half-expected, that they were both fitted with the Yaran equivalent of the saddle. Coley grinned without humor; and looked back toward the town.

"Thanks for nothing," he told it. And he turned to boost the girl into one of the saddles. She went up easily, as someone who had ridden one of the beasts before. He untethered her animal, passed the single rein back up into her hand, then unhitched and

mounted the other beast himself. There was a knife
tied to its leather pad of a saddle.

They headed off down the road into the descending
sun.

They rode until it became too dark to see the road
before them. Then Coley stopped and tethered the
animals. He helped the girl down and unsaddled the
beasts. The saddles came off—and apart—quite easily. In fact, they were the simplest sort of riding
equipment. The equivalent of the saddlecloth was a
sort of great sash of coarse but semi-elastic cloth that
went completely around the barrel of the animal and
fastened together underneath with a system of hooks
and eyes. The saddle itself was simply a folded-over
flap of leather that hook-and-eyed to the saddle cloth.
Unfolded, Coley discovered the saddle was large
enough to lie on, as a groundsheet; and the unfolded
saddle cloth made a rough blanket.

He and the girl lay down to sleep until the moon
rose. But Coley, not unsurprisingly, found sleep hard
to come by. He lay on his back, gazing up at the
sprinkling of strange stars overhead, and thinking
hard.

It was not hard to realize he had been suckered
into something. Coley had expected that. It was harder
to figure out what he had been suckered into, and by
whom, and why. The presence of the knife on his
saddle pointed the figure at the Consul; but to suppose the Consul was in league with the humanoids
ran counter to Coley's experience with a half a dozen
non-human worlds. He was not inexperienced with
aliens—his speciality was designing and adapting
human-type tools for the grasping of alien append-
ages. He was only inexperienced with humanoids.
Lying on his back, he narrowed his eyes at the stars
and wished he had found out more about the Consul.

Four hours after sunset, by Coley's watch, the moon
rose. Coley had expected one sooner, since Yara was
supposed to have two of them. But then he remembered hearing that the orbits of both were peculiar so
that often neither would be visible over any given

spot for several nights hand-running. He roused the girl, who got up without protest. They saddled and rode on.

Coley tried from time to time to get the girl to talk. But, although she would look at him when he spoke to her, she would not say a word.

"Is this something you did to yourself?" he asked her. "Or something they did to you? That's what I'd like to know."

She gazed solemnly at him in the moonlight.

"How about nodding your head for yes, or shaking it for no?" ... He tried speaking to her in Yaran. When that failed, he tried upper middle English, and what he knew of Arcturan's local canting tongue. On a sudden chilling impulse, Coley urged his beast alongside hers, and, reaching out, pressed on her jaw muscles until she automatically opened her mouth. In the moonlight, he saw she still had her tongue.

"It's not that," he said. He had remembered certain ugly things done around the Spaceport district of Venus City. "So it must be psychological. I'll bet you were all right when you left the compound." He found himself clenching his teeth a little and thinking, for no obvious reason, of Ansash. To get his mind off it, he looked at his watch again.

"Time to stop and rest a bit, again," he said. "I want to get as far as possible across this desert at night, but there's no use killing ourselves right at the start."

He stopped the beasts, helped the girl down and unsaddled.

"A couple of hours nap," he said. "And then we go." He set his watch alarm and fell asleep.

He woke up to broad daylight and hooting voices. Automatically, he leaped to his feet. One ankle tripped him and threw him down again. He lay there, half-propped on one elbow, seeing himself surrounded by a bunch of young Yarans.

His hand slipped quietly to his belt where he had tucked the knife from the saddle. To his astonishment, it was still there. He let his hand fall away from it, and pretending to be dazed, glanced around under half-closed eyelids.

Sara Illoy was not to be seen. Of the young Yarans around him—all of them uniformly dressed in a sort of grey loose robe or dress, tightly belted at the waist—the large majority were male. None of them seemed to be paying any great attention to him. They were all hooting at each other without words and—well, not dancing so much as engaging in a sort of semi-rhythmic horseplay with each other. Most of the males carried knives themselves, tucked in their belts; and some had tucked in beside the knives a sort of pistol with an exaggeratedly long slim barrel and a bulbous handle.

Farther off, he could occasionally glimpse between the bounding and whirling bodies some of the riding animals, tethered in a line and contentedly twitching up grass. Coley measured the distance between himself and the beasts, speculated on the chance of making a run for it—and gave the notion up.

A thought about the girl occurred to him.

"But right now, kid," he thought silently to himself, "if I had the chance, it'd be everyone for himself and the devil take the hindmost. I wasn't raised to be a shining knight."

At the same time he admitted to himself that he was glad she wasn't around to see him, if he did have a chance to make a break for it—no reason to rub in the fact that she would be being abandoned. Then he went back to worrying about his own skin.

Coley had discovered in the gutters and back alleys of Venus City when he was young that the best cure for being afraid was to get angry. He had learned this so well that it had become almost automatic with him; and he began to feel himself growing hot and prickly under his shirt, now, as he lay still with his eyes half-closed, waiting. There would be a chance to go out fighting—he did have the knife.

Suddenly—so suddenly that he found himself unprepared for it—the roughhousing and hooting stopped and he found himself jerked to his feet. A knife flashed, and the tension of the rope binding his ankle fell away. He found himself standing, loosely surrounded by Yarans; and through the gaps between them he could see the line of riding animals clearly and close.

He almost took the bait. Then, just in time, he recognized what was before him as one of the oldest traps known to civilized beings. He had seen exactly the same trick played back in Venus City. He had played it, himself. The idea was to tempt the victim with the hope of an escape, to tempt him into running; and when he did, to chase and catch him again, cat-and-mouse fashion.

With this sudden realization, confidence came flooding back into him. The alienness of the situation melted away and he found himself back in familiar territory. He stretched up to his full height, which was half a head taller than the tallest of the Yarans surrounding him; and smiled grimly at them, his eyes skipping from individual to individual as he tried to pick out the one that would be the leader.

He almost fell into the error of picking out the largest of the Yarans around him. Then he thought of a surer index of rank, and his eyes swept over the male Yarans at belt level, until they halted on one whose belt held two pistols, with matching butts. Coley smiled again and strode calmly forward toward the Yaran he had picked out.

With a sudden rush the Yarans spread out into a circle, leaving Coley and the male with two pistols inside. Coley halted within double his arms' length of the other, and hooked his thumbs into his own belt. His eye met that of the Yaran before him sardonically.

Up until now, the Yaran had not moved. But, as the circle reached its full dimension and went still, his right hand flashed to the butt of one of his pistols. In the same instant, Coley dropped to one knee. His knife flashed in his hand and glittered suddenly as it flew through the air.

And the Yaran fell, clutching at the knife in his chest.

A chorus of wild hoots went up; and when Coley glanced up from the male he had just knifed, the others were scrambling for their riding animals.

Within seconds, they were mounted and gone, the dust of the desert rolling up behind them to mark their trail. Of the long line of riding animals, only two were left.

And, peering around the farther of these, was the girl.

Coley buried the Yaran he had killed, before he and the girl took up their road again.

Coley had expected the desert to be a man-killer by day. It was not—for reasons he did not understand, but guessed to have something to do with its altitude, and also the latitude in which this part of Yara lay. Still, it was hot and uncomfortable enough, and they had neither food or water with them. Luckily, later on in the day they came to a wayside well; the water of which, when Coley tasted it gingerly, proved to be sweet enough. He drank and handed the dipper to the girl.

She drank eagerly as well.

"Now, if we could just happen on something to eat," Coley told her. She showed no sign that she understood him, but, later in the day, when they came to the nearer foothills of the coastal mountain range, she rode off among the first trees they came to. When he followed her, he found her eating a black-skinned fruit about the size of a tangerine.

"Here, what are you doing?" shouted Coley, grabbing the fruit out of her hand. She made no protest, but picked another fruit from the small, wide-branched small tree or bush beside her. Seeing her bite into it without hesitation, Coley felt his alarm dwindle.

"I suppose they fed you some of these while you were there," he growled. He sniffed the fruit, then licked at it where the pulp was exposed. It had a rather sour, meaty taste. He took a tentative bite himself. It went down agreeably. He took another.

"Oh, well—what the hell!" he said. And he and the girl filled themselves up on the fruit.

That night, when they camped on the very knees of the mountains themselves, Coley lay stretched out under his animal-blanket, trying to sort out what had happened to them and make some sense from it.

The situation was the wildest he had ever encountered. If certain elements in it seemed to be doing their best to kill him (and undoubtedly the girl as well) off, other elements seemed just as determined to keep them alive. Tannakil had been a death-trap if they had lingered there after nightfall; he knew this as surely as if he had seen it written in Basic on one of the wooden walls there. But Tamakil had apparently provided the riding animals for their escape.

Those Yaran youngsters back there on the desert had not been fooling either. Yet they had ridden off. And the desert had been no joke; but the well had been just where it needed to be—and how come those fruit trees to be so handy, and how did the girl too recognize them, even some way back from the road?

Unthinkingly, he half-rolled over to ask her. Then it came back to him that she would not be able to answer; and he frowned. There was something about this business of the girl herself that was funny, too. . . .

Thinking about it, he fell asleep.

The next day, they pushed on into the mountains, finding pleasanter country full of shaggy-barked, low green trees, and green ground-covering of tiny, thick-growing ferns. They climbed steadily into cooler air, and the road narrowed until it was hardly more than a trail. The mountain tops ahead, at least, were free from snow, so that whatever happened, they would not have to contend with mountain storms and low temperatures, for which neither of them was dressed or equipped.

Then an abrupt and dramatic change took place. The road suddenly leveled out, and then began to dip downward, as if they had come into a pass. Moreover, it was now wider and more carefully engineered than Coley had ever seen it before. And more than that, after a little while it began to sport a crushed rock topping.

They were walled in on both sides by steep rock, and were descending, apparently, into an interior mountain valley. Suddenly they heard a sharp hooting noise, twice repeated, from up ahead of them; and around the curve of the mountain road came a double line of Yarans mounted on running riding animals. The leading Yaran yelled a command, the riding animals were reined in and skidded to a halt; and one mounted Yaran who was holding a sort of two-handed bellows with a long, ornately carved tube projecting from it, pumped the device once, producing a single additional hoot which at this close range hurt Coley's eardrums.

These mounted Yarans were dressed in short grey kilts with grey, woolly-looking leggings underneath that terminated in a sort of mukluk over each foot, and bulky, thick, green sweater-like upper garments with parka-type hoods which they wore thrown back on their shoulders. They did not hold the single reins of their riding animals in their hands, but had them loosely looped and tied leaving their hands free—the right one to carry what was truly a fantastically long-barreled version of the bulbous-handled pistols Coley had encountered in the desert, the left one to be carried in a fist against the left hip, the elbow stylishly cocked out. They were all riding in this position when Coley first saw them; and the sudden sliding halt did not cause a single fist to slip. There was also both a short and a long knife in each man's green belt.

"Permissions?" snapped the Yaran on the lead animal; and continued without waiting for an answer. "None? You are under arrest. Come with me." He started to turn his animal.

"Wait a minute—" began Coley. The other paused, and Coley noticed suddenly that his belt was not green, like the others, but yellow. "Never mind," said Coley. "We're coming."

The yellow-belted Yaran completed his turn, nodded to the one with the bellows, and an ear-splitting hoot shook the air. One moment later Coley found himself and the girl on their animals in a dead run for the valley below, with mounted Yarans all about them. Forgetting everything else, Coley grabbed for the front edge of his saddle flap and concentrated on hanging on.

They swept around a curve and down a long slope, emerging into a sort of interior plateau area which looked as if it might be a number of miles in extent. Coley was unable to make sure of this—not only because most of his attention was concentrated on staying on his mount, but because almost immediately they were surrounded by circular small buildings of stone, which a little farther on gave way to hexagonal small buildings, which yet further on gave way to five-sided, then square, then triangular edifices of the same size. Beyond the triangular buildings was an open space, and then a large, stone structure of rectangular shape.

The bellows hooted, the troop slid to a stop. The yellow-belted Yaran dismounted, signalled Coley and the girl to get down as well, and led them in through a door in the large, rectangular building. Within were a good number of Yarans standing at tall desks arranged in a spiral shape within a large room. The yellow-belted Yaran went to one of these, apparently at random from all Coley could discover, and held a whispered conversation. Then he returned and led them both off through more doors and down halls, until he ushered them into a room about twenty feet square, furnished only with a pile of grey cushions neatly stacked in one corner, and one of the tall desks such as Coley had seen arranged spirally in the large room behind them. A male Yaran, dressed like all the rest except that he wore a silver belt, turned away from the room's single large window, and came to stand behind the tall desk.

"West Entrance. No permissions, Authority," spoke up the yellow-belted one behind Coley.

"Now, wait a minute—" began Coley. "Let me tell you how we happened to come this way—"

"You—" said the silver-belted Yaran, suddenly interrupting. "You speak the real language."

"Of course," said Coley, "that's part of why we happen to be here—"

"You are not one of the real people."

"No. I—"

"Confine yourself to simple answers, please. You are Human?"

"Yes," said Coley.

"A Human, speaking the real language, and here where you have no permission to be. A spy."

"No," said Coley. "Let me explain. Yesterday, our Consul . . ." He explained.

"That is your story," said the silver-belted Yaran. "There's no reason I should believe it—in view of the suspicious circumstances of your being here, an obvious Human, speaking the real tongue and without permission to be here. This young female will be taken into protective custody. You, as a spy, will be strangled."

"I wouldn't do that, if I were you," said Coley, "The old persons down on the coast have their own ideas about how to deal with Humans. If I were you, I'd at least check up on my story before I stuck my neck out by having a Human strangled."

"This is the Army," retorted the silver-belted Yaran. "The old persons down on the coast have no authority over us. They have nothing whatsoever to say about what we do with spies caught in restricted areas. I want you to understand that clearly." He stared at Coley with motionless black eyes for a long moment. "On the other hand," he continued, "it is, of course, regular Army routine to check up on the stories of spies before strangling them. As I was just about to say, when you interrupted me. Consequently, you will be allowed the freedom of the commercial area adjoining the military establishment under my command here. I warn you, however, against attempting to spy any further, or trying to leave the area without permission. The female will still be taken into protective custody."

He turned to the one in the yellow belt.

"Take him to the commercial area and turn him loose," he ordered. Numbly, Coley followed the yellow-belted Yaran out, casting a rather helpless glance at the girl as he passed. But the girl seemed as blandly unconcerned about this as she had about almost everything else. The Yaran with the yellow belt led Coley out of the building, had him remount, and rode with him to a far side of the camp where they passed a sort of gate in a stone wall and found themselves among a cluster of wooden buildings like those Coley had seen at Tannakil.

Here, the yellow-belted Yaran turned his animal and scooted back into the military compound on the run, leaving Coley sitting alone, on his beast, in the center of a cobbled street.

It was past noon when Coley was turned loose. For more than a couple of hours of the short Yaran day, he rode around the commercial area. It was actually a small town, its buildings set up as permanently as the ones in the military area. What he saw confirmed his original notion that, much as the human sort of army is the same everywhere, the human sort of civilian population that clings to its skirts is pretty much the same, as well. The town—a sign at its geographic center announced its name to be Tegat— revealed itself to be a collection of establishments for the feeding, drinking, and other pleasuring of off- duty soldiers. So had the spaceport district been, back at Venus City. True, the clients of the district had not exactly been soldiers; but there was much similarity between the uniformed breed and the men who worked the starships

Once more, as he had in that moment back on the desert, Coley began to feel at home.

He considered his wealth, which consisted in Yaran terms of his muscle, his knife, and the animal he was riding, and then he stopped a passing Yaran, a civil- ian type in an unbelted grey robe.

"Who around here lends money?" asked Coley. "And just how do I go about finding him."

The Yaran looked at him for a long moment with- out answering, and without any expression on his face that Coley could interpret. Then his thin mouth opened in the swarthy face.

"Two streets back," he said. "Turn right. Twelfth building, second floor. Call for Ynesh."

Coley went back, found the second street and turned right into it. This turned out to be little more than an alley; and Coley, moreover, found he had trouble telling where one building left off and another started, since they were all built firmly into each other. Finally, by counting doorways and making a hopeful guess, he entered what he believed was the twelfth building and, passing a couple of interior doors, strode up a ramp and found himself on a landing one floor up. Here there were three more doors. Coley stopped, perplexed; then he remembered that his instructions had been to *call* for Ynesh.

"Ynesh!" he yelled.

The door on the furthest right flew open as if his voice had actuated some sort of spring release. No one came out, however. Coley waited a moment, then walked face first into a hanging drape. He pushed his way past the drape and found himself in a circular room containing cushions and one tall desk behind which a middle-aged Yaran in an unbelted figured green robe was standing. One tall window illuminated the room.

"Live well," said the Yaran, "I am Ynesh. How much would you like to borrow?"

"Nothing," said Coley—although his empty stomach growled at this denial of the hope of the wherewithal to buy something to put in it. Ynesh did not stir so much as a finger that Coley could see, but suddenly three good-sized Yarans in belted, knee-length robes of blue-grey appeared from the drapes. They all had two knives in their belts.

"Don't misunderstand me," said Coley, hastily, "I wouldn't have come here unless I meant to do some business. How'd you like to make some money?"

Ynesh still stood without moving. But the three with knives disappeared back into the drapery. Coley breathed more easily. He walked forward to the desk and leaned close.

"I suppose," he said to the Yaran, "there's some sort of limit set on how much interest you can charge, and how much you can lend the ordinary soldier."

Ynesh parted his thin lips.

"For every grade an amount of credit commensurate with the pay scale for that grade. The interest rate is one tenth of the principal in the period of one year, proportionately decreased for shorter lengths of time. This rate and amount is set by the military Authority in Chief. Everyone but a Human would know that, Human."

"Call me Coley," said Coley.

"Gzoly," replied the Yaran, agreeably.

"You wouldn't want to risk going above the amounts or charging a greater interest rate, I take it?" said Coley.

"And lose my license to lend?" said Ynesh. He had not pulled back from Coley. They were talking, Coley suspected, with more cozy intimacy than probably any Human and Yaran had talked to date. It was marvelous what the right sort of topic could do to eradicate awkwardness in communication between the races. "I would hardly be sensible to do that, Gzoly."

"What if somebody else would take the risks for you—say, take your money and lend it without a license, quietly, but for better than the usual rates of interest, in any amount wanted?"

"Now who, Gzoly, would do that?" said Ynesh.

"Perhaps certain soldiers wouldn't object to acting as agents," said Coley. "They borrow the money from you and relend to their fellow soldiers at higher rates? Under the blanket, no questions asked, money in a hurry."

"Ah, but I wouldn't be able to lend each one of them more than his grade-amount of credit, since it would surely be traced back to me," said Ynesh, but in no tone that indicated that he considered the topic closed. "Moreover, where would be the extra profit? I'd have to lend to them at legal rates." He paused, almost imperceptibly. The effect was that of a silent shrug. "A pity. But that is the Game."

"Of course," said Coley. "On the other hand, there are no rules set up for me. I could lend them as much as they wanted, at any rate I wanted. And also since

I'm a Human, you could lend me the money originally at a higher-than-legal rate of interest."

"Ah," said Ynesh.

"I thought the idea would meet with your approval," said Coley.

"It might be worth trying in a limited way, Gzoly," said Ynesh. "Yes, I think it might. I will be glad to lend you a small trial sum, at, say, a fifth part in yearly interest."

"I'm afraid," said Coley, straightening up from the desk, "that you happen to be one of those real people who would cut open the insect that spins the golden nest. A fifth in interest would force me to relend at rates that would keep my agents from finding any borrowers, after they had upped their own rates to make their cut. I'm afraid I couldn't do business with you unless I borrowed at no more than a ninth part."

"Ridiculous. I'm laughing," said Ynesh, without cracking a smile or twitching a facial muscle. "If you're one of those people who always like to feel they've beaten a little off the price for form's sake, I'll let you have your first sum at five and a half."

"Goodbye," said Coley.

"Now, wait a minute," said Ynesh. "I might consider . . ." And the classical argument proceeded along its classical lines, terminating in a rate to Coley of eight and three-quarters part of the principal on a yearly basis.

"Now, the only question is," said Ynesh, after the rate had been settled, "Whether I can trust you with such a sum as I had in mind. After all, what proof have I—"

"I imagine you've heard by this time," said Coley, drily. "The military Authority has confined me to this area. "If I try any tricks you won't have any trouble finding me."

"True," said Ynesh, as if the thought had just struck him for the first time. . . .

Coley went out with money in his pocket and intrigued the Yaran who sold food in one of the eating and drinking establishments by ordering a large number of different items and sampling them all in gingerly fashion. The search was not a particularly pleasant one for Coley's tastebuds; but he did eventually come up with a sort of a stew and a sort of a pudding that tasted reasonably good—and assuaged a two days hunger. He also tried a number of the Yaran drinks, but ended up gagging on their oily taste and settled for water.

Then, having eaten and drunk, he glanced around the establishment. Not far off across the room a Yaran soldier with the green belt of the lower ranks was seated glumly at a table holding an empty bowl and a stick of incense that had burned itself completely out. Coley got up, went over and plumped down on a stool at the same table.

"Cheer up," he said. "Have a drink on me. And tell me—how'd you like to make some money . . . ?"

It took about a week and a half for Coley's presence in the commercial area and in the military establishment to make itself felt. Early the third day, Coley discovered where the girl was being held—in a sort of watchtower not far from the main gate. However, there was no getting in to her and obviously she could not get out—though from the few glimpses Coley had had of her uninterested face when it occasionally showed itself at the window of the tower when he was watching, it was a good question whether she even wanted to.

Otherwise, however, things had gone well. Every day had become a little more comfortable. For one thing, Coley had discovered that the Yaran meats, in spite of their gamey taste, were quite satisfying if soaked in oil before, during, and after cooking. In addition to this, business was good; Coley having noticed that gambling was under as strict regulations as the lending of money, had thoughtfully started a chain-letter scheme to start the financial picture moving.

A desert takes no more thirstily to one of its infrequent rain showers than the Yaran soldiers took to both of Coley's schemes. The local money situation literally exploded; and ten days after Coley's arrival, he was escorted to the office of the Yaran Authority who had originally passed sentence upon him.

The Authority in his silver belt was as inscrutable as ever. He waited until he and Coley were alone together.

"All my officers are in debt," he said to Coley. "My common soldiers are become a rabble, selling their equipment to illegal buyers for money. The army treasury has been broken into and robbed. Where is all our money?"

"I couldn't tell you," replied Coley, who was being perfectly truthful. He knew only where about a fifth of the area's hard cash was—carefully hidden in his room. As for the rest, Coley suspected other prudent souls had squirreled most of the rest out of the way; and that in any case the sum the Authority had in mind was entirely illusory, resulting from vast quantities of credit multiplying the actual cash reserves of the area.

"I will have you tortured to death—which is illegal," said the Authority. "Then I will commit suicide—which is shameful but convenient."

"Why do all that?" said Coley, enunciating clearly in spite of a slight unavoidable dryness of the mouth— for though he had planned this, he realized the extreme touchiness of the situation at this stage. "Let me and the girl go. Then you can declare a moratorium on all debts and blame it on the fact I absconded with the funds."

The Authority thought a moment.

"A very good suggestion," he said, finally. "However, there's no reason I should actually let you go. I might as well have a little fun out of all this."

"Somebody might find out, if I didn't actually escape with the girl. Then the blame would fall on you."

The Authority considered again.

"Very well. A pity," he said. "Perhaps I shall lay hands on you again, some day, Human."

"I don't think so," said Coley. "Not if I can help it."

"Yes," said the Authority. He went to the entrance of the room and gave orders. Half an hour later, Coley found himself, his belongings, and the girl hurrying on a pair of first-class riding animals out the far end of the pass, headed down toward the seacoast. The early sunset of Yara was upon them and twilight was closing down.

"Great hero," breathed the girl in Yaran. Coley jerked about and stared at her through the gathering gloom. But her expression was as innocuous as ever, and for all the expression there was on her face, it might have been somebody else entirely who had spoken.

"Say that again," said Coley.

But she was through speaking—at least for the present.

Coley had managed to get away with the money hidden in his room. He wore it in a double fold of heavy cloth—a sort of homemade money belt—wrapped around his waist under his shirt; and a few coins taken from it supplied himself and the girl with a room for the night at a way-station that they came to that night after the second moon rose in the sky. The coins also supplied Coley with food—raw meat which he cooked himself over the brazier filled with soft coal which the way-station help brought in to heat the room. He offered some to the girl, but she would not eat it; and if he had not thought of the notion of ordering in some fruit, she might have gone to sleep without any food at all. The last thing he saw, by the dim glow of the dying coals in the brazier was the girl half-curled, half-sitting in a far corner of the room on some cushions and looking in his direction steadily, but still without expression or a word.

The following morning, they left the way-station early. Coley had been wary that in spite of his decision the military Authority might have sent men after them. But evidently the Yaran mind did not work that way. They saw no signs of any threat or soldiers. By mid-day, between the clumps of bush-like fern that covered the seaward side of these mountains, they began to catch glimpses of the coast below them, and when they stopped to rest their animals in a spot giving them an open view of the lowlands, it was possible for Coley to make out the glittering spire of the traffic control tower in the Human Compound.

He pointed. "We're almost home," he said, in Basic. The girl looked at him interestedly for a long second.

"Hawmn," she said, finally.

"Well!" said Coley, straightening up in his saddle. "Starting to come to life, are you? Say that again."

She looked at him.

"Say that again," repeated Coley, this time in Yaran.

"Hawmn," she said.

"Wonderful! Marvelous!" said Coley. He applauded. "Now say something else in Basic for the nice man."

"Hawmn," she said.

"No," said Coley. "You've said that. Try something else. Say—say—" He leaned toward her, enunciating the words carefully in Basic. "Friends, Romans, Countrymen—"

She hesitated.

"Frendz, Rawmans, Cundzrememns—" she managed.

"Lend me your ears—"

"Lenz me ur ears—"

"Come on, kid," said Coley, turning his own riding animal's head once more back onto the downtrail, "this is too good to let drop. I come not to bury—"

"I cauzm nodt do burrey—"

They rode on. By the time they reached the first gate of the walled town, as dusk was falling, the girl was reciting in Basic like a veteran. The guard at the gate stared at the strange sounds coming from her mouth.

"What's the matter with her? You can't go in, Human; the gate's already closed for the night. What's your business in Akalede?"

Coley gave the Yaran a handful of coins.

"Does that answer your questions?" he asked.

"Partly—" said the guard, peering at the coins in the falling dusk.

"In that case," said Coley, smoothly, "I suppose I'll just have to wait outside tonight; and perhaps some of my good friends inside the city, tomorrow, can fill out the answer for you. Although," said Coley, "perhaps a fuller answer may not be quite what you—"

"Pass, worthy person," said the gateman, swinging the door wide and standing back deferentially. Coley and the girl rode on into the city of Akalede.

The streets they found themselves in were full of Yarans pushing either homeward, or wherever Yarans went at sundown. From his experience with the commercial area outside the military compound, Coley suspected a majority of the males at least were on their way to get drunk. Or drugged, thought Coley, suddenly remembering he had not been able to drink enough of things Yaran to discover what it was in their potables that addicted the populace to them. He had seen Yarans become stupefied from drinking, but what kind of stupefaction it was, he suddenly realized, he had not the slightest idea. This made him abruptly thoughtful; and he rode on automatically, trying to chase down an elusive conclusion that seemed to skitter through his mind just out of reach.

His riding animal stopped suddenly. Coming to himself with a start, he saw he had ridden full up against a barricade that blocked the street.

"What the—"

His bridle strap was seized and he looked down at a kilted Yaran whose clothes bore the cut, if not the color of the army.

"Human, you're under arrest," said the lean face. "Where do you think you're going?"

"To the Compound," said Coley. "I and this female Human have to get back—"

"Permissions?"

"Well, you see," said Coley, "We—"

But the Yaran was already leading him off; and other kilted Yarans had fallen in around the mounts of Coley and his companion.

* * *

Coley stood, cursing inwardly, but with a bland smile on his face. Behind him, the girl was silent. The heavy drapes of the room in the building to which they had both been brought did not stir. The only thing that stirred was the lips of the rather heavy-set, obviously middle-aged Yaran standing behind a tall desk.

"You have made a mistake," said the middle-aged Yaran.

Coley was fully prepared to admit it. The middle-aged native before him was apparently a local magistrate. As such, he had made it obvious that it was up to him whether Coley and the girl were to be allowed through the barricades into the restricted area of the city that lay between them and the Human Compound. And Coley, judging by his past experience with these people, had just made the mistake of trying to bribe him.

"I am, you see," went on the magistrate, "one of the real people who actually plays the Game. But perhaps you don't know about the Game, Human?"

Coley rubbed his dry lips in what he hoped was a casual gesture.

"A little about it," he said.

"You could hardly," said the magistrate, leaning on the high desk, "know more than a little. Understanding in its full sense would be beyond you. You see—we real people, all of us, hope to reach Old Age." He paused, his black eyes steady on Coley. "Of course, I am not speaking of a physical old age, an age of the body, which is nothing. I am speaking of true Old Age, that highest level of development that is winnable."

"That's pretty much how I heard it," said Cole.

"Few of us," said the magistrate, going on as if Cole had said nothing, "very few of us make it, and we do it only by playing the Game to perfection."

"Oh. I see," said Coley.

"It does not matter if you do," said the magistrate. "What matters is that I offer you this explanation, leaving it up to you to use, misuse or ignore it as you will. Because, you see, there is one thing required of a player of the Game." He paused, looking at Coley.

"What?" said Coley, filling the gap in the conversation

"Consistency," said the magistrate. "His rules of living—which he chooses for himself—may be anything, good or bad. But having adopted them, he must live by them. He cannot do himself the violence of violating his own principles. A person may adopt selfishness as a principle; but, having adopted it, he may not allow himself the luxury of unselfishness. He must live by the principles chosen in youth— and with them try to survive to years of maturity and wisdom." He paused. "If he falters, or if the world kills or destroys him, he has lost the Game. So far—" he leaned a little closer to Coley—"I have neither faltered nor been destroyed. And one of my principles is absolute honesty. Another is the destruction of the dishonest."

"I see," said Coley. "Well, what I meant was—"

"You," went on the magistrate, inexorably, "are one of the dishonest."

"Now, wait! Wait!" cried Coley. "You can't judge us by your standards. We're Human!"

"You say that as if it entitled you to special privileges," said the magistrate, almost dreamily. "The proof of the fact that the Game encompasses even you is the fact that you are here caught up in it." He reached below the table and came up with a sort of hour-glass, filled not with sand but with some heavy liquid. He turned it over. "This will run out in a few moments," he said. "If before it has run out you come up with a good reason why you should, within the rules of the Game, be allowed on into the Human Compound, I will let you and the female go. Otherwise, I will have you both destroyed."

The liquid from the little transparent pyramid at the top of the timing device began to run, drop by drop, down into the pyramid below. The liquid was clear, with no reddish tint, but to Coley it looked like the blood he could feel similarly draining out of his heart. His mind flung itself suddenly open, as if under the influence of some powerfully stimulating drug, and thoughts flashed through it like small bursts of light. His gutter-bred brain was crying out that there was a gimmick somewhere, that there was a loophole in any law, or something new to get around it—The liquid in the top of the timer had almost run out.

And then he had it.

"How can you be sure," said Coley, "that you're not interrupting a process that greater minds than your own have put in motion?"

The magistrate reached slowly out, took the timer from the top of the desk and put it out of sight behind the desk top.

"I'll have you escorted to the gates of the Human Compound by one of our police persons," he said.

Coley was furious—and that fury of his, according to his way of doing things, hid not a little fear.

"Calm down," said his jailer, one of a squad of star-marines attached to the embassy, unlocking the cell door. "I'll have you out in a minute."

"You'd better, lint-picker," said Coley.

"Let's watch the names," said the star-marine. He was almost as big as Coley. He came inside and stood a few inches from Coley, facing him. "They want you upstairs in the Consul's office. But we got a couple of minutes to spare, if you insist." Coley opened his mouth—then shut it again.

"Forget it," growled Coley. "Shoved into jail— locked up all night with no explanation—you'd be hot, too. I want to see that Consul."

"This way," said the jailer, standing aside. Coley allowed himself to be escorted out of the cell, down a corridor, and up a fall-tube. They went a little way down another corridor and through a light-door into the same office Coley had been in before. Some two weeks before, to be precise. The Consul, Ivor Ben was standing with his back to the hunched, smoke tube in his fingers, and a not pleasant look on his aristocratic face.

"Stand over there," he said; and crossing to his

desk, pushed a button on it. "Bring in the girl," he said. He pushed another button. "Let Ansash in now."

He straightened up behind the desk. A door opened behind Coley; and he turned to see the girl he had escorted from Tannakil. She looked at him with her usual look, advanced a few steps into the office, as the door closed behind her, and then halted—as if the machinery that operated her had just run down.

Only a couple of seconds later, a door at the other end of the room opened, and Ansash came in. He walked slowly into the room, taking in Coley and the girl with his eyes.

"Well, hello there," said Coley. Ansash considered him flatly.

"Hello," he said in Basic, with no inflection whatsoever. He turned to the Consul. "May I have an explanation?"

The Consul swiveled about to look at Coley.

"How about it?"

"How about what?" said Coley.

The Consul stalked out from behind his desk and up to Coley, looking like some small rooster ruffling up to a turkey. He pointed past Coley at the girl.

"This is not the woman I sent you to get!" he said tightly.

"Oh, I know that," said Coley.

The Consul stared at him.

"You *know* it?" he echoed.

"He could hardly avoid knowing," put in the smooth voice of Ansash. "He was left alone with this female briefly, when I went to fetch his beloved. When I returned, he had vanished with this one."

The Consul, who had looked aside at Ansash when the other started speaking, looked back at Coley, bleakly and bitterly.

"That" went on Ansash, "is the first cause of the complaint I brought you this morning. In addition to stealing this real person, the Human, Coley Yunce, has committed other crimes upon the earth of Yara, up to the including murder."

"Yes," breathed the Consul, still staring at Coley. Coley looked bewildered.

"You mean she's no good?" he asked the Consul.

"No good? She isn't Sara Illoy, is she?" exploded the Consul.

"I mean, won't she do?" said Coley. "I mean— she looks pretty human. And she talks fine Basic—" He stepped over to the girl and put a friendly hand on her shoulder. "Recite for them, Honey. Come on, now—'Friends, Romans—'."

She looked up into his face and something that might almost have been a smile twitched at her expressionless mouth. She opened her lips and began to recite in an atrocious accent.

"Frendz, Rawmans, Cundzrememns, I cauzm nodt do burrey Shaayzar, budt do brayze ymn. Dee eefil dwadt memn dooo—"

"Never mind! Never mind!" cried the Consul, furiously; and the girl shut up. "You must have been out of your head!" he barked, and swung about on Ansash. "Very clever, my friend," he grated. "My compliments to Yara. I suppose you know the real Sara Illoy came back of her own accord, the day after this man left."

"I had heard some mention of it," said Ansash, without inflection.

"Very clever indeed," said the Consul. "So it's a choice between handing this man over to your justice to be strangled, or accepting a situation in which contact between our two races on this planet is permanently frozen in a state of Middle-Age restricted contact and chicanery."

"The choice is yours," said Ansash, as if he might have been remarking on the weather.

"I know. Well, don't worry," said the Consul, turning to fling the last three words at Coley. "You know as well as I do I have no choice. Human life must be perserved at all costs. I'll get you safely off-planet, Yunce; though I wouldn't advice you to go boasting about your part in this little adventure. Not that anyone would do anything but laugh at you, if you did." He turned to look at Ansash. "I'm the real loser as you all know," he added softly. "Yara'll never rate an Ambassador, and I'll never rate a promotion. I'll spend the rest of my professional life here as Consul."

"Or," put in Coley, "in jail."

Three heads jerked around to look at him.

"What kind of a sucker do you take me for?" snarled Coley, spinning around upon the girl. His long arm shot out, there was a very humanlike shriek, and the girl staggered backward, leaving her blonde locks in Coley's fist. Released, a mass of chestnut hair tumbled down to frame a face that was suddenly contorted with shock.

"I learned to look for the gimmick in something before I could walk." He threw the blonde wig in the direction of the Consul's desk. "This set-up of yours stunk to high heaven right from the beginning. So the girl's gone! How'd she get out of the Compound in the first place? How come you didn't call in regular help from the authorities back at Sol? You were all just sitting back waiting for a tough boy you could use, weren't you?"

He glared around at the three in the room. None of them answered; but they all had their eyes on him.

"I don't know what kind of racket you've got here," he said. "But whatever it is, you didn't want the Humans to win the Game, did you? You wanted things to stay just the way they are now. Why?"

"You're out of your head," said the Consul, though his face was a little pale.

"Out of my head!" Coley laughed. "I can *feel* the difference between Ansash and you, Consul. You think I wouldn't notice that the girl I was with was a Yaran, almost right off the bat? And who could suppose I would need a knife when I left Tannakil, but the man who knew I could use one? How come I never saw her eat anything but fruit? A native Yaran wouldn't have restricted her diet." He leaned forward. "Want *me* to tell *you* what the deal was?"

"I think," said the Consul, "We've listened to enough of your wild guessing."

"No you haven't. Not on your life," said Coley. "I'm back among Humans, now. You can't shut my mouth and get away with it; and either you listen to me, or I'll go tell it to the star-marines. I don't suppose you own them."

"Go ahead, then," said the Consul.

Coley grinned at him. He walked around the Consul's desk and sat down in the Consul's chair. He put his feet on the table.

"There's a world," he said, examining the rather scuffed toes of his boots with a critical eye. "It seems to be run on the basis of an idea about some sort of Game, which is practically a religion. However, when you look a little closer, you see that this Game thing isn't much more than a set of principles which only a few fanatics obey to the actual letter. Still, these principles are what hold the society together. In fact, it goes along fine until another race comes along and creates a situation where the essential conflict between what everybody professes to believe and what they actually believe will eventually be pushed into the open." Coley glanced over at the Consul. "How'm I doing?"

"Go on," said the Consul, wincing.

"The only thing is, this is a conflict which the race has not yet advanced far enough to take. If it came to the breaking point today, half the race would feel it their duty to go fanatic and start exterminating the other half of the race who felt that it was time to discard the old-fashioned Games Ethic." He paused.

"Go on," said the Consul, tonelessly.

"Now, let's suppose this world has a Consul on it, who sees what's happening. He reports back to Sol that the five stages of the Game consist of (1) trying to rid yourself of your enemy by refusing to acknowledge his existence, as a child ignores what it does not like. (2) By reacting against your enemy thoughtlessly and instinctively, as a youth might do. (3) By organized warfare—young manhood. (4) By trickery and subtlety—middle-age. (5) By teaching him your own superior philosophy of existence and bringing him by intellectual means to acknowledge your superiority—old age.

"The only trouble with this, the Consul reports, is that the Yaran philosophy is actually a more primitive one than the human; and any attempt to conquer by stage five would induce a sort of general Yaran psychosis, because they would at once be forced to admit a philosophical inferiority and be *unable* to admit same."

"All right, Mr. Yunce," said the Consul. "You needn't go on—"

"Let me finish. So Sol answers back that they sympathize, but that they cannot violate their own rigid rules of non-interference, sanctity of a single human life, etc., for any situation that does not directly threaten Humanity itself. And this Consul—a dedicated sort—resolves to do the job himself by rigging a situation with help from one of the more grown-up Yarans and a young lady—"

"My aide-de-camp," said the Consul, wearily. Coley bowed a little in the direction of the girl.

"—a situation where a tough but dumb Human sets out inside the Rules of the Game, but so tears them to shreds that the Game-with-Humans is abandoned and set aside—where it will rot quietly and disappear as the two races become more and more acquainted, until it gradually is forgotten altogether. Right?"

Coley looked at him. They looked back at him with peculiarly set faces. Even the Yaran's face had something of that quality of expression to it. They looked like people who, having risked everything on one throw of the dice and won, now find that by gambling they have incurred a sentence of death.

"Fanatics," said Coley, slowly, running his eyes over them. "Fanatics. Now me—I'm a business man." He hoisted himself up out of his chair. "No reason why I shouldn't get on down to the pad, now, and catch the first ship out of here. Is there?"

"No, Mr. Yunce," said the Consul, bleakly. The three of them watched him stalk around the desk and past them to the door. As he opened the door the Consul cleared his throat.

"Mr. Yunce—" he said.

Coley stopped and turned, the door half open.

"Yes?" he said.

"What's—" the Consul's voice stuck in his throat. "Wait a minute," he said. "I'll give you a ride to your ship."

He came around the desk and went out with Coley. They went down and out of the Consulate, but all during the short ride to the Compound's landing pad for the big interspace ships, the Consul said not another word.

He was silent until they reached the ramp leading up to the ship then in ready position.

"Anywhere near Arga IV?" Coley asked the officer at the ramphead.

"No, Sirius and back to Sol. Try the second ship down. Deneb, and you can get a double transfer out of Deneb Nine."

Coley and the Consul walked down onto the ramp leading up to the entrance port on the second ship, some twenty feet up the steel sides.

"Farewell," said Coley, grinning at the Consul and starting up the ramp.

"Yunce!" the word tore itself at last from the Consul's lips.

Coley stopped, turned around and looked a few feet down into the older man's pleading eyes.

"What can I do for you?" he said.

"Give me a price," said the Consul.

"A price?" Coley, grinning, spread his hands. "A price for what?

"For not reporting this back on Sol. If you do, they'll have to take action. They won't have any choice. They'll undo everything you did."

"Oh, they wouldn't do that," said Coley. He grinned happily, leaned down and slapped the smaller man on the shoulder. "Cheer up," he said. The Consul stared up at him. Slowly, the older man's eyebrows came together in a searching frown.

"Yunce?" he said. "Who....? Just who are you anyway?"

Coley grinned and winked at him. And then he burst into a loud laugh, swing about and went trotting up the airlock ramp and into the ship, still laughing. At the airlock, he stopped, turned, and threw something white that fluttered and side-slipped through the air until it fell on the concrete pad by the Consul's feet. The consul leaned over and picked it up.

It was a folded sheaf of paper, sealed with a melt-clip with no identifying symbol upon it. On one side it was stamped TOP SECRET.

The Consul hesitated, broke it open and looked at it. What stared back up at him was that same report he had written back to the authorities on Sol five years before, concerning the Yaran Game of Five and its possible disastrous conclusion. Clipped to it was a little hand-printed note in rather rakish block capitals.

'WHEN SEARCHING THROUGH GOVERNMENT LISTS DON'T LOOK A GIFT HORSE IN THE MOUTH.'

Scratched in the lower right hand corner of the mouth, as if in idle afterthought, was a small A4.

Inch by manmade inch, our corridor of moments grows.
Each succeeding mason toils in confident belief that
"after me cometh a builder" until the end of time.

Guided Tour

Please keep close—
We enter by this new pale arch of hours
Into the greystone corridor of years,
Which at this end is still under construction.
Please note the stained glass windows which depict
A number of historic episodes.
A legal green here—further back they're purple—
Before that, bright iron, bronze, and last—grey flint,
From which the hall drives its general tone.
One legend goes that at the furthest part,
Where it begins, there's only two small stones
Placed one on top the other for a start
By some half-animal—but others think
The whole was laid out from the very first
By some big architect whose spirit still
Directs construction. Well, you take your pick.
. . . And now, I thought I heard somebody ask
About our future thoughts for building on.
Well, there's now building quite a fine addition
Of plastic, steel and glass, all air-conditioned,
Also there's planned a nucleonic part
Built up from force-fields. But beyond *its* end

We butt, unfortunately, on a space—
A pit, or void, through which the right of way
May be disputed, and is still in doubt. . . .

Here is an excerpt from Cloud Warrior *by Patrick Tilley, coming from Baen Books in August 1985:*

With Jodi in the lead, the three Skyhawks flew in a silent descending curve that took them over the line of the Laramie Range. Jodi's intention was to come around behind the advancing Mutes, firing a lethal burst into their unsuspecting backs before slamming the throttle forward and jinking away under full power, returning from different directions at low level to pick off the remainder. In previous actions against the southern Mutes she had found that they were as terrified of "cloud warriors" as they were of the "iron snake" and, if subjected to a determined, vigorous attack, usually turned tail and fled for cover.

Like the execs to whom she reported, Jodi had not allowed the idea that Mutes might possess magical powers to take root in her mind. The interaction of earth-forces—ground and air temperature, humidity, atmospheric electricity, and the movement of air masses over differing terrain—were part of a logically constructed system of cause and effect that could be recorded, analyzed and understood. Like Hartmann and his officers, Jodi had found it strange—and slightly unnerving—that the mist and low cloud that had formed overnight around and above the train should still persist several hours after sunrise. And not only persist; actually appear to move with the wagon train when it had begun its advance. Jodi was not an expert, but she preferred to think that there was a simple, rational, meteorologically sound explanation for what had occurred.

Back in Nixon-Fort Worth, she had been irritated by Steve Brickman's probing questions about the rumors of so-called Mute magic. Odd things had happened in the past, but when the facts were considered carefully and coolly—as in the incidents investigated by the Assessors—it was clear that most of the things people claimed had happened either hadn't happened at all, or were nothing more than strange coincidences. A haphazard conjunction of events which, in the heat of battle, had seemed extraordinary. Despite the odd, occasional doubt, Jodi had clung stubbornly to the official viewpoint. She refused to consider the possibility that "summoners" really existed. The idea that the Plainfolk clans had people who could manipulate the weather at will was clearly ridiculous.

As this thought passed through her mind, Jodi heard an ominous rumble of thunder. She looked up through the clear-view panel in the wing. The sky was clear. But it had been hot and humid for days. When that happened, you often got a buildup of pressure and static, and then . . .

Jodi checked the movement of the rifle mount and the ease with which she could pull the weapon into her shoulder and take aim, squeezing off imaginary shots on the uncocked trigger at rocks on the slopes of the mountain below. Satisfied, she stretched out her arms and pointed three times at Booker and Yates. They veered away obediently, opening out the formation to fly three wingspans from their section leader. As they assumed their new positions and turned their faces toward her, Jodi raised her right hand and brought it down in a slow chopping motion over the nose of her Skyhawk. It was the signal to go into what was known as a free-firing attack.

With their propellers windmilling silently behind their backs, they swooped down over the western flank of the Laramie Mountains like three giant birds of prey. The tops of the forest of red trees that carpeted the lower slopes rushed up to meet them.

To the south, The Lady continued to advance cautiously, still blinded by the heavy mist. Unknown to Hartmann, the wagon train had wandered two or three miles off course. What he took to be the eroded remains of Interstate 80, which had once run from Cheyenne, through Laramie and then westward to Rawlins, was actually a dry, shallow river bed. As they followed its winding course northwestward, Hartmann noted that the ground on either side was rising steadily. He made his second mistake of the day in thinking that they were passing through a cutting.

From the hour before dawn when the mist had formed around the wagon train, a small group of Mutes camouflaged with scrub had been trailing it, sending reports of its progress to Mr. Snow by runners at regular intervals. Mr. Snow knew of Hartmann's navigational error. Indeed, with the knowledge Cadillac had given him, Mr. Snow had reached into Hartmann's mind and had created the confusion that had made the mistake possible and then prevented the wagon master from realizing what he had done. The rumble of thunder that Jodi had heard when she turned west over the mountains had been a trial blast by Mr. Snow, clearing his throat for the big event.

Escorted by ten Bears, Mr. Snow ran, Mute-fashion, some way behind the two large groups that Jodi had spotted. Cadillac and Clearwater had been ordered to stay hidden in the forest with the She-Wolves, the M'Call elders, the den-mothers, and the children. The remaining Bears were moving under cover of the trees to a point nearer the wagon train. This much larger group constituted the clan's strategic reserve and would be committed to the battle as conditions required.

The whole of Mr. Snow's remarkable mind was concentrated on the task he had set himself. He had produced a cloud and sown a degree of confusion in Hartmann's mind, but he was worried about his ability to summon, control, and ultimately survive the immense power he was about to draw from the earth and sky. As a consequence, the soundless volley of rifle fire that mowed down the running warriors around him came as a complete surprise.

A bullet struck him in the head, sending him sprawling to the ground. Miraculously, the needle-pointed round hit a cluster of knuckle-bones threaded on one of the plaited loops of white hair. The force of the impact drove them against his skull, shattering two in the process, and knocking him temporarily senseless. As his body rolled onto its back amidst his wounded and dying escort, he saw the three blue arrowheads flash overhead.

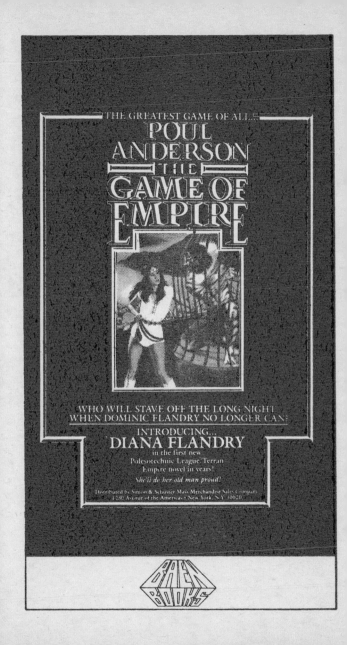